Silver ▮▮▮ & Silver Mink

H
C

OF

EROTIC DOMINATION

If you like one you will probably like the rest

A NEW TITLE EVERY MONTH
NOW INCLUDING EXTRA BONUS PAGES

Silver Moon Books Ltd
PO Box CR25 Leeds LS7 3TN

Silver Moon Books Inc
PO Box 1614 New York NY 10156

*Distributed to the trade throughout North America by
LPC Group, 1436 West Randolph Street, Chicago, IL 60607
(800) 826-4330*

Silver Moon Books of Leeds and New York are in no way connected with Silver Moon Books of London

If you like one of our books you will probably like them all!

Write for our free 20 page booklet of extracts from early books - surely the most erotic feebie yet - and, if you wish to be on our confidential mailing list, from forthcoming monthly titles as they are published:-

Silver Moon Reader Services
PO BOX CR 25 LEEDS LS7 3TN
or
PO Box 1614 NEW YORK NY 1016

or leave details on our 24hr UK answerphone
0113 287 6255

<u>New authors welcome</u>

ANGEL OF LUST first published 1998

Copyright Lia Anderssen

The right of Lia Anderssen to be identified as the author of this book has been asserted in accordance with Section 77 and 78 of the Copyrights and Patents Act 1988

CONTENTS

ANGEL OF LUST

a full length new novel by

Lia Anderssen

author of Bikers Girl,
Bikers Girl on the Run,
The Hunted Aristocrat
Bush Slave

BONUS PAGES

ANGEL OF LUST by Lia Anderssen

Chapter 1

Charlotte Lamb stood at the kerb and watched as the cab approached. Sure enough, as the black cab drew up beside her, she saw Marie's smiling face staring from the window. She was wearing a tight red dress that was cut low across the bosom and was so short that her stocking tops were visible. Charlotte, Charlie to her friends, admired her friend with a tinge of envy.

"You look gorgeous tonight, Marie," she said. "Dressed to kill, eh?"

Marie laughed. "Something like that." She was blonde and slim, with a stunning body, and she knew how to look good. "I'm out to get laid tonight."

"Marie!" Despite knowing her friend well, Charlie found it hard to disguise the shock in her voice.

"Well it's all right for you," replied Marie. "Come the weekend Jon will be back and you'll be getting it regularly."

Charlie didn't reply. Instead her mind went back to the thoughts that had filled her head when she had been dressing, less than half an hour ago.

She remembered how she had stood in front of the full-length mirror in her bedroom and had run her eyes down her naked body. There was no doubt about it, she had told herself, any man who encountered her thus would like what he saw. Charlie was, by any standards, beautiful. She stood about five foot three inches in her bare feet, her body slim and in perfect proportion. Her breasts were firm and inviting, the size and shape of ripe grapefruits. They were tipped by large nipples which, even when not erect, stood out proudly. Her waist was narrow, her hips not too broad, her pubic hair trimmed short so that it formed a triangle, beneath which the pink of her sex lips made a neat cleft. Her legs were long and shapely, tapering to small ankles and beautiful feet. In anybody's terms, Charlie had a body to kill for.

Her face, too, was classically beautiful, with high cheekbones, a pert nose and a small, eminently kissable mouth. Her eyes were bright green, their innocent stare belying the desires that lurked behind them. The whole was framed by dark, wavy hair that hung down below her shoulders.

Charlie paused long enough to assure herself that she was irresistible, then turned away from the mirror and opened the top drawer of a chest. She rummaged inside for a moment, pulling out a matching bra and pants. She put the bra on first, scooping her full breasts into it and adjusting the straps so as to show off her cleavage to full advantage. Once satisfied, she stooped down and stepped into the panties, pulling them up her legs. Again she paused to examine her reflection. The bra was white and lacy, cut so low that it barely covered her nipples. The panties were extremely brief, with a transparent panel up the front through which her dark pubic thatch was clearly visible.

Charlie sighed. There was no doubt that the underwear was extremely sexy, and would increase the pulse rate of any red-blooded man who saw her in it. But she knew that no man would see it. For all the sex she was likely to have that night she may as well be wearing woolly combinations.

On top of the chest was a photograph in a frame, and she picked it up and examined it. It showed her with a handsome man, the pair of them smartly dressed, with flakes of confetti still sticking to their shoulders. She had married Jon two years before, when she was seventeen and he was twenty-four. Then he had seemed a fascinating and glamorous man, working as an engineer on the oil rigs off the Gulf of Mexico and bringing in a considerable salary. There had been a degree of mystery about him, and she had enjoyed the lifestyle they led, out every night at parties and discos and holidaying in the Caribbean and Mediterranean.

It hadn't been long, however, before the novelty had begun to wear off. The trouble with Jon's job was that it meant him being away for months at a time. Charlie had rapidly become bored with her solitary existence.

What had surprised her, though, was how much she missed the sex. When she had married Jon she had been a virgin, and it was he that had introduced her to the joy of carnal desires, releasing a passion that she had not realised existed in her. No sooner had he awakened her body to these pleasures, however, than he had begun to leave her for long periods. At first it hadn't seemed too bad, but she soon realised that her own cravings were far greater than those of a normal woman. Night after night she had lain in bed, the heat between her thighs preventing sleep, her mind populated by images of naked men, their rampant penises filling her. When she had managed to sleep, her dreams were filled with erotic fantasies, in which she was forced to walk naked amongst groups of fully-clothed men who would grab and fondle her body, pinning her down and publicly fucking her whilst their companions watched, awaiting their turn. Charlie would wake from these dreams in a state of agitation, her body on fire with desire, and would lie masturbating in the darkness, longing for the feel of Jon's big cock inside her.

After two years, her desires had not changed. Simply the realisation that, as her current situation continued, those desires could be no more than dreams.

Now, here in the cab with Marie, Charlie's thoughts returned once more to the subject of her husband. For a while now, she had been preoccupied by another photograph that stood beside that of her wedding day. It depicted a much more youthful Jon, sitting astride a powerful motorcycle, dressed in brightly coloured leathers. Charlie knew that he had once been a member of a biker gang, and that he had been carefree and lawless then. At the time she had married him she had been happy that that life was now part of her past.

Recently, however, she had realised that an aspect of Jon's character had been inextricably linked with the gang, and that his experiences with them had been extremely important to him. It had soon begun to occur to her that maybe reuniting him with the machine might rekindle his fire for her and recapture some of their earlier lust. She knew the bike was still at the back of the garage. Every time he came home he would take it out and polish it, starting the engine and listening carefully to its note. The leathers were still there too, hanging in the back of the wardrobe encased in polythene. She sometimes took them out and looked at them, wondering what Jon had been like then. It was a phase in his life that he seldom spoke of now, though she knew he had been happy.

For some time now Charlie had suspected that there was another woman, though she had no firm proof. It was her intuition that told her that Jon wasn't being completely frank with her. He would be evasive when she asked him what he had been doing, giving vague replies, and he was often not in when she rang his hotel in the evenings. There were other things, too. When he came home, his case would be neatly packed, the shirts carefully folded, revealing a feminine touch. Occasionally she would catch a whiff of perfume on the clothes he brought back for washing, and once she had discovered a smear of lipstick on one of his shirts. Jon was seven years older than her, and she knew he had had a number of lovers before meeting her. Now it looked as though he had returned to his old ways, much to her frustration.

The club was crowded and noisy. By the time she had had a couple of drinks Charlie was feeling much better. They had been befriended by a pair of personable lads, who were telling the most outrageous jokes, having both girls in fits of laughter. It was just as she remembered the days when she and Jon had been courting

As the evening wore on, the couples began to pair off, Marie dancing with the taller of the two, a dark-haired lad called Tom, whilst Charlie was left chatting with his friend Al. She was anxious not to be too forward with the young man, but Al proved an attentive companion, ensuring that her drink was regularly refilled and keeping her amused. Quite soon she found herself warming to him.

After a while the smoke and noise of the club began to give Charlie a headache, and when Al suggested they go outside for a while she was quite amenable to the idea.

They stepped out into a lovely night, the full moon drifting in and out of the clouds, the air both warm and fresh. Charlie breathed it in gratefully. She was feeling a little drunk and was glad of the chance to clear her head. Beside the club was a small park and that was where they headed. Soon they were strolling through it hand in hand. For a while, Charlie found herself forgetting her problems, happy to walk through this peaceful night with an attractive partner, suddenly feeling like a teenager again.

When Al turned to kiss her it seemed the most natural thing in the world, and Charlie responded eagerly, allowing him to snake his tongue into her mouth. Even when he pushed her off the path and up against a tree, pressing his body against hers, she made no complaint, and the sensation of his fingers running down her back and squeezing the soft globes of her backside brought no more than sighs of pleasure from the frustrated girl.

In her heart she knew she was letting him go too far, and that trouble would ensue. Yet still she didn't stop him as she felt his hand move higher, gliding over her flank and up to cup her breast, kneading her soft mammaries through her dress. When he wormed his fingers down her front and closed them about the warm flesh beneath, making her nipple harden she sighed with pleasure at his touch.

The two of them remained as they were for some time, their lips locked together whilst he continued to explore the softness of her breasts. Then she felt his other hand slide down her body and onto her thigh, creeping beneath the hem of her dress and up to her crotch, and she realised what was happening.

"No!"

She pulled back from his embrace, pushing his hands away from her as she did so.

"Come on, babe," he said. "You know you want it."

"No!" she said again, pulling away from him.

"What's the problem?" he asked.

"I'm married."

"Then why the hell isn't he the one out here with you?"

"He's away."

9

"Well that's all right then." He moved close to her once more. "What the eye doesn't see..."

"No!" This time she was more violent as she shoved him away.

"Shit darling, I'm not going to hurt you. I just wanna fuck. Don't you?"

"No."

But it wasn't true. She did want to fuck. She wanted to badly. Her sex was running with lubrication and her whole body was trembling with desire. Yet she couldn't bring herself to submit. Something deep inside her told her she must remain faithful to Jon, even though she was certain that he was not faithful to her.

"Look darling, do you want to have some fun or not?" His voice was sounding impatient now. "There's plenty more babes in there."

"Go and find one then," she said defiantly.

"Suit yourself, bloody prick teaser," he snarled. And with that he turned on his heel and strode back toward the nightclub.

Charlie watched him go, cursing the circumstances of their parting. She had really liked him, and would have enjoyed having sex with him. For a second she was tempted to call him back, but she didn't.

She felt lousy. To have been taken so high, then to drop so suddenly was awful. She straightened her dress, running her fingers over the gusset of her panties and feeling the wetness there. God, she needed fucking! She only hoped Jon would be in an amorous mood when he returned.

Charlie didn't want to go back into the club just yet. Apart from anything else, she feared that she would see Al making another conquest. She decided to walk right round the park, in the hope that her ardour would have cooled down by the time she reached the gate once more. She set off at a slow pace, her head down.

She had been walking for about ten minutes when she heard the sound. She froze in her tracks, listening hard. There was somebody whispering close by. The voices seemed to be coming from amongst the trees, about ten yards off the track. Charlie stopped and strained her ears. Then she heard a giggle, followed by the rustle of clothing.

Intrigued, she crept off the track toward the spot from which the sounds were coming. As she came closer she was just able to discern two figures standing close to a tree. She froze, straining her eyes to make out what was going on.

At that very moment the clouds parted and the moon shone through. At once Charlie crouched down behind a bush, peering over the top. Then she gave a sharp intake of breath.

It was Marie.

She was standing with her back against the wall, clad in only bra and panties, her dress lying discarded beside her. Tom was standing in front of her, his body pressed against her, his mouth over hers. Marie had her arms up about his neck pulling him down to her. As Charlie watched he reached behind her and unhooked the catch on her bra. He stepped back slightly, pulling it down and revealing the pale globes of her breasts. They were big, larger than Charlie's, the nipples puckered and brown. He took one into his palm at once, lowering his head and closing his lips over the nipple.

"Mmmm. Oh shit that's good," murmured Marie as he sucked at her, his other hand rubbing and kneading her heavy globes. Charlie stayed still and quiet, a mixture of envy and arousal filling her as she watched her friend's seduction. She thought once more of Al, and the fact that she too could have been enjoying the caresses of a randy young man, and she cursed her ill luck.

All of a sudden, Tom dropped to his knees and his hands went to the waistband of Marie's panties. In a moment he had slid them down her thighs and off, leaving her totally naked. Charlie was transfixed, eyeing her friend's body with fascination. It was beautifully shaped, the full breasts, slim waist and rounded hips in perfect proportion. The dark triangle of pubic hair drawing attention to her slit which, as she stood with her legs parted, was clearly visible even in the restricted light of the moon.

Marie seemed quite unworried about her nakedness in so public a spot, the expression on her face one of sheer pleasure as Tom worked his hands up her thighs and sought out her sex.

"Ah!"

Marie gave an audible cry as Tom's fingers slid into her slit. She spread her legs wider, her back pressed against the tree, her hips thrust forward. Charlie found her hand sliding down to her own crotch as she watched him work her, his fingers making a wet sound as they slid in and out of her love hole. The craving inside her was growing with every second, and her envy knew no bounds.

"Oh Christ Tom, let's fuck," Marie said suddenly. "I can't wait any longer."

Even as she spoke, she pulled him to his feet and her hands went to his trousers, fumbling with the fastener and sliding down his zip. His cock sprang free from his pants almost at once, jutting up pale and thick from his groin.

Charlie watched, licking her lips as she saw the great spear of flesh that was about to penetrate her friend. Her hand was up her skirt now, rubbing back and forth over the smooth wet nylon of her panties. This time it was Marie's turn to drop to her knees as she took Tom's cock in her hand and began to masturbate him, whilst her mouth closed over the bulbous end of his tool.

She sucked hard, the slurping sounds clearly audible to Charlie. Marie's head was moving back and forth, her hair almost covering her face as she concentrated on his erection. Charlie wished desperately that her own mouth was filled in a similar manner, or, even better, her vagina and she slid her hand down inside her panties, masturbating in earnest now.

Marie allowed Tom's cock to slip from between her lips. Then, glancing up at him, she lay back on the grass and, raising her knees, spread her legs wide.

"Come on Tom," she said. "I really need it now."

Charlie strained forward to watch as Tom lowered himself over her friend's prostrate body. She saw Marie reach down and take hold of his cock, guiding it towards her open slit. Then it was lost from view as he buried it inside her.

He started to fuck her, his white backside pumping up and down. Marie's moans were of pure ecstasy, and Charlie felt a pang of jealousy as she imagined the sensation of Tom's rampant tool inside her. She felt her own love bud, now hard as a nut as her fingers rubbed over it, the wetness leaking out onto her thighs. She reached into her bra, taking her protruding nipples between finger and thumb and teasing them into erectness.

She couldn't take her eyes off the couple, her ears filled with their lovemaking, her mind obsessed with the sensations her friend must be feeling. She began to make mewing sounds, her mouth clamped shut to try and reduce the noise as she frigged herself hard.

Tom and Marie came simultaneously, the noise they made enough to rouse half the neighbourhood as their climaxes overcame them. Charlie was glad of the sound, since it drowned that of her own orgasm as she finally reached her peak, her fingers bringing her off in a way that was both relieving and frustrating as she realised how more satisfying was Marie's.

She watched until Tom's behind had ceased moving, and he had collapsed over her friend. Then, smoothing down her dress, she stole away, her face crimson with guilt.

Chapter 2

Charlie paced up and down her living room in an agitated manner, quite unable to relax, her mind buzzing with thoughts. Ever since she had witnessed the seduction of her friend on the previous night she had found herself unable to think of anything else, her mind obsessed with the image of Marie being fucked. It seemed to her the most erotic thing she had ever seen. Somehow the fact that they had done it in public made it even more exciting, as if the danger of being seen had added to the thrill. Charlie had masturbated twice after she had arrived home, yet had woken as aroused as ever, her consciousness dominated by the image of the couple.

For the tenth time she consulted her calendar. It was two days before Jon was due back. Two days of further enforced abstinence. And even when he returned she couldn't be sure of having her desires satisfied. He was probably screwing his other woman right now. Why should he bother with Charlie?

She thought of Jon in bed with his mistress, and was suddenly seized with anger. If he could do it, why the hell couldn't she? Why was it that her conscience had prevented her fucking with Al when she had wanted to so badly? It simply wasn't fair.

All at once she badly wanted revenge. To get her own back on him for his infidelity. If only there were something she could do to show her own defiance. Perhaps she should go back to the nightclub and pick up a man, and this time really let him have his way with her?

She sighed. That wasn't the answer, and she knew it. It would simply make her as bad as him, and leave her feeling guilty.

She wandered up to her bedroom. Maybe she would feel better if she frigged herself again, though she doubted it. She picked up the wedding photo, studying his face and trying to recapture the pleasure of their early days together. But all she could feel was anger. Then her gaze fell on the picture of him astride his motorcycle.

Charlie caught her breath. The motorcycle! His most treasured possession, possibly even more so than her. What would he think if she were to take it out? To run it into town and risk it being damaged, or even stolen? She knew he would be shocked beyond belief. In fact, in a way, he would be more put out at the idea of her riding his precious bike than if he was to find she had been unfaithful to him.

Charlie's eyes gleamed. It was a great idea. After all she knew how to ride a motorcycle. One of her boyfriends at school had had a small machine and had taught her. Whilst his bike was not exactly on a par with Jon's gleaming machine, the principle must be the same. It was simply a matter of balance.

Then another thought struck her. His leathers! That prized motorcycling outfit that he coveted so much. What would he think if she went out in that? On a sudden impulse she pulled open the wardrobe door and dragged out the suit, pulling off the protective cover. She laid it on the bed and stood back, studying it.

It was black all over, dotted with gleaming silver studs. On the back was the image of a white ghost with wide, staring eyes, the word 'SPIRITS' picked out in capitals beneath. She took the leather in her hands, rubbing it between her fingers. It was of the finest quality, and a shiver ran through her as she imagined it caressing her bare skin.

All at once her mind was made up. She would do it. She would take his precious machine out on the road. And what was more, she would wear his leathers. They were a little bit large for her, but that would not be a problem. At once she started to pull off her blouse and jeans.

Stripped to her panties she began to rummage in her drawer for something to wear under the suit. She pulled out a pair of shorts and a T-shirt, then hesitated. Why bother to wear anything underneath? Why not enjoy the sensation of the leather against her bare flesh? The idea sent a shiver of excitement through her, and she tossed the garments back in the drawer. Then she picked up the biker's suit.

The soft leather felt wonderful against her skin, her nipples hardening at once as she zipped it up to her neck. Her panties were of a thin silk material, so that it was almost as if, even at her crotch, the suit was pressed against her bare flesh. The smell of the leather, too, added to the sensation and she found herself quite turned on as she fastened the collar and cuffs.

She stopped in front of the mirror. The suit was cut too loose to show off her figure. In fact it was hard to determine her sex, since the chest of the leathers disguised the fullness of her breasts. This was fine by her, though. A woman on a motorcycle would be too conspicuous. With her hair tucked inside her helmet, though, she might well pass for a man.

She took the helmet from the closet, then made her way downstairs and out of the house. She pulled open the garage door. There, parked against the wall, was the bike. Charlie took hold of the plastic cover draped over it and dragged it off. Then she paused, staring at the machine.

It was a large and powerful bike, all gleaming chrome, with

exhaust pipes that curled out from the cylinders and swept upwards at the back. The handlebars were short and low, the tank
wide. She straddled the seat, surprised at the size of the machine. Her feet barely touched the ground, and she knew she
would have to be careful to keep it upright once it was off the
stand. She gathered her hair, twisting it into a makeshift bun,
then pulled on the helmet, fastening it at her neck. She was ready.

She took the ignition key from her pocket and placed it in
the lock, then she eased the kick start out and pressed down on
it with her foot. At first it didn't move, and she was obliged to
stand and put all her weight on it to turn the engine.

One kick, two, and then the engine roared into life, the sound
almost deafening in the small garage. She revved it a couple of
times, then, with a mighty effort, lifted the bike off its stand.
She pressed down on the gear pedal and eased out the clutch.
All at once she was moving, steering carefully out of the garage
and down the drive.

She swung out onto the road and opened the throttle. With a
roar the machine shot forward, and it was all she could do to
keep hold of the handlebars as the tyres bit into the road surface.
She eased off at once, then changed up a gear.

Charlie took the bike round all the side roads she knew,
accustomising herself to it. It was much larger and more powerful than she had expected, but the controls were light and before
long her confidence returned. Soon she felt sure enough to pull
out onto the main road and open the throttle, thrilling at the way
it performed.

She headed off up the highway, the speedo reading a steady
eighty miles an hour. To Charlie it felt wonderful, the wind rushing past her face, the throb of the powerful machine between her
legs giving her a sensation that was almost sexual. For a while
she was able to forget her troubles, zooming along the highway,
weaving around the cars and then opening her throttle so that
they were left far behind.

She wasn't sure how far she had gone, ten miles, maybe fifteen, when she spotted the small cafe beside the road. Shifting
down through the gears, she pulled off into the car park. She

stopped by the door, kicking down the side-stand and killing the motor, then she climbed off. She was surprised to find herself almost trembling with excitement and exhilaration, and her hands shook as she undid the strap on her helmet.

She strode into the cafe, letting her hair fall down, aware of the eyes that stared at the unusual sight of the young girl in bikers' leathers. The cafe was scruffy. Most of the clients were truckers and they nudged one another and grinned at her as she made her way to the bar. They were rough-looking and unshaven, and Charlie found herself unexpectedly turned on by their attention. She wondered what they would say if they knew she was nearly naked under the leather suit.

She drank her coffee sitting in a corner of the cafe. It was bitter and strong, but it tasted good to her as she felt her heartbeat gradually return to normal after the excitement of the ride. She stayed no more than ten minutes, then donned her helmet and strode back out to the bike.

This time it started first kick, and she revved high as she swung out of the cafe car park and back onto the open road, gunning the engine as she roared away.

So intent had she been on controlling the machine in front of all the truckers, Charlie hadn't noticed the other two motorcycles parked in a lay-by opposite the cafe. Nor had she seen the two men sitting astride them. Had she done so she might have been struck by the similarity of their leathers to her own, even down to the depiction of a ghost and the word 'SPIRITS' written across their backs. They had noticed her, though, and she was barely round the next bend before they had kicked their engines into life and, swinging their machines in a U-turn across the road, set off in pursuit of her.

Chapter 3

Charlie felt good, sitting astride the powerful motorcycle as it roared up the highway. There was something intensely sexual about the heavy machine that throbbed between her legs and the feel of the leather against her bare skin. She smiled to herself as she twisted the throttle, passing a line of cars and just dodging back onto her own side of the road in time to avoid an oncoming juggernaut. This was a freedom she had never imagined, and suddenly she felt her own woman for once, able to go where she wanted and liberated from the ties of being wife and housewife.

She spotted a small side road leading off the highway and took it, cutting across the front of a small car that hooted angrily at her as she zoomed away. The road was quiet and winding and she leaned the bike low into the corners, speeding along through the countryside.

She had been going for more than a mile before a flash of sunlight in her mirrors revealed the two bikers on her tail. At first she thought nothing of it, simply winding on more power as she swept through the bends. Then she realised that they were catching her, and the first inklings of doubt entered her mind.

She tried again to go faster, but they too increased their speed. Charlie was riding to the limit of her ability now, leaning dangerously low into the corners, her footrests scraping the road, yet still the other machines seemed to be closing on her.

She still had a good few hundred yards on them, and she resolved to make use of the lead, searching for somewhere she might be able to pull over and conceal herself whilst they passed. Up ahead she spotted an open gate that led into a wood and, waiting until the last moment, she braked heavily.

The machine snaked from side to side as she hung on grimly to the handlebars. She leaned over hard and headed the bike up the track, her rear tyre skidding sideways on the gravel. It was a narrow, bumpy path, the trees leaning close on either side, and it was all she could do to keep control. Once again she found herself struggling with the weight of the machine, and when the path took a right angle bend Charlie just couldn't hold it, sprawling onto the grass as the bike slid between the trees.

The leathers, her helmet and the softness of the grass protected her from any injury, and she sprang to her feet at once, rushing across to where the bike lay and heaving it up onto its wheels. A quick inspection revealed no damage apart from a few grass stains on the fairing, and she gave a sigh of relief. Then she heard the roar of powerful engines and realised with a shock that she hadn't shaken off her pursuers and that they were, even now, heading up the path behind her.

She straddled the bike at once and kicked frantically at the kick-start. But the accident must have flooded the engine, and it refused to start.

The two bikers came into sight at the far end of the track. She knew that they had spotted her at once, and she heard them throttle back as they closed in and came to a halt on either side of where she sat, still trying vainly to start her machine. Then a hand reached across and, before she could stop him, the man had snatched her key from the ignition.

"Give me that," she exclaimed, grabbing at it, but he was too quick for her, and she found herself trapped between them.

"Put the bike on its stand and get off," said the man on her right.

Charlie had no choice. Reluctantly she kicked down the stand and climbed from the machine. They were in a small wooded glade some distance from the road, and there was nobody around.

The biker took off his helmet. He had long dark hair which framed a handsome face, his chin covered with stubble, his eyes a piercing blue.

"What the hell are you doing riding around in our colours?" he demanded.

"Colours?"

"Zep's talking about the leathers," said the second man, who had also removed his helmet, revealing a shock of fair hair and a thick beard. "They're in our colours. That's our logo on the back. You're no Spirit."

"I borrowed them."

The man called Zep's eyes narrowed. "Take your helmet off," he ordered.

Charlie hesitated. Then she reached up and undid the strap at her neck. She pulled off the helmet, shaking her hair down.

"Shit... it's a fucking babe!"

For a moment she thought that the revelation of her sex would save her. However, it wasn't to be. In a very short time the men's initial surprise evaporated and she felt the hostility return.

"Babe or not," said the one called Zep, "you're not entitled to wear those colours."

"What's so important about them?" she asked.

"Everything," rejoined the biker. "You gotta serve an apprenticeship with the Spirits before you can wear those. Even more so if you're a babe. We make it pretty tough for a girl to be entitled to wear our colours. Most chicken out on the first day."

"So you're breaking the rules, baby," said his companion. "And we've got ways of dealing with anyone who does that."

Charlie took a step backwards. This whole thing was rather getting out of control. "What are you going to do?" she asked, trying to keep the tremor from her voice.

"First of all, get those leathers off."

"I can't."

The biker moved closer to her. "You've got no choice," he said. "The longer you stand there wearing them, the madder it makes me and Lou here. And we're not nice people when we get mad."

"But I..."

The biker called Lou reached into his pocket and pulled out a motorcycle chain.

"The colours," said Zep quietly.

Charlie looked from one of the men to the other, then back again. Their faces were grim. There was no doubt about it, they meant business. Slowly she crouched down and began unlacing her boots. She slipped them off. The grass felt cool and soft against her bare feet. Then, turning to face away from the men, she reached for the zip at her neck and pulled it all the way down. She hesitated for a second, then shrugged the suit off her shoulders, allowing it to fall to the ground. She stepped out of it and glanced down at herself. Her breasts jutted prominently forward, the brown nipples hard from the constant chafing against the leather. The panties were tiny and inadequate, a tuft of dark pubic hair visible above the low waistband. She hugged an arm across her chest and then, blushing brightly, turned to face the men again.

Zep gave a low whistle. "Not exactly dressed for the occasion, were you darling?"

"I need some clothes," she replied.

"I can see that. You should have thought about that before you started riding round in Spirit colours. Give them to me."

Covering her breasts as best she could, Charlie crouched down and picked up the leathers. She handed them to the biker.

"Right," he said. "We're gonna cut these up, then we're going to trash the bike."

"No!" exclaimed Charlie in alarm. "You mustn't do that."

"We've got to. We swear an oath when we join the club that if we find anyone wearing our colours when they're not entitled, their bike and their leathers are history. It's only because you're a chick that we're not going to smash your teeth as well."

"But you mustn't destroy them, they're not mine. They're my husband's."

"Husband eh? What does he think to you riding round the countryside like that?"

"He doesn't know. He's away. He used to be a Spirit years ago. I just borrowed his bike. He'll kill me if he finds out. He's in Mexico. He works there. But he'll be back on the weekend."

Zep eyed her scantily clad figure. "A guy shouldn't go away and leave a gorgeous chick like you on her own," he said. "Still, there's nothing else for it. Only a Spirit is entitled to wear those colours and you're not one. We've got to trash the bike."

The two men stepped towards the gleaming machine, but Charlie hurled herself in front of it, spreading her arms out in a protective gesture that she knew left her lovely breasts uncovered before their hungry gazes.

"No!" she said again. "You can't."

Zep stopped, an exasperated look on his face.

"Listen," he said, "this is nothing personal darling. It's just something we've got to do. It's the rules. Now don't make us have to hurt you."

"There must be some other way."

"There isn't. Only Spirits can wear those leathers."

"What if I became a Spirit?"

Zep laughed. "You?"

"Why not?"

"You couldn't become a Spirit. There's an apprenticeship. It takes months. What about your husband?"

"He goes away for months at a time. He need not know. Let me become a Spirit."

"No way."

"Please. I beg of you. There must be a way. Please at least let me become an apprentice." She gazed into his eyes, a look of desperation on her face.

"Listen darling," said Zep. "You don't know what an apprenticeship is like. You're treated bad as a slave. And you have to do as you're told. No matter what it is."

"Oh."

Charlie's heart sank. She couldn't possibly contemplate that. She was in real trouble now. What on earth was she to do?

All at once she noticed that the two men had stepped back and, turning away from her, had begun talking quietly to one another. She felt a chill as she realised what was happening. She had begged them to let her join, and now they were taking her pleas seriously. But there was no way she could possibly behave in the way they had suggested, could she?

Zep turned back to her. "All right," he said, grinning. "We've decided. From now on you're an apprentice Spirit, with all that that entails."

Charlie's eyes widened. "No!" she said in alarm. "I can't."

"Sure you can. By the look of you you're finding the idea pretty exciting."

Charlie dropped her eyes, and saw with surprise that her nipples were still hard. It couldn't be the leather any more, surely? With a shock she suddenly realised that the situation was turning her on, and that Zep's words were exciting her. She felt herself redden as she realised how obvious this must be to the men.

"But I..."

"Look, bitch, you're in. Whatever you do we're gonna find

where you live and come for you. Now, do you want the bike trashed as well? 'Cause that's what we'll do if you don't start obeying orders."

Charlie was trapped and she knew it.

"All right" she said in not more than a whisper. "But if I agree to become an apprentice, will you leave me alone to re-turn the bike and leathers?"

"How long do you need?"

"I... I could join you when my husband goes away. In a week."

Charlie could scarcely believe she was saying what she was. But she knew now that she had no choice, and that her destiny was in the hands of these two.

Zep cocked his head on one side.

"How do we know you're serious?"

"I'm serious."

"You accept that you're an apprentice, right?"

"Yes."

"And you'll obey our orders?"

She lowered her eyes again. "Yes."

He narrowed his eyes. "All right," he said. "Show us your snatch."

"My what?"

"Your cunt. Take off your knickers and give us a look."

"What? I can't! Not here."

Lou sneered. "I think this one could do with a little training in how to obey her superiors, Zep."

"Let's see how she reacts to seeing those leathers converted into a two-piece."

"No!" Charlie glanced about herself nervously. "What if someone came along and I had nothing on?"

"Then they get lucky and see your tits and cunt," said Zep. "Listen baby, you've got five seconds to get your knickers off, or we'll see to it that someone does see you. Fancy being dropped off outside that diner starkers?"

"What?"

"You'd better believe we'd do it."

"But you can't."

23

"Then flash your fucking cunt!"

Charlie stared from one to the other of them. Her heart was hammering in her chest. To ask her to remove her panties was an outrageous suggestion, particularly coming from a stranger. But they were obviously serious.

All at once a shiver of excitement ran through her as she realised how aroused she was becoming at the thought of showing her naked body to the bikers. It was opening a door on her an aspect of her sexuality which she had always tried to keep firmly closed - the desire to exhibit her body. Now the memory of that desire came back to her in a rush as she recognised that some perverse alter ego within her wanted to bare all before the bikers.

Trembling she let her hand drop to her panties.

She hesitated for a second, staring at the pair. Her thumbs hooked through the waistband. Then she slid them down her thighs and off over her feet. She immediately raised the tiny wisp of material to cover her sex.

"Give them to me."

"Please?" she whimpered.

"Give them to me!"

Slowly, reluctantly, she raised her hand, exposing the dark bush of her pubic hair to the two bikers.

Zep took the panties from her and tossed them carelessly aside.

"Now show us!"

"I've done what you asked."

"Show us the lot!"

Charlie gave a small cry of despair.

"Must I?"

"Spread them!"

Charlie let her eyes drop. Then she leant slowly back against the bike and spread her legs, aware that this would reveal the pink gash between her thighs.

"That good enough for you?"

"Just fine," grinned Lou. "Now, smile!"

By the time Charlie realised he had a camera in his hand it

was too late. The shutter clicked and he had captured the image of her, her legs spread, her open sex in clear view of the lens.

"No!" she cried. But already he was taking another, and as she lunged at the camera Zep caught her, pinning her arms back whilst Lou continued to snap photos of her naked form.

Charlie struggled as hard as she was able, but the biker was too strong for her. She was devastated. To think that this man would have pictures of her in the nude. Pictures he could, and probably would, show to his friends.

"That's not fair!" she shouted as he slipped the camera back into his pocket.

"Course it is," said Zep, releasing her arms and pushing her back against the bike again. "Now get those legs open."

For a moment a flash of defiance showed in Charlie's eyes. Then she realised the futility of it and slowly planted her legs apart once again.

Zep grinned. "All right," he said. "When does your husband go away again?"

"A week on Sunday."

I'll pick you up on the Sunday night. You'll have to stay with us, we're going on the road."

"On the road?"

"Yeah, on the road. You got that?"

She gave a sigh of resignation. "I'll be there," she whispered.

"And you realise you'll be expected to do as you're told?"

"I did just now, didn't I?"

"There'll be guys wanting to go further than that, though."

"You mean..."

"Fuck you is what I mean."

"F-fuck me?" Charlie could barely believe what he had said, but she managed to meet Zep's eye as he stared at her.

"That's it. Like us, right now."

"What?"

"But only if you ask nicely."

"But you can't. Not here."

Zep moved closer, towering over her. Then he took hold of her chin, pulling her face round so that her eyes met his.

25

"Listen girlie," he growled. "Stop telling me what I can and can't do. Now stand perfectly still whilst I get a feel of those tits of yours."

Charlie tried to draw back, but the bike was behind her and there was nowhere to go. Her instincts told her to fight him off, or at least to cover herself, but she knew that would make things worse, so she stood as still as she was able.

A broad grin on his face, Zep reached a hand out and ran it over her breast, his fingers kneading the flesh roughly, tweaking her solid nipples so that she gave a little squeak of pain.

"You like it really though, honey don't you?" he said.

Charlie didn't answer, but her eyes told all. Somehow his rough treatment was kindling a fire inside her like she hadn't felt for years and a warm feeling was beginning to envelop her belly as he mauled at her.

"Check out her crotch!" laughed Lou.

Once again Charlie fought her instincts and didn't move, her hands still placed on the bike behind her. Zep slid his hand lower, his eyes still fixed on hers. For Charlie the tension was electric, her nudity and the sensation of his hands on her bare flesh sending spasms of passion through her, so that she knew her sex lips were wet with her juices.

"Oh!"

The exclamation escaped her lips as she felt his rough fingers slide down her slit, seeking out the hard nut of her clitoris and rubbing it hard. This time her legs almost gave way beneath her as a surge of arousal shook her small body and, quite against her will, she found herself pressing her hips forward against his hand.

"Shit," he said. "Bitch is wet as hell."

"Probably wants fucking."

"Only if she asks nicely."

"What about it girlie?" said Zep. "You gonna ask? We never fuck a chick unless she asks nicely."

Charlie stared from one to another, her hips still writhing lewdly as he fingered her. They were clearly going to make this whole thing as humiliating as possible.

"Well?" said Zep. He pulled out his fingers and stood back, staring into her eyes.

Charlie bit her lip.

"Fuck me," she said quietly.

"Pardon?"

"Fuck me," she said again, her face crimson.

Zep shook his head. "You'll have to do better than that. Show me you really want it. Ask me properly."

"But I..."

"Make me want to fuck you darling," he said slowly.

Charlie knew what he meant. It was like a game Jon had liked her to play to get him horny. She took a deep breath, then fell into her act, looking down at her lovely, naked body, then up into the eyes of the two bikers.

"Why don't you fuck me?" she said. "Both of you? I really want it."

Then, her heart drumming hard, she slid a finger down between her legs, teasing out her hard little love bud. "Feel how wet I am."

Charlie could barely believe what she was doing. Only the night before she had turned a man down through some kind of sense of fidelity to Jon, yet here she was, naked and abandoned with two strangers and acting as if she was dying to feel their cocks in her. And as she masturbated she knew that she really did want them. She wondered what it was that had changed the way she was thinking. It must be the coercion that had done it, the need to gamble something to save his precious motorcycle. Somehow it was as if it was for his sake that she was doing this, and that made it okay. This time, when Zep stepped forward, brushing her hand aside and reaching for her crotch there was no resistance. Instead she moaned and thrust her hips forward against his hand.

"That's better," he said

Then she felt her own hand grabbed and she turned as Lou placed it on his crotch. He felt hard down there, and suddenly she didn't need to pretend to be a slut any more. She closed her fingers about the bulge, rubbing it hard.

27

"Suck him," ordered Zep. He took her shoulders and pressed her down to her knees.

Charlie was on a kind of autopilot now, totally focused on giving the two men pleasure, her own modesty and recalcitrance suspended, giving herself like she knew a whore must do to a customer. She turned to Lou, taking hold of his thighs and pulling him closer to him, so that the rough denim of his jeans rubbed against her nipples, stimulating them still further. She reached for his fly, pulling down his zip and delving inside. His cock was trapped in his briefs, and she grabbed the waistband and pulled them down. At once it sprang to attention, standing proud from his groin, thick and pink.

She wrapped her fingers about his shaft, feeling it twitch as the blood coursed through the thick, blue vein that ran up its length. She began to work her hand back and forth, and was rewarded by a gasp from the Biker as she did so. She drew back the skin and examined his glans. It was large, deep purple in colour, and it glistened with his secretions. Suddenly she felt an overwhelming desire to taste him.

She moved her head forward, then opened her mouth and closed her lips over the end. He smelt and tasted of arousal, and a shiver ran through her as she sucked hard at him, her head moving back and forth as she did so. She reached into his jeans and cupped his balls. They were puckered and tight, as if poised to deliver their contents into her mouth at any moment.

Suddenly Charlie felt her thighs grasped and pulled backwards. Then a hand came between her legs from behind, making her give a muffled gasp as strong fingers closed over her sex.

"Spread your legs, slut," ordered Zep.

Charlie obeyed at once, pressing her behind backwards and presenting what she knew to be perfect access to her open love hole.

Zep continued to finger her lovely young frame as she ground her hips down on his hand, whilst still fellating Lou. Charlie knew her behaviour was totally wanton, but she was beyond caring now, and when she felt something thick and hot press against the flesh of her backside, then work down the crack, she took it in her stride. She wanted to turn round and see the rock-hard cock that was manoeuvring its way toward her gaping cunt, but Lou had taken hold of her head and was forcing his erection further down her throat as the urgency in him increased.

Zep slipped his cock over the tight star of Charlie's anus, and lower still as she thrust backwards. He was at the very entrance to her love hole now, and pressing hard. She felt the flesh resist momentarily, then he was inside her.

"Mmmf!"

Once again the mouthful of thick flesh muffled Charlie's exclamation as she felt Zep's cock slide into her, forcing the walls of her sex apart. He rammed his stiff rod home with a series of short jabs that left the naked girl breathless, continuing to press into her until she felt sure she could take no more. Her limited experience of men had not prepared her for a weapon as large as Zep's, and she couldn't believe the way it filled her so thoroughly, pressing home until at last she felt his wiry pubic hair hard against the flesh of her backside.

He began to fuck her, thrusting his hips forward so violently that Charlie had to cling to Lou's legs to keep her balance. It was the most extraordinary experience she could imagine, his hefty truncheon pumping back and forth inside her whilst Lou maintained a similar onslaught from in front, his balls slapping against her chin, the saliva running down her neck and onto her breasts as she sucked and wanked him.

Charlie's breasts shook back and forth as the bikers pounded into her small, naked frame. Suddenly she felt free from all constraints, able at last to give herself totally without guilt, her entire being consumed by lust as she felt her orgasm build.

Lou came first, a hoarse cry escaping his lips as the spunk gushed forth from his cock. Charlie gagged for a second, coughing out a gob of creamy semen that trickled down her chin and neck and onto her bare breasts. Then she closed her lips about his twitching erection once more, sucking hard and savouring the taste of his semen as she gulped it down. It was the first time a man had ever come in her mouth, and she slurped the hot, viscous fluid down with enthusiasm, determined to consume as much as she could.

At that moment there was a grunt from behind her, then Zep was coming too, his cock throbbing as spunk gushed into her vagina. Suddenly the wanton youngster could hold back no longer and she gave a groan as a shattering orgasm overcame her. Her hips pumped back and forth violently and uncontrollably as she felt her cunt filled with Zep's semen. It was as if she was coming for the first time, and she wanted to scream with elation as they shook her body with their thrusts.

The climax seemed to go on forever, both bikers continuing to ram their cocks into her until she almost collapsed with the shuddering pleasure that enveloped her.

At last the two men began to slow, the spurts that sprang from their cocks ebbing as they shot their loads. Charlie held her position, milking every last ounce from them, sucking and thrusting until there was no more to take. Then, as the two of them withdrew, she flopped down onto the ground, rolling onto her back and staring up at them, her lips, neck and breasts shiny with spunk, another white stream escaping from between her widely spread legs and trickling down her thighs.

Zep grinned at her as he tucked his cock back into his pants.

"Not a bad start," he said. "You might make a Spirit yet."

Chapter 4

Jon's visit was not a particularly auspicious occasion for either of them. He arrived morose and taciturn, and said little on that first night. His one attempt at lovemaking was a cursory affair, rolling over and taking her one morning, thrusting and grunting until he came, then flopping to one side and falling asleep once more, leaving Charlie frustrated and unfulfilled.

Now, more than ever, she was convinced he was having an affair. There were more lipstick stains on the collars of his shirts and she had found a packet of condoms at the bottom of his wash bag. Charlie was not able to conceive, having been sterilised some years before due to a medical condition, so there could be no other reason for him to have them.

The discovery made her angry at first, and she wanted to confront him, but then she thought of Zep and Lou, and what had happened that day in the wood, and she knew that she couldn't. She comforted herself with the knowledge that the week would pass quickly, and that she would soon be alone again.

Normally, after such a visit she would have been glad of her solitude, despite her sexual frustration, but this time things were different. She had made a promise to the bikers, and the time had come for her to honour it. Now, as the hour drew nearer, she paced up and down the carpet of her bedroom, her eyes constantly straying to the clock. She had never felt so nervous in her life. Were they really coming for her?

After returning from her encounter with the bikers she had persuaded herself that they wouldn't hold her to her promise - then the package had arrived.

It came early in the day, pushed through the letterbox whilst she was out seeing Jon off at the airport. When she opened it a small pair of shorts and a skimpy top had fallen out, along with a scrap of paper: 'Be ready at seven thirty. Wear these and nothing else. Z.'

She could scarcely believe it was really going to happen. That they actually wanted her to go through with her apprenticeship with the Spirits, the initiation and - everything.

She stared down at the shorts and top, which lay on the bed untouched. She was wearing only a short dressing gown, and had been meaning to get dressed. But somehow she couldn't bring herself to put on her clothes. It was as if she knew she should don the biker's garments.

The ringing of the doorbell made her jump. She froze where she was and silence descended, the only sound the pounding of her heart. Then it rang again. She tiptoed to the bedroom door and gazed down at the hallway. There, silhouetted in the frosted glass of the front door was the figure of a man.

The doorbell rang a third time. Then a voice called.

"Come on, let me in. I know you're in there."

"Go away. I'll call the police."

"Go ahead. I'm committing no crime."

"They'll make you go away."

"I'll go. Once I've told them about you."

"They won't believe you."

"They'll believe this."

There was a bang as the letterbox flap went and something dropped onto the doormat.

"Go ahead, pick it up."

Charlie crept nervously down the stairs. She crouched and picked up the object that lay by the door. Then she gave a cry of dismay.

It was a photograph of her, in full, clear colour. She was stark naked, leaning back against the motorcycle, her legs spread, an expression of unmistakable arousal on her face.

She had completely forgotten the photographs. Her heart sank as her eyes took in the image.

"Copies of that will be spread all around town by morning," he said. "Along with a full account of your behaviour in the woods."

"You can't."

"Oh yes I can. And I will unless you open this door."

"Go away."

"Suit yourself. I'll just drop a few copies through your neighbours' doors on my way out."

"No! Wait!" Charlie was trapped and she knew it. "I'll open the door then. But I'm not coming with you."

She went to the door and unlocked it, pushing it open. Zep stood there, grinning down at her.

"That's better," he said. "Not dressed yet?"

"I'm not coming."

He stepped inside, closing the door behind him.

"Oh you're coming all right. Now get changed."

"You can't make me."

"Oh can't I? Watch this."

Before she realised what was happening, he had taken hold of her dressing gown. In a single movement he tore it in two, throwing the halves to the ground. Charlie was completely taken by surprise, suddenly naked before him, clutching desperately at her private parts.

"Now get changed," he ordered.

"I won't."

"I've got plenty of ways to persuade you. Besides are you planning to stand around starkers?"

Charlie glanced down at her bare body. He was right, she had to put something on. With a sigh she turned and made her way up the stairs.

He followed her into her room and sat and watched as she struggled into the garments the bikers had sent. Charlie, her face red, avoided his gaze as she pulled them on.

She paused before the mirror to examine her appearance. The top was cut low across her breasts, the thinness of the material clearly showing the darkness of her nipples as they pressed against the garment, their shape perfectly outlined. Even to the most casual observer her lack of a bra would have been obvious. Beneath she wore a pair of tiny denim shorts, pulled so tight into her crotch that wisps of pubic hair were visible. The roughness of the material biting into her sex in a way that was uncomfortable and -.

She turned to face Zep, who eyed her up and down approvingly.

"Bring your passport and a toothbrush," he said. "You won't need anything else."

"I said I'm not coming."

He rose and took her by the arm, turning her toward the mirror again.

"You want to come, though, don't you?" he murmured.

"Of course not."

"Come on baby. You know how horny the whole idea makes you. Why not live a little? You won't get harmed. Hurt maybe, but maybe you'll enjoy even that."

"Would you really show the photos?"

"You bet your life. You agreed to become an apprentice, and that's not the kind of promise a girl goes back on."

"But these clothes. Couldn't I have some underwear?"

He grinned. "What do you think? Now, come on, baby. I'm in a hurry. Be downstairs in two minutes."

He went out and descended the stairs.

Charlie felt numb. Scarcely aware of what she was doing, she put her passport and toothpaste into a washing bag. Then she took a last glance at the image of the scantily clad girl who looked back at her from the mirror. This was it. Once she went downstairs there was no turning back... she picked up the small bag and set off for the front door, her heart pounding.

"You ready?"

"Ready as I'll ever be."

His bikc was parked in the road. He swung a leg over and pulled it upright. Then he kicked the engine into life. He gave a wave of his head, indicating that she was to climb on behind.

She wanted to ask if they shouldn't be wearing crash helmets, but decided against it. Instead she mounted the seat, wrapping her arms about his body and placing her feet on the footrests, He gunned the motor, then they were speeding off up the road.

Charlie held onto Zep, her breasts pressed into his back as he leaned the machine hard into the corners. The throb of the engine against her almost bare crotch felt wonderful, and at once she felt the juices flow inside her as she clung tight to the muscular young man in front.

They rode for about ten minutes, weaving through the streets of the town towards one of its less salubrious areas. Soon they were riding between dull terraced houses outside which stood rusting wrecks of cars. Then Zep turned down a side street and suddenly they were slowing.

They came to a stop outside what looked like an old church hall. All around were large, powerful bikes like Zep's. He killed the engine and kicked down the stand. Then they both climbed off.

"In there," he said, indicating the front door of the building.

"Where are we?"

"Headquarters. Stop asking questions. In fact don't speak

unless you're spoken to. And call me Sir."

She glanced at him, thinking for a moment that he must be joking, but his face was stern.

"Yes Sir," she said.

He pulled the door open and pushed her inside. She stood in the entrance staring about her.

The hall was quite large, with a stage at one end, at which sat four men, all clad in leathers identical to Zep's. On the floor were a number of tables surrounded by chairs, and here sat still more bikers. There were about thirty of them altogether, about five of whom were young women. The tables were strewn with beer bottles and ashtrays and there was a smell of smoke in the air. Charlie gazed about her, feeling suddenly very conspicuous in her skimpy outfit.

There was a hubbub of noise when she first entered, but this quickly died away as all eyes were turned in her direction. She felt her cheeks redden under their gazes, and was suddenly overcome by a desire to escape. But the presence of Zep close behind her told her that there was no chance.

Zep took her arm and led her forward between the tables. Still their occupants were silent as they eyed the nervous youngster. There was a flight of steps at the edge of the stage, and it was towards these that she found herself being led. She climbed them slowly, Zep close behind her. He led her to the table where the four men were sitting, bringing her to a halt just in front of them, so that she stood sideways on to the crowd below.

The man sitting furthest from her wore a silver star on his chest. There was an air of authority about him that convinced Charlie he must be the gang's leader. He had long, lank hair that hung down to his shoulders. His face was hard, the nose slightly crooked as if he had once been a boxer. He eyed her up and down, then turned to Zep.

"This is her, is it?"

"This is the one."

"And she wants to be an apprentice?"

"That's what she says."

"Give you any trouble?"

35

"Bitch tried to back out. But when she saw the pretty picture she changed her mind."

"Tried to back out eh?" He turned to her. "What's your name girl?"

"Charlie."

Whack! The man sitting closest to her suddenly pulled a thin horsewhip from his belt and dealt Charlie a stinging blow to her thigh, making her cry out with pain.

"Say Sir when you speak to Mamba," he ordered. "Show some respect for our leader."

Charlie reeled for a moment, shocked by this sudden unexpected show of violence, the tears rising in her eyes.

"Ch-Charlie Sir," she stammered.

"I don't know, Zep," said the man called Mamba. "D'you think she's tough enough? After all, one little stroke with the whip and the bitch is practically bawling. What'll she do when we give her ten? Or twenty?"

"Twenty?" gasped Charlie

"Apprentices have to be disciplined sometimes. Didn't Zep tell you that?"

"I... Yes, of course he did Sir." Charlie stared at the whip. Twenty strokes from that? She wasn't at all sure if she could take it.

"Well, I guess we'll find out soon enough. After all, you're already due a lashing for trying to back out tonight."

"What?" Charlie felt an odd feeling at the pit of her stomach on hearing the words.

"Ten strokes I think. On your behind."

"You can't," she said wide-eyed. "Not ten strokes."

"One more sound out of you, bitch, and I'll make it twenty."

Charlie opened her mouth to speak, then closed it again. She was totally flabbergasted. She watched as the man who had struck her picked up the weapon from the table. Ten strokes! Unconsciously she ran her hand over her behind. The denim wasn't going to provide much protection from the cruel looking whip. She turned to Zep, but he had retired to the corner of the stage and was watching with a blank expression.

The four men rose from the table and moved it back from the edge of the stage. Then the man with the whip beckoned to Charlie to step in front of it. He was a tall, muscular man, his hair cropped into a skinhead. He wore three rings in his ear, and another through his nose, and his neck bore a purple tattoo of a spider's web. On his chest was emblazoned the name 'Fredo'.

"You accept ten strokes?" he asked her.

Charlie hesitated.

"I..."

"Better accept," he said darkly.

Charlie's shoulders slumped. "Yes Sir." She whispered.

"Remove your shorts."

Charlie's eyes widened. Remove her shorts? In front of all these people? She glanced round at the grinning faces below her, then back to Fredo. He was standing, hands folded, a stony look on his face.

Charlie knew this was a turning point. To have to remove the shorts, to be forced to bare her cunt and backside to all these people, would be the most embarrassing and humiliating thing imaginable. Yet if she refused she knew they would force her. She must choose now between submission and rebellion, to come quietly and allow her masochistic nature to carry her through this ordeal, or to suffer the torments of constant coercion. There was only one sensible choice, and she had no doubt what it was.

Slowly she dropped her hands to her shorts. She undid the metal button at the waist, then slid down the heavy zip, revealing the black triangle of her pubic hair. The shorts were very tight and she had to ease them over her hips. Then they dropped to the floor and she stepped out of them. A cacophony of cheers and wolf whistles rang about the room as she did so.

She glanced down at herself. She had been careful to trim her bush that afternoon so that it formed a perfect triangle, the hairs cut very short, allowing the white of her mound to show through and leaving her thick pink sex lips bare and visible. At the time she had thought she might be preparing herself to be seen by one of the gang. Now her face glowed red as the entire room took in her charms.

Fredo picked up the shorts and flung them down from the stage. Then he tapped the table top with his whip.

"Bend over this."

Charlie turned and faced the table. She moved close to it so that she could feel the edge of the wood against her pubis. Then she bent forward, pressing her body down against the hard surface.

"Spread your legs."

Slowly she obeyed. She heard chairs scraping back in the room as the bikers stood for a better view of her bare bottom. She closed her eyes, imagining the sight she must make, her behind stretched tight, her anus and vagina visible to all.

There was a hush in the room now, a tangible tension filling the air as all eyes were fixed on the hapless girl. Then she felt the leather of the whip tap against the flesh of her backside.

She turned her head, watching as Fredo drew back the whip. Then she gritted her teeth.

Swish! Whack!

The whip descended with devastating force, landing across her rear cheeks with a crack that echoed about the room. For a second Charlie felt nothing. Then the pain came, a dreadful, stinging pain that brought a sudden flow of tears to her eyes.

Swish! Whack!

Almost before she could think a second blow fell, the whip biting deep into the flesh of her behind and doubling the agony that was already almost unbearable.

Swish! Whack!

This stroke struck her at the top of her thighs, just below the curve of her backside, leaving a thin white stripe across her pale flesh that almost immediately darkened to red.

Swish! Whack!

Charlie's knuckles were white as she gripped the edge of the table. All her instincts told her to cover her behind with them, and it was only by an extreme act of willpower that she resisted doing so, a sweat breaking out over her body as the punishment continued.

Swish! Whack!

Swish! Whack!

There was no part of her behind that wasn't burning with pain now, yet still the blows kept falling. The tears were running down her cheeks and splashing onto the table, yet still she made no sound, determined not to show any weakness. Instead she concentrated on the eroticism of her position, stretched across the table naked from the waist down, her most private places on open display.

Suddenly, as the image of herself formed in her mind, another quite unexpected emotion began to grip her, one that even began to override the pain of the beating. To her shock and surprise, Charlie realised that she was getting turned on.

Swish! Whack!
Swish! Whack!

Each blow landed with deadly accuracy, thrusting Charlie's small frame forward against the wood. But now there was a new sensation. Her love bud was swelling, and the force of the strokes was driving it down against the rough edge of the table, sending extraordinary thrills through her that made her gasp with lust.

Swish! Whack!

Charlie fought to keep her emotions under control. How was it that she could feel this way, her backside criss-crossed with the stripes of the whip, yet her mind filled with the most erotic images? All she could think of was Fredo, thrusting the whip into her vagina and frigging her before the eager crowd.

Swish! Whack!

Charlie was barely aware that the punishment had finished. She lay, prostrate across the table, her hips thrusting against the wood as she tried desperately to excite her clitoris. It was fully a minute before she became aware of what she was doing, her backside moving back and forth as if she were impaled on the cock of some invisible lover.

Gasping with lust, her face bright scarlet, she lifted herself up from the table top, the act making her backside sting anew. She looked down at the spot where she had been lying and was mortified to see a wet stain on the edge, a dribble of moisture running down the wood and dripping onto the stage. She rubbed her eyes, wiping away the tears that had formed there, then stood, her mind consumed by arousal and pain, waiting to see what would happen next.

What did happen was unexpected. Mamba pulled a bottle of beer from a case beneath the table and, snapping off the lid, handed it to Charlie. She took it from him and gulped it down gratefully, draining the bottle and bringing a low cheer from the crowd. She was still standing with her back to them, reluctant to turn, not only because that would give them a view of her bare sex, but also because she was still deeply embarrassed by her reaction to the beating. She hoped someone might offer her her shorts back, but nobody did.

"So," said Mamba at last. "You can certainly take the pain of a beating. I don't think I've ever seen a reaction quite like yours. Have you finished or would you like to frig yourself a bit more?"

Charlie didn't answer.

Then Mamba said something that made her heart sink even further.

"Take off your top."

She should have guessed that even being knickerless wouldn't be enough for them, she reflected. They wanted to see her stark naked. All at once she felt a cold feeling in the pit of her stomach as she realised that they were about to discover her deepest secret, the latent exhibitionism that she had been suppressing all this time. She knew how her body would react to being displayed before all these men, and she knew too that the reaction would be obvious.

"The top," said Mamba impatiently.

Slowly Charlie reached for the hem of her top. She paused, gazing down at herself, her heart pounding. Then, in a single movement, she pulled it over her head. She clutched it to her chest, reluctant to uncover herself, but one look from Mamba told her that she must. Her eyes downcast, she handed it to the bikers' leader. Then she stood, her pale breasts jutting proudly, the nipples half erect as the sense of the eyes on her body began to arouse a perverse excitement in her.

"Turn and face the front."

"Please..."

"Do it!"

Charlie obeyed, her face glowing as she bared all to those watching.

Mamba eyed her strangely.

"You wanted to do that didn't you?"

"Of course I didn't," she mumbled

"But you did. There's something strange about the way you've been reacting to all this. What is it? Tell me what it is that makes a sweet little thing like you so obviously excited."

"I... I can't. I don't know Sir."

"I think you do know. Tell me now. Tell the whole truth. He slid his hand down her belly. At once she went to push it away.

Whack!

He slapped her behind with the flat of his hand, making her cry out.

"Stand still!"

She bit her lip, then let her arms fall to her side.

"Legs apart!"

Hanging her head, she obeyed. Then she felt his hand on her belly once again. He ran it down over her mound and rubbed her clitoris lightly, making her groan aloud.

"Tell me what makes you excited," he said. "Tell me properly, using words that make you ashamed, but that turn you on. That's what I want to hear."

Charlie looked at him, then out at the bikers, who were silent, hanging on every word. She knew exactly what he wanted her to say, but could she bring herself to say it in front of all these people? She'd never even admitted to Jon that one perverse side of her nature. She sighed. Mamba would know if she lied, and he's expect her to embellish her words as well. A simple yes or no would never satisfy him. It would be dreadful, but it seemed she had no choice.

She whimpered slightly as he continued his intimate caress.

"Now let's hear what gets our little naked newcomer turned on. Because you're really horny right now, aren't you?"

"Yes Sir" she muttered.

"I thought so. When Zep and Lou fucked you that day in the wood they said you came like you were on heat. That was no act, was it? Your orgasm was genuine."

"Yes Sir" she said. "They really made me come."

"So tell me what turns you on so much."

"I don't know."

"Yes you do. You know you do. Now admit it."

"It's..."

"Yes?"

"It's being seen like this, Sir. It's having men look at me."

"I thought so," put in Zep. "Back there in the wood, you were really hot for it as soon as I made you take off your leathers, weren't you?"

"Yes Sir. As soon as you looked at my bare body. As soon as you saw I was hardly wearing anything underneath."

Mamba shook his head. "The perfect girl for a biker's apprentice. One who loves to show off her body. It's giving you a real thrill right now that all these people can see your breasts and that tight little cunt of yours. It makes you want to be fucked doesn't it?"

"Yes Sir" she admitted again.

"Tell me you like it."

"I... I like it."

"Like what?"

"You know. I like to be looked at."

"Tell me exactly what you like, little slut. Tell me what it is that thrills you so."

Charlie hung her head in shame.

"I like having men see me with nothing on, Sir," she said quietly

"With nothing on?"

"With no clothes on. Nude. Like I am now."

"Nothing at all? Not even, say a brief bikini?"

"Nothing. I like it when they see me completely bare. No dress, bra or panties. I like showing everything," she glanced down at her body.

"Showing what?"

42

"You know what, Sir. You can see."

"Tell me. Tell me what you want the men to see."

"My... my breasts. I want men to look at them. To see my nipples. How hard they get. And..." she blushed.

"And what?"

"And my vagina, Sir. With my legs open like I am now. I want men to see how wet my vagina is."

"Even strangers?"

"Especially strangers."

He grinned. "A girl who wants men she doesn't even know to see her tits and cunt? That's extraordinary. Most women reserve such privileges for their lover. Aren't you ashamed of your lack of modesty? Any normal girl would be devastated by having people see her in such a state."

"Of course I'm ashamed, Sir. But when men look at me and see I'm nude I just get excited"

"And having, as you say, nothing on, makes you want to be fucked. Admit it."

"It's true."

"But I still think you have more to tell me," said Mamba.

Charlie sighed. "Haven't I said enough?"

"I think you've shown your body to men before. Tell me about it."

"I'm too embarrassed," she muttered.

"That's good. Now tell us the first time you showed yourself to a man."

Charlie took a deep breath. "When I was sixteen, Sir," she said. "At the gym"

"Go on."

"We used to have to go to this gym every week from school. It was an old building with wooden cubicles to change in. One day I was sent back to the changing rooms after the class had started and I came across two of the gym attendants. There was a crack in the wood and they were looking through it. When they saw me they pretended they were checking the paintwork. Then they went away and I took a look."

"And?"

"And I could see right into the cubicle. Quite clearly. And it was my cubicle. They must have watched me get changed."

"And had you been naked?"

"No Sir. But I'd been in my underwear. They'd seen me in my bra and pants."

"But surely that was not enough for you?"

"No Sir."

"Go on."

"All that week I couldn't get it out of my mind. And I couldn't understand how excited it made me. I knew I had to go back and use that compartment again. And I knew I had to show them everything."

"You actually planned to strip naked with these men watching?"

"Yes Sir."

"Tell me what happened."

"The next week I used the same cubicle. I took off my dress and just stood there in my underwear listening to the other girls as they went off to play netball. When they'd gone it went quiet, and I could hear the men outside. I knew they were looking at me."

"You were certain they were there?"

"Absolutely."

"And?"

"And... And so I took off my bra, Sir."

"Facing them?"

"No Sir. I was too scared, so I turned away. I unhooked it and slipped it off. Then I threw it down behind me. I stood there looking down at my breasts. The nipples had gone hard and I was so excited. I knew I just wanted to show myself. To have the men see me bare breasted."

"So you turned round."

"Yes Sir. I just turned and stood there, my hands by my side, knowing they were looking at me."

"And you were excited?"

"Very excited."

"But they still hadn't seen everything."

"No Sir."

"So?"

"I nearly didn't do it. My hands were shaking so much I could hardly get hold of my panties. I just pulled them off and stood there. Like I am now. Letting them see me."

"And what was their reaction?"

"They were laughing, Sir. I could hear them. They laughed at me."

"Yet you stood there, a sixteen year old beauty, stark naked and being mocked by these men?"

"I didn't care. I was just so aroused."

"So what did you do about your arousal?"

"Nothing."

"I think you did do something. Tell us Charlie."

"I... I played with myself, Sir"

"What?"

Her colour deepened. "I masturbated."

"Where they could watch you?"

"Yes Sir."

"Go on."

"There was a bench that ran the length of the wall behind where I was standing. I sat down on it. I was shaking so much I thought my legs would give way. I wanted them to see everything, so I spread my thighs apart. Then I touched my bud."

"Your bud?"

"My clitoris, Sir. It was all swollen and I touched it with my fingers. I was wet down there and it felt wonderful to touch it. I thought of the men watching, then I couldn't help myself. I slid my fingers into my vagina and began to move them back and forth."

Charlie looked out at the bikers. The room was completely silent, all eyes fixed on her. Mamba ran his hand down her belly again and teased her clitoris. For a moment she feared she would come then and there, but she managed, with an effort to keep control.

"So you sat there and frigged yourself?"

"Yes Sir. I could hardly believe I was doing it. All my classmates were off playing an innocent game of netball and here was I, completely naked and flaunting myself in front of a group of gym instructors."

"A group? You said there were two."

"There were at first. But they must have told their friends. I think there were about six of them in the end. I could hear them talking and laughing."

"Yet you went on with the show?"

"Yes Sir."

"Did you come?"

"Yes Sir. Twice. I couldn't stop myself. Then I heard the girls returning and I had to stop."

"Did you ever go back?"

"No Sir. When I came out the cubicle all the men were standing and watching me, nudging one another and pointing. I felt so ashamed. So I never went to another gym class and I left the school soon afterwards."

Mamba shook his head.

"That's quite a story. Have you ever told it to anyone else?"

"No Sir."

"You should. You're a sexy little chick. And I suspect there's more to tell about that past of yours. Other shameful stories. Am I right?"

Charlie looked at him. "Yes Sir."

"We'll look forward to hearing them," he said. "Meanwhile there still remains the subject of your initiation."

Charlie stared at him. She had assumed that the beating was her initiation, but clearly that was just a foretaste. There was obviously more to come.

"I think we should ask the gang," he said. "Let's see if there's any suggestions."

Charlie gazed out at the onlookers. As she did so a chair scraped back. She looked across to where a red-headed girl had risen to her feet. She was taller than Charlie, with a slim waist and large breasts that pressed against the front of her leathers.

"Yes Zana?" said Mamba.

"What about a town ride?" said the girl. "After what she's

46

just told us, it should be right up her street."

"An interesting suggestion," said Mamba, grinning. "But is it enough?"

"It is if we send her out low."

Mamba's grin widened. "I think you've got it, Zana," he said. "Does everyone else agree?"

There was a general nodding of heads. Charlie looked from face to face, confused. Whatever it was, she knew that it wouldn't be long before she found out.

Chapter 5

Charlie stood, quietly watching, as the bikers drank and chatted. It was about fifteen minutes since her beating, and the fire in her backside had ebbed to a throbbing ache. She was standing at the side of the stage, still quite naked, waiting to find out what humiliation would be foisted on her next. She knew something was going on. The girl Zana, along with Zep, had left the room soon after they had decided on the mysterious town ride, and the rest of the gang were clearly awaiting their return with some enthusiasm.

Suddenly the door at the far end of the room opened, and the pair re-entered. Conversation stopped as they made their way up onto the stage. Zep was carrying a piece of paper and, as he unfolded it on the table, Charlie recognised it as a street map.

Mamba beckoned her forward, and she moved closer to the table, still acutely aware of her lack of covering.

"You are familiar with the town, I think?" asked Mamba.

"Yes Sir."

"Good. You are going to take a ride round the streets, following the route marked."

Charlie gazed down at the map. Someone had used a highlighter pen to trace a path from where they were into the centre of town, where it twisted through the streets, covering all of the major roads before taking a new route back to the hall.

"Do you think you can remember all that?" asked Mamba.

"Yes Sir."

Charlie was puzzled. What was so difficult about riding a bike around the town? Surely anyone could do it.

"Zana's machine is parked outside," Mamba went on. "The keys are on the table."

Charlie picked up the keys, then looked down at herself, and all of a sudden she realised. They were going to make her do it without her clothes. She was going to have to ride round the town in broad daylight without top, skirt or panties. Perhaps that was what Zana had meant about sending her out low, though she couldn't really make any sense of the expression.

"Outside," said Mamba.

Charlie turned, making her way to the steps and descending to the floor of the hall. She wound between the tables, looking neither right or left, her face as red as her behind. As she did so, the bikers rose and followed her.

When she reached the front door, Charlie paused. What if there were someone out there? After all, they were in a normal street. Dare she stroll out stark naked? But she knew she had no choice now and, turning the handle, she stepped out onto the street.

For a moment she was alone there, feeling conspicuous and vulnerable, the pavement hard beneath her feet, the evening sunshine feeling warm on her naked flesh. She glanced up and down nervously, finding it difficult to suppress the desire to cover her breasts and crotch with her hands. Then the bikers were crowding out after her and she stepped out into the road, where a single motorcycle stood apart from the rest.

Zep took her arm and led her to the machine. It was large and powerful, just like the rest, and Charlie eyed it with trepidation.

"On you get," he said.

Charlie straddled the machine. It was odd to feel the warm softness of the saddle against her bare skin, and she winced in pain as she settled into the seat.

"Right," said Mamba. "You are to follow the route exactly

as instructed. There will be people out there making sure you do exactly as you are told. Otherwise you are completely on your own, and will receive no assistance from anybody here, no matter what happens. Do you understand?"

"Yes Sir."

"Off you go then."

Charlie kicked the machine into life. The engine seemed unnaturally loud to her as it echoed from the house fronts, and she expected people to emerge from the buildings at any moment, though nobody did. She took a final glance around the bikers, all of whom were watching her closely, then she slipped the bike into gear and roared off down the street.

For Charlie it was a very strange experience, to be stark naked on the public highway, her charms on open view. As she pulled up to a junction she saw her reflection in a darkened shop window opposite and she paused momentarily to examine herself. She made an extremely erotic sight, her pale nudity a stark contrast to the normal black suit of a biker. Her firm breasts stood out conspicuously, the nipples slightly upward pointing and hard with the thrill of what she was doing. The handlebars on the bike were set high, so that she sat upright and affording a full-frontal view of her body, the dark vee of her pubic bush perfectly visible.

For a moment she contemplated escape. After all, the bike was a fast one, and she'd have a head start. But she knew they would catch her, and that it would be the worse for her afterwards. The pain in her behind was proof enough of that. Then there were the photographs...

Despite the overwhelming fear in the pit of her stomach, Charlie felt a sudden thrill as she swung the machine out into the road and headed toward the town centre. How many people would see her naked body during her ride? How many men would ogle her bare breasts and sex, and remark on the criss-cross of red weals that covered her backside? As usual she couldn't understand exactly why the idea excited her so, but all at once the exhibitionist in Charlie came to the fore and she sat proud in the saddle, thrusting her breasts forward, almost as if she wanted to be seen, to flaunt her naked charms.

So far she had seen nobody in these scruffy residential alleys, but now she spotted a pub up ahead with a number of drinkers standing in the street or sitting at trestle tables. As she came closer she saw them turn toward the sound of the approaching bike, then stare in disbelief at its gorgeous young rider as she sailed past them. She glanced in the mirror and saw that a number of them had run out into the street behind her and were pointing and laughing. All at once she momentarily forgot her fears and laughed too, exhilarated by the power of the machine that throbbed between her legs and by the effect that the men's eyes had had upon her.

She took one hand from the handlebars and slid it down beneath her legs, Her clitoris was hard as a nut and protruding between her sex lips so that its wetness was visible. She rubbed it, gasping with pleasure. As she did so she passed a group of people queuing outside a cinema. They stared in disbelief as she gently masturbated herself.

She grasped the bars again, afraid that she might trigger an orgasm which would make her riding unsteady. She was coming closer to town now, and the streets were becoming busier. She passed some cars going the other way, their drivers' eyes wide as they took in her nudity. Everyone she encountered had a similar reaction. A glance, followed by an expression of disbelief and a nudging and pointing as she swept by.

Charlie was beginning to feel good. Somehow, with the power of the machine beneath her, she felt safe, able to outrun anyone who tried to apprehend her. All at once it felt wonderful to be naked amongst all these people, to flaunt her body, yet to feel protected from them.

She was nearly in the town centre, now, and the pavements were busier still. Then she saw the lights ahead of her were on red, and she slowed, suddenly feeling more vulnerable.

She came to a halt. A young couple were crossing the road in front of her and both stopped short, the man's eyes bulging, the woman clearly surprised and outraged. She took her partner's arm and dragged him away as he stared back over his shoulder.

Charlie blushed crimson, though the close encounter had thrilled her.

A car pulled up beside her, and still the lights were on red. She glanced to one side. There were four men inside, all scruffily dressed and all staring at her. The window beside her was wound down and a man stared out.

"Nice tits, darling," he said.

The man behind also opened his window.

"Who's been thrashing your behind love? I wouldn't mind doing that myself."

"Fancy a quick fuck sweetie?" said another. "You're dressed for it."

A hand reached out and Charlie realised how close they were. She tried to draw away, but the bike was too heavy. The hand closed over her breast, sending a sudden shiver through her. Charlie didn't want to admit it to herself, but inside she felt incredibly excited at her situation. She remained stock still, not looking at the men, but making no move to stop the hand that was mauling her breast, safe in the knowledge that the moment the lights changed she could outrun the car easily. To right and left she could see people coming toward her, pointing and shouting to one another. Another few seconds and she knew she would be engulfed by a crowd. Then the lights changed and she dropped the clutch and roared away, her body tingling with excitement at the man's touch. The episode could have lasted no more than thirty or forty seconds, but it had increased her arousal tremendously and she felt the wetness seep from her vagina onto the saddle as she swept through the streets, past the closed shops and the staring people.

She was nearly through the centre of town now, and was, much to her surprise, feeling almost relaxed, beginning to congratulate herself on how well she had done.

Then the engine died.

It happened suddenly. One second she was in confident control, the next she was staring down in dismay as the machine rapidly lost its momentum.

She glanced about her. Fortunately she had just turned into

an empty street, though she knew the men in the car were still pursuing her and might turn the corner at any moment. She began to feel the panic rising in her. Goodness knows what would happen if they caught her. There was no doubt that they wanted her body, and how could she possibly prevent them taking it? She looked about desperately for somewhere to go.

Then she spotted a small alley up ahead. It wasn't much, but at least it would offer her some cover from the main road. But would her momentum allow her to reach it? At once she pulled in the clutch, and headed for it.

The bike had barely enough speed to negotiate the turning, and it coasted to a halt a few yards down the alley. She heard the car approaching and held her breath, uncertain whether they had seen her. But it went past without reducing speed, much to her relief.

She stared about her. It was a narrow alley that led between two buildings, with a wall at the far end. It was quite deserted, so she was at least safe for the moment, though the more she considered her predicament, the more dismayed she became. Unless she found a way to restart the machine, she was in a real mess. There was no way she could get back through the streets unseen. If caught she faced possible arrest, or worse.

Yet she was surprised to realise that the idea of being arrested was far from being the main cause of her dismay. What really worried her was the thought of failing the Spirits. All at once she realised just how much she feared the power of the gang. Meeting them was the most frightening experience of her life. Ever since she had surrendered herself in the wood that day she had thought of little else, and the treatment she had received that evening had had more of an effect on her than she could believe possible. Their power over her was something extraordinarily strong, and she knew that, for her own sake, she had to get back to them, no matter what.

She kicked the bike over a few times, but the engine remained stubbornly silent. Then it occurred to her to open the filler cap and check the tank. She gazed inside, but could see nothing. She tried shaking the bike from side to side, listening for he sloshing of the fuel in the tank, but there was silence. There was no getting away from it, the bike had no fuel.

She pondered this piece of intelligence. The bikers must have known that the machine wasn't going to make it round the town and back to the headquarters, yet they had sent her anyhow, knowing full well that she would be stranded naked in the middle of town. Indeed, it was pure luck that she had found the alley when she had. If it had happened a few moments earlier, when she had been waiting at the traffic lights, who knows what might have happened. This was clearly part of her test, and she realised for the first time how dangerous the bikers were, and how willing to take an almost ultimate risk with her.

She climbed from the machine and looked about her. The alley was narrow and dark, with high walls on either side. Behind her was the road, with cars swishing by every few seconds. Ahead was a dead end, nothing more than a few oil drums stacked against a wall. Having no better plan, she made her way up to the end.

It was a complete cul de sac, with no way out apart from over the wall. Charlie glanced about her, then vaulted up onto one of the oil drums. She was able to see clearly over the wall now, and she surveyed the scene before her.

Immediately in front of her was a stretch of wasteland, in the centre of which was an abandoned factory. Beyond she could see the car park of a large superstore, with cars bustling in and out. To her right were the backs of shops. Then, on her left, she spotted something that made her draw in her breath.

There, on the edge of the wasteland, was a low building outside which were parked a number of cars, many of which had body parts or wheels missing. In the side of the building were a pair of double doors which were wide open. Through them Charlie could see a ramp on top of which was a car. Beneath she could just discern a figure moving back and forth.

It was a garage, and garages generally had petrol.

Charlie gazed down at her naked body, then across at the garage. There was little doubt she could get to it without being seen, but once there she knew she would have a real problem hiding herself. She glanced back at the silent motorcycle, and thought of the Spirits waiting for her back at the clubhouse. She had to get back to them, and the bike was her only means of doing so. She had to get some fuel.

Drawing a deep breath, she levered herself onto the top of the wall, then dropped down onto the other side.

Chapter 6

Charlie picked her way carefully across the wasteland, crouching low to avoid being seen. The ground was littered with rubbish, the broken bottles and sharp metal edges threatening to scratch or puncture her bare skin at any moment. She was getting closer to the garage with every step, and could clearly see the men working inside. There were two of them. Beneath he ramp was a man about twenty-five years old, his hair almost shaved, a gold earring gleaming in one of his ears. Beyond him, standing at a workbench, was a tall Negro, his face turned away from her. Both were clad in grey, greasy overalls. A radio was playing loud pop music somewhere in the back of the workshop.

Charlie's heart beat harder as she approached the entrance. She was amongst the cars now, less than ten yards from the garage entrance, yet still the men had not noticed her, both intent on what they were doing. She crouched for a moment behind the last of the cars, watching them as they worked. She glanced down at herself once more. It seemed extraordinary to be standing there, totally nude, and about to expose herself to these two men.

It was at that moment that she spotted the open store room off to her left. It was empty apart from an array of gallon cans. Charlie's heart leapt. Perhaps here she would find the fuel she required, and maybe she could escape the gazes of the two young mechanics. Dropping into a crouch she made her way around the cars and towards the open door.

She hesitated before entering, suddenly intimidated by the bright neon lights inside the room. Crouched where she was, the cars provided the cover she needed, but beyond the doors there was no cover, and her nakedness would be impossible to hide.

She took a deep breath, stepped out from behind the car and scuttled across to the entrance. She headed straight for the line of cans and began lifting them. The first three were empty, but the fourth felt almost full. Crouching down she unscrewed the cap and checked the contents.

Petrol!

Giving a little sigh of relief she screwed on the top once more and, lifting the can, turned toward the entrance.

She almost ran into the security guard before she saw him.

"Where the hell are you going with that?"

Charlie stopped short, speechless with surprise. He was a tall man, in his late forties, his hair streaked with grey. He wore a blue uniform with a peaked cap, and in his hand he carried a truncheon.

Charlie immediately tried to cover her private parts, holding the can in front of her crotch whilst wrapping her other arm across her breasts.

"Where the hell do you think you're going with that can?"

"I'm... I need some petrol."

"That's not all you need by the look of you. What have you done with your clothes?"

"My motorcycle ran out of petrol."

"So you took off all your clothes?"

"I wasn't wearing any."

"What, not even a pair of knickers?"

Charlie's face glowed. "Nothing at all... it was a kind of bet..." She put the can on the ground and covered her pubis with her hand. "Keep the petrol," she said. "I'll find another way. I have to go."

The security guard held up a hand.

"Hold it!" he ordered. "You're not going anywhere. Get up against that wall."

"I..."

"Move!" he barked, wielding his truncheon. "Stand against the wall, your hands up, palms flat against the surface."

This time there was an air of authority in his voice that Charlie dare not disobey. Hurriedly she padded across the floor of the garage to the wall. Then, reluctantly, she took her hands from her body and placed them against the wall above her head, the surface feeling cool and rough under her fingers.

"Spread your legs. I'm going to search you."

"Search me? But how could I possibly..."

Whack! He brought his truncheon down hard across her still tender behind, making her cry out with pain.

"Just keep quiet, slut," he ordered. "You were stealing. And showing your tits and cunt off like some common whore. I have a right to check you for weapons before handing you over to the police."

"The police? Oh please don't do that."

"Then behave yourself. I can see that pretty behind of yours has already had a thrashing tonight. Don't ask me to give it another. Now spread those legs."

Slowly, her face crimson with shame, Charlie obeyed, placing her legs wide apart, only too aware of the view she was presenting to him.

"Now stand still whilst I search you."

He moved his palms up he flanks, his rough fingers tracing the curve of her thighs over her hips and up to her rib cage. Charlie shivered as he ran his hands over her soft young skin.

He moved closer, his arms encircling her, and she closed her eyes as she felt him reach for her breasts. He took one in each hand, squeezing them roughly, his fingers travelling over her nipples which, to Charlie's extreme embarrassment, puckered to hard little knobs almost at once.

"Hmm, nothing false about those," he murmured as he stood, caressing them.

"Please..."

"Quiet, bitch," he snarled. "Just do as you're told. Now there's only one other place you could be hiding something, and you know where that is, don't you?"

Charlie whimpered slightly, but said nothing as his hands left the soft plumpness of her young breasts and moved down her body.

"Press your arse back!" he ordered. "Let me get at your cunt."

Charlie closed her eyes. She knew she had to obey. But she knew too that her vagina was wet with her juices, and that his touch would simply serve to increase her arousal. And she was only too aware that this shameful secret would be revealed the moment he felt her down there. Slowly she widened her stance then, with a supreme effort of will, she pressed her backside back, presenting him with the access he desired to her most private place.

He ran a hand down the crack of her backside and slid a finger into her vagina. At once a shudder ran through her small body and she felt the muscles of her sex close about his finger, as if drawing it into her.

"Christ you're sopping," he murmured, working his finger back and forth and feeling the way her sex lips convulsed. Charlie said nothing, her humiliation complete, her arousal now obvious.

"When were you last fucked?"

"Pardon?"

"You heard me. When did you last have a cock in you?

"I... last week."

"No wonder you're so fucking horny. Get down on your knees."

"What?"

Thwack! He pulled his fingers from inside her and brought the truncheon down hard against her backside once more.

"Move!"

Charlie obeyed at once, turning to face him and dropping to her knees in front of him. She looked up at him through lowered eyelashes, acutely aware of the thrust of her breasts as she awaited his orders

"Now, you dirty little whore," he murmured. "If you don't want me to call the police you'll co-operate. Understand?"

"Yes," she whispered.

"Suck my cock."

The words took Charlie by surprise, and she glanced up at him, her beautiful eyes questioning.

"You heard me."

Charlie looked down at his crotch. Even in his tight jeans the bulge there was obvious. Trembling, she reached out a hand and felt the hardness.

"Get on with it."

Charlie reached for his zipper and, her hands shaking, slid it down. She stared at it for a moment, trying to gain the courage to go further. Gently she eased the flaps of his fly apart and tentatively reached inside. His cock was straining against the thin material of his briefs, and she could feel its heat through the material.

"Get it out, come on!"

Charlie took hold of the waistband of his briefs and slowly pulled them down. All at once his cock sprang out, long and hard. She stared at it. It was a beautiful cock, the veins running up the sides standing out proudly, the foreskin forced slightly back revealing the smooth fat glans and the large eye.

"Suck it!"

Her heart fluttering, Charlie leaned forward until the tip of his penis was almost touching her lips. Then, after a moment's hesitation, she opened her mouth, took him inside. He smelt and tasted of male, and, as the scent dominated her senses she felt a desire to satisfy him. Charlie couldn't understand the urge, but she knew it was something deep in her psyche that was only now coming to the fore. Something that made her want to obey. At once she began to suck hard at his cock.

The man reacted with a groan of pleasure, thrusting his hips forward against her mouth so that she almost gagged. Charlie's reaction was to suck all the harder, one hand wrapping about his shaft and beginning to wank him whilst the other delved into his fly and caressed his balls.

He took hold of her hair between his fingers, fucking her face with gusto, his stiff member forcing her lips apart. Charlie responded with equal enthusiasm, her tongue flicking back and forth over his glans as he worked it in and out.

He came with a grunt, and suddenly Charlie's mouth was filled with hot, viscous spunk. His ejaculation took her by surprise and at first she could scarcely contain him, the fluid leaking from the side of her lips as she struggled to gulp it down. He seemed to be full of sperm, his balls twitching as spurt after spurt filled her mouth. Charlie drank it down, swallowing his seed greedily, draining him until there was no more and his rod began to soften. Only then did he pulled his cock from between her lips and tuck it back into his pants. Charlie stayed on her knees, gazing up at him, a dribble of his spunk trickling down her neck and onto her breast.

He grinned. "Not bad," he said. "I guess I won't need to be calling the police after all."

Charlie gave a sigh of relief at these words.

"But there's still the problem of your bike."

All at once Charlie was crestfallen again. In the excitement of fellating the guard she had forgotten the seriousness of her plight, but now it came back to her.

"Couldn't you let me take some petrol?" she asked. "After what I just did?"

He shook his head. "Not mine to give," he said. "You could always ask the mechanics, though."

"Who?"

"The two guys working next door. I'm sure they'd help if you asked nicely."

"Oh."

"You want me to call them?"

"But I'm naked. Couldn't I borrow your jacket or something?"

He shook his head again. "Not allowed to take this off. Company rules. Now, do you want me to call them?"

She lowered her eyes. More than anything else she longed for some clothes, even the simplest garment to hide her nakedness. The thought of two more men being treated to the sight of her defenceless young body appalled her. But what could she do?

"All right," she whispered.

"Hey Bob, Steve. There's a lady here needs some help."

"What the hell's the matter?"

The young mechanic with the skinhead rounded the corner of the garage, then stopped short, his mouth open. Charlie's face turned scarlet as he stared at her bare breasts and crotch.

"Lady's in trouble," said the guard.

The man shook his head in disbelief.

"Come on girl," ordered the guard. "Get on your feet and tell Steve what you want."

Charlie rose from her knees and, keeping her eyes cast down, she walked toward the man, her arms hanging at her side. She had contemplated hiding herself behind her hands, but there seemed little point. She felt her face burning as she approached him, all her charms on open display. His eyes roved over her body, taking in the firmness of her breasts, the stiffness of her nipples and the dark patch of hair at her crotch. Suddenly she remembered the streak of sperm that ran down to her nipple. She wished she had wiped it away, but it was too late now.

"I need your help," she said.

"What the..."

"I need fuel for my bike."

Still he continued to stare open-mouthed at the picture of loveliness that stood before him.

"But you're starkers."

"Have you always been that observant, or did you go on a course?" said the guard sarcastically.

"But..."

"Close your mouth or you'll catch a fly."

"I asked if you'd give me some petrol," said Charlie, an edge of desperation creeping into her voice.

"Dirty little slut doesn't care who gets a look at her," said the guard. "Look at her now. I reckon flashing her tits and cunt makes her horny"

The man shook his head. Then his eyes narrowed.

"Wait a minute. Don't I know you?"

Charlie stared at him in alarm. "I don't think so."

"Sure I do. Your husband's the guy who works on the oil rigs. Jon something. We drink in the same pub. I've seen you there with him."

Charlie didn't know what to say. This was dreadful. What if he were to tell Jon he had found her like this?

"Hey, Bob! Come and take a look at this!"

The young black man, who she had seen earlier in the garage, suddenly appeared, then stopped short.

"Shee-it. What the hell's going on?"

"It's Jon's wife. You know, the guy in the pub. The one that used to be a biker."

"Hell, you're right," he said. "I've seen her out with him. Sexy little thing. I always fancied getting a look at those gorgeous tits."

"Well the lady's showing them now all right," grinned Steve. "Jon know you're out like that?"

"No. And please don't tell him," pleaded Charlie.

"I guess that depends on how I feel," he said. "And as for the petrol, if you can't pay money, you pay some other way."

Charlie stood, still staring at him. Well at least he wasn't beating about the bush. The message was perfectly clear. If she wanted the fuel, she'd pay with her body.

"You want to fuck me?" she asked quietly.

"I do, as you so elegantly put it, want to fuck you."

"What if I say no?"

"Then you find your petrol somewhere else."

"You'd turn me out in this condition?"

"I could always call up Jon and tell him you were in trouble."

"No, please don't."

"Wait a minute," said Bob, moving closer to Charlie. "What's that on your tit?"

Charlie looked away.

"Tell him," said the security guard.

"It's sperm," she said quietly.

"Whose?"

She indicated the guard.

"What? How?"

61

"I-I sucked him off. Just now."

Bob gave a low whistle. "Now you're talking my language. Well baby, how about that fuck?"

Charlie's shoulders slumped in defeat. She looked about her.

"Where can we go?" she asked quietly

"There's an office at the back."

"All right then."

"Now you're being sensible. I just gotta wash my hands. You go through and make yourself comfortable."

He stood aside and Charlie peered past him. At the back of the garage was a half glazed door, with another window next to it. It didn't look as though it would offer much privacy, but Charlie realised that beggars couldn't be choosers. Not for her the soft silk sheets of seduction, simply a scruffy office in the back of a garage with two other men watching her. Slowly, her cheeks burning, Charlie moved past the men, ignoring the low whistle as they took in the red stripes that decorated her behind. She opened the door and stepped through. There was a light switch beside it and she clicked it on.

The office was a basic affair. The naked light bulb illuminated a wooden desk strewn with papers behind which stood a chair. In the corner was a filing cabinet and an old workbench. The wall was adorned with calendars, most of which depicted naked young women. Charlie studied them, and decided that the models had nothing to offer that she hadn't. She perched on the desk and glanced out at the young mechanic who was still staring at her.

Bob emerged from a washroom at the side of the workshop and strode into the office, closing the door behind him. Then he turned and moved closer to her, and his hand reached out for her breast. She said nothing as it closed over the soft flesh, but she knew that the way her nipple suddenly stiffened told him all he needed to know.

"Shit, you're something else," he murmured, his hand squeezing her firm mammary.

He placed an arm behind her back and pulled her closer to him, his lips closing over hers. At once she felt his tongue probing against her lips and she parted them, allowing him to lick at hers.

The kiss was long and passionate, his hands continuing to caress her breasts as he devoured her. All at once she was more turned on that she could imagine, and, as she sucked hard at his tongue, she felt a warm moisture invade her crotch.

He slid his palm off her breast and began moving it slowly down her flank, his mouth still locked against hers. The feel of his strong hand against her soft young flesh was wonderful, and her breath shortened as he moved his fingers down her rib cage and over her belly, inching downwards toward the centre of her desires. When he found the bud of her clitoris with his fingertip her whole body shook, her gasp muffled by his kiss. He probed gently at her, his index finger sliding down her slit and penetrating her in the most intimate way possible.

Charlie responded by pressing her hips forward, urging him deeper inside her, her fingers digging into his overall.

He broke off his kiss and stood back slightly, gazing deep into her eyes as he worked his finger back and forth. Charlie moaned softly as he masturbated her, her arousal increasing with every second. She glanced out of the office window to where the other mechanic stood, his eyes fixed on her body, taking in the swell of her breasts, the curve of her waist and the way she spread her legs wide, pressing her hips urgently forward against the black man's fingers.

Charlie couldn't believe her own wantonness. To be sprawled across the desk of this scruffy office, surrendering her naked body to a total stranger whilst another watched was an unthinkably outrageous thing to do. Yet here she was, not just surrendering but revelling in the rough treatment from the mechanic.

She glanced down at his crotch and saw that the bulge there was bigger than ever. All at once she wanted to see his manhood, and to taste him. The overall was fastened by a zip that ran all the way down the front, and she reached for the man's collar, taking hold of he tab on the zip and pulling it downwards. The garment fell open, revealing a bare, broad chest beneath. She ran her fingers over it, marvelling at the solid strength of his pectorals. He was wearing a pair of small blue briefs and as she moved her hand down and over the front of them she could see that they were straining almost to breaking point, his cock growing stiffer by the moment. She took hold of the waistband, as she had the watchman's earlier. Then she had been shaking with nerves, but now her fingers trembled with desire as she dragged his pants down, watching as his manhood sprang into view. It was half erect, growing longer and thicker all the time as it uncurled itself before her eyes. She wrapped a hand about the shaft, shivering slightly as she felt how hard he already was. Then she leaned forward, pulling his cock toward her mouth.

She closed her lips about his bulbous glans, savouring the taste and smell of him as she probed her tongue into his foreskin and sought out the smooth, hard bulge beneath. Now it was his turn to gasp as she drew him deep inside, her mouth filled with stiff, twitching cock as she sucked hungrily at him, her fingers kneading his bulging ball sac.

"Oh shit that's great baby," he murmured. His hands wandered over her breasts as she fellated him, her head working back and forth, her hand wanking his thick shaft. She glanced up at his face through raised eyelids and saw the expression sheer pleasure.

She lifted her head, allowing him to slip from her mouth. His cock glistened with saliva, the end bobbing up and down as she watched it.

"Get over to that workbench, you little whore," he ordered.

Charlie scuttled across to where he was pointing. It was an old bench, the surface covered with dust and oil, and she stood close to it, then looked back at him, her eyes wide and questioning.

"Bend forward over it."

Charlie looked down at the bench. It was filthy. Under normal circumstances she wouldn't have gone near it.

But these were not normal circumstances.

Slowly she lowered her body over the bench, shivering slightly as she felt the hard wood against the tender flesh of her breasts. She pressed herself down, trying to ignore the smell of oil and grease, her body bent at the waist so that her lovely young behind was presented to the man.

"Spread your legs.".

She obeyed, opening herself to him, then glanced back at him. He was standing watching her, his fist closed about his cock, working the foreskin back and forth.

"Show me what you've got."

Reluctantly Charlie raised her backside, aware of the perfect view of her sex and anus that she was giving him.

He ran his fingers gently over the red stripes that covered her behind.

"You been a naughty girl then?" he asked.

She said nothing, but Bob just moved forward, and a tremor ran through Charlie's body as she felt his stiff organ press against the yielding flesh of her sex. He placed a hand over her slit, his fingers forcing the lips apart and revealing the wetness within. Then he pressed his hips forward, and all at once he was inside her, his thick black cock invading her wet sex.

He pressed hard, sliding ever deeper into the prostrate girl. Charlie spread her arms out, gripping the edge of the desk as he drove into her, until he could go no further.

He began to fuck her with slow, even movements, his cock sliding back and forth over the walls of her sex, bringing hoarse grunts of pleasure from her. He took hold of her hips, gripping her tight as he worked his meaty cock in and out of her hot, throbbing vagina. Each stroke almost drove the breath from her lungs as he pressed his strong body against her small naked form, but Charlie didn't care. This was sex at its most basic, with no ties or emotions, simply a rampant dick and a helpless chick.

His thrusts began to increase in urgency, his hips banging hard against hers, hammering her against the hard edge of the desk. Charlie bit her lip, barely able to suppress the cries that were trying to escape her as the onslaught continued.

All at once the rhythm of his fucking changed, his thrusts becoming more jerky as she felt his muscles become tense. She sensed his breath shortening, then he gave a hoarse cry and suddenly her vagina was filling with sperm.

Her own hips jerked as she felt him shoot his load into her, then she too was coming, her cries ringing round the small office as she gave vent to a shameful rush of pleasure. The advent of her orgasm seemed to fill him with new energy, and his pace quickened for a moment as he continued to spurt hot semen into her, his hands gripping her thighs hard. Time after time she felt his rod jerk inside her, each jerk releasing another gob of spunk into her throbbing sex. Charlie clung tightly to the bench, waves of passion flowing through her with every twitch of his organ until at last he was spent. His body collapsed over hers, his breath hot on the back of her neck.

They lay there locked together for some time, both breathing heavily. Then he slipped his great organ from her and stepped back.

Charlie straightened and glanced down at herself, Her breasts and belly were streaked with grease and grime, her hair a mess. A long dribble of sperm was leaking from her vagina and running down her leg. She knew she must look a dreadful sight.

At that moment she heard a voice close to her ear.

"My turn I think."

She looked round, then gasped with surprise as she saw the other mechanic standing beside the desk. He was naked, his stiff cock jutting from his groin. Rhythmically jerking up and down.

"She's all yours," said Bob, rising to his feet.

"No," she said. "Not both of you!"

"It's either that or we tell your old man we've been enjoying that tight little cunt of yours," said Bob.

Charlie opened her mouth to protest, then closed it again. Steve stepped forward and glanced down at his erection. Slowly Charlie reached out and took hold of his cock.

"Spread your legs, slut," he ordered.

Her eyes avoiding his, Charlie lowered herself to the benchtop on her back. Then she pulled him forward between her thighs, groaning slightly as he slid his erection into her.

Chapter 7

Charlie's mind was a whirl as she manoeuvred the motorcycle through the streets of the town. She was still naked and, even in the gathering twilight, her lack of clothing was quite clear to passers-by. But she barely noticed the pointing and catcalls all about her, revving the bike's engine and speeding away from any car that came too close.

Bob had followed her back across the wasteland, she carrying her precious can of fuel. The bike had been precisely where she had left it, the alley still deserted. Charlie's feelings about being accompanied had been mixed. With Bob beside her she didn't fear attack, but she knew there would be a price, and she was concerned, but not surprised when he made her lie across the back of the bike's saddle whilst he fucked her for a second time.

Before she had left she had begged for the loan of a spare pair of overalls, but they had simply laughed at her.

"I could just wear them as far as the bike," she had said.

"Nah!" Bob had replied. "We like the sight of those pretty tits and cunt. And that freshly whipped arse."

And so she had remained naked, her cheeks glowing with embarrassment as they commented on her lovely young body.

Bob had his way with her, and afterwards he watched as she filled the bike's tank and kicked it into life. Then he pulled her face to his, giving her an intimate kiss, his hands roving over her exposed young body before he allowed Charlie to slip it into gear and drop the clutch, leaving him staring after her as she swung out into the road.

Now, as she came closer to the bikers' clubhouse, she began to feel the trepidation rising inside her once again. She had been gone more than an hour on what should have been a twenty-minute ride. She knew she would be questioned on her return, and she knew too that they would get the truth out of her. Even if she tried to lie, the grease stains on her skin and the spunk that was still tricking out of her onto her thigh would be evidence enough as to her lascivious behaviour. For a moment it crossed her mind that there was nothing to prevent her going home, turning her back on the awful existence offered by the bikers and returning to a more normal life. But even as the idea crossed her mind she knew it wouldn't work. They would hunt her down for sure, and then it would be the worse for her. Whether she liked it or not, she knew she would have to go through the ordeal of being a biker slave sooner or later, and she might as well get on with it.

She tried not to look at two men who stood at the roadside, their mouths agape as they watched this vision of naked beauty sweep past them. Then she swung right down the road that led to he clubhouse.

She pulled up outside the door and killed the engine. There was nobody around and she paused for a few seconds glancing about her. She was parked beneath a bright street lamp, so that any passer-by would be able to see her charms. She dismounted and turned, to find Zana standing in the doorway, staring at her. Charlie dropped her eyes, glancing down at her naked body, her pale breasts jutting forward, her thighs streaked with semen.

"Been having fun?" asked Zana.

Charlie didn't answer.

"What's that on the seat of my bike?"

Charlie turned to see a pool of white semen on the saddle where she had been sitting.

"Well, what is it?"

"It's sperm," Charlie mumbled.

"Whose?"

"I don't know. They were mechanics."

"They? You mean there was more than one?"

"Three."

"Jeez, you don't waste time do you? Well get their spunk off my saddle. Use your tongue."

Charlie stared at her for a moment longer. Then, she turned and went back to the bike.

"Go on, lick it off!"

Slowly Charlie bent over the bike and licked the thick, glutinous fluid from the seat. Its taste and smell reminded her of the two men from whom it had come, and she was shocked to feel a new thrill run through her as she swallowed it down.

Zana moved closer to her, running a gloved hand over her breast.

"You're something else," she said quietly. "Maybe you'll make a Spirit after all."

And with that she turned and strode back into the clubhouse with Charlie following behind.

Inside it was warm, the air thick with smoke. There was a hubbub of chatter above the music, but at the sight of Charlie it died, and all eyes turned towards her.

Charlie stopped, staring about her for Zep. He was standing on the platform, at the back, watching her as she made her entrance. Then she saw that Mamba was beckoning to her. Her heart sank as she made her way toward him.

She mounted the platform slowly, only too aware of her nudity, and of the added shame of the spunk that was matted in her pubic hair and formed long silvery streaks down the inside of her thighs. She stopped in front of Mamba, who eyed her up and down.

"So Zana sent you out low," he said.

"Sir?"

"She omitted to fill her fuel tank."

All at once the meaning of his words were clear. Charlie could barely believe that it had been a deliberate act to strand her naked in the middle of town, but here was the proof.

"Yes Sir," she said.

"Yet you managed to find some fuel?"

"Yes Sir."

"How did you pay for it?"

"I..." Charlie glanced nervously about the room. The music had been switched off now, and all eyes were fixed on her.

"Well?"

"With my body, Sir," she whispered.

"Speak up."

"With my body."

69

"You fucked to get the fuel?"

"Yes Sir."

"Tell us about it."

Charlie was forced to reveal, to the smallest detail, her encounter with the two garage mechanics. Mamba questioned her closely, making her describe the office and the bench, how she was positioned, and the three orgasms she had enjoyed at the hands of the men, as well as how she had sucked off the guard. The room sat in total silence as she told her tale, right up to the point of licking the spunk from the seat of the bike. For Charlie the experience was dreadfully humiliating, yet the recollection of the fucking she had received stirred something in her as she told her tale.

When she finished nobody in the audience spoke. Mamba, who had stared her in the eye throughout her recounting of the tale, turned to the men who sat with him, and a low conversation ensued. Charlie simply stood silent, staring out at the rest of the bikers, wishing desperately that they would allow her some clothes. At last Mamba turned back to her.

"You've made a good start, young lady," he said. "We have decided to allow a vote of club members to decide whether you can invest as a Spirit apprentice. Once invested, you will obey the rules of the Spirits, and will defer to all club members. Do you understand?"

"You mean I'm not already an apprentice Sir?"

"Not until the vote is taken."

Charlie gazed about her in desperation. "Couldn't you vote against?" she pleaded. "Let me go home?"

"The members will vote as they think fit," said Mamba, and soon every hand in the room was raised.

"That settles it," said Mamba. "You are now officially an apprentice. You will come away with us tomorrow, and will remain in our power for the following weeks. Do you understand?"

Charlie stared round at the motley group she was allying herself with. They were a mixed band, some scruffy and longhaired, some with piercings all over their faces and ears, others with long hair and thick beards. They were far from the types she was accustomed to mixing with socially. Yet she was about to be placed in their hands. She glanced down at her naked body. They had already shown that there were no limits to the power they would wield over her, and the throbbing in her behind was proof enough of their methods.

"I understand Sir," she muttered.

Mamba nodded. "Good," he said. "Now there is the matter of a master during your apprenticeship."

At this point a chair scraped back in the middle of the room and a man rose to his feet. He was a giant of a man, with lank, greasy hair and he wore quite the scruffiest jeans and waistcoat Charlie had ever seen. He took a long swig from a beer bottle, belched loudly, then raised his voice.

"Give the bitch to me. I'll knock some sense into her."

Mamba eyed him. "Why you, Garth?"

"'Cause I'm the most senior Spirit here apart from the committee. It's about time I got an apprentice to fuck."

The words brought an odd feeling to Charlie's stomach. Clearly this was to be no ordinary apprenticeship.

"It's not just a case of fucking her, Garth," said Mamba. "She needs schooling in obedience and becoming a Spirit."

"I'll show the slut how Spirits behave," slurred the man. "Just let me at her."

Mamba stared at him for a moment, then shook his head. "No," he said. "Since Zep found her, he should be her guide during the apprenticeship."

"Why the fuck should he?" asked Garth angrily.

"Because I say so!" There was a dangerous edge of anger in Mamba's voice, an edge that made Garth pale slightly.

"All right," he grumbled. "But he'd better be prepared to fight for her when the time comes."

"Zep knows the code," said Mamba. He turned to Charlie. "You will defer to Zep in all things. Do you understand?"

"All things?"

Mamba glared at her. "That's what I said. Are you deaf?"

"No Sir"

"Then answer me. Zep is your master, understand?"

"Yes Sir."

Charlie glanced at Garth, who was glaring up at her, then across to Zep, who had said nothing during the proceedings. He stared at her, stony-faced and she felt her cheeks redden, suddenly shy of the tall, handsome biker who had brought her to this strange world.

"Take her round to greet the members," ordered Mamba.

Zep stepped forward and took hold of Charlie's hands. Without warning he pulled them behind her, and she suddenly felt the cold steel of handcuffs closing about her wrists. She raised her voice in protest, only to receive a hard slap on her bare behind. Zep took hold of her elbow and led her roughly down from the stage.

"You must greet every gang member with a kiss," he ordered.

Charlie stepped up to the first table, where a large man with a black beard and substantial belly sat with one of the girl bikers. She leaned forward to kiss him, and was suddenly made acutely aware of her vulnerability, her breasts dangling before his eyes. The man reached up and cupped the soft flesh as his lips closed over hers and his tongue snaked into her mouth.

When he finally broke away, Charlie turned to the girl, a slim dark-haired biker with a gold ring through her nose. Charlie went to kiss her on the cheek but, to her surprise, found her head being pulled down by the girl, the kiss every bit as passionate and intimate as that she had received from the man. Charlie's emotions were in turmoil as this leather-clad beauty licked at her tongue, her hands roaming over the soft flesh of her breasts. She had never experienced any form of intimacy with a woman before, and was astounded at the arousal it kindled within her as the intimate embrace continued. By the time they separated, Charlie's sex was flowing with juices and her desires were stronger than ever.

Zep continued to lead her round the room, each of the bikers kissing her intimately and taking the opportunity to feel up her luscious young body. Fingers probed at her breasts, sex and anus.

Charlie knew that at some point she would have to greet

Garth, and she wasn't looking forward to it. She tried hard not to show her distaste as she was led up to where he was sitting, but it wasn't easy. At close quarters he was no more attractive than he had been from the stage. As soon as she was close enough he grabbed her and pulled her down onto his lap, closing his lips over her own. His chin was covered with stubble, scratching the softness of her lips as he ground his mouth down on hers. He mauled her body with heavy hands, pinching her nipples until she squealed with pain and ramming his fingers crudely into her vagina. Every fibre of her being told her to struggle and free herself from this lout of a man, but she managed to keep her feelings at bay, knowing that to show her distaste would be to arouse the wrath of both Zep and Mamba.

When at last Garth had had his fill, he shoved her sprawling onto the floor. Charlie scrambled to her feet, shaken but glad that particular part of her ordeal was over. She couldn't get his image from her mind, though, and even after she had moved away from his table, she was acutely aware of his eyes on her as she continued her tour about the room

The ordeal went on. By the time the last of the bikers had greeted her, Charlie was close to tears as Zep led her back onto the stage, where Mamba passed her a beer. She waited whilst her cuffs were undone, then swigged it down thirstily, placing the empty bottle on the table and staring questioningly at Mamba.

"Take her upstairs and show her to her room," said Mamba. "I'll be up shortly."

Zep took Charlie's arm and dragged her to the back of the stage, where a staircase led upwards. Charlie threw a final glance over her shoulder at the bikers as she was taken away, still not quite able to believe what was happening to her.

At the top of the stairs was a narrow corridor. Zep took her to the end and opened a door. It led into a bathroom, a plain room with tiled floor and two shower cubicles at one end. He picked up a cake of soap and threw it to her.

"Here," he said. "Clean yourself up."

Charlie stepped into the shower cubicle. There was no door, and she turned back to look at Zep. He clearly wasn't about to leave, so she resigned herself to being watched, turning on the tap and letting the water cascade over her skin.

As she began to wash, she realised for the first time how dirty she had become. It wasn't just the semen that had leaked from her sex and left patches of grime on her thighs and down her legs. Her body was covered in greasy handprints from the two mechanics, as well as from the bikers who had been groping her. She rubbed hard at herself, cleaning every speck from her soft young skin.

When at last she was satisfied, she switched off the tap and turned to Zep, who threw her a towel. She dried herself carefully, then he took her out. Almost opposite was another door and he opened it. It was a tiny room, with one small, barred window set high in the wall. There was a single bed, that almost took up all the floor space. It seemed more like a cell than a bedroom.

"Lie down," said Zep.

"But..."

"Do as you're told!"

Charlie obeyed, stretching out on the low bed. It wasn't particularly soft, but it felt comfortable all the same. Then, to her surprise, Zep reached beneath it and pulled out leather manacles attached to short chains. He began fastening them about her wrists.

"Please don't chain me, Sir," she said.

"Quiet," he growled. "Speak when you're spoken to."

He fitted the leather bands about both wrists, then did the same to her ankles, tightening the chains so that Charlie's body was spread, open and helpless before him. Once she was secure, Zep sat down beside her on the bed, his voice softer now.

"There's no way to escape," he said.

"Then why the chains? And the barred window?"

"You're a Spirit apprentice now," he said. "You have to accept what we do to you without question. Besides, Mamba likes having the women tethered."

"Mamba?"

"Hush!" He placed a hand on her lips. "You ask too many

questions. Now you've done very well this evening. The best I've ever seen. I'm proud of you."

With that he rose to his feet and slipped out the door, closing it behind him. Charlie heard the key turn in the lock.

Charlie lay, staring up at the ceiling, contemplating his words. They had been spoken softly, with a genuine warmth. Despite his apparent indifference she was beginning to feel a real empathy with the tall biker, and to be in his power gave her an odd sense of security.

She gazed about her at the bleak room. She wondered what Jon would say if he could see her now, a slave to this group of outlaws, chained naked in their headquarters, her body available to anyone who chanced upon her. Yet he must have seen the training of apprentices when he too was a Spirit. How had he behaved when the likes of Zana had been, like her, a young recruit?

She drifted off into a light sleep that was haunted by erotic dreams in which the two mechanics pursued her naked through the streets of the town. The sound of a key in the lock awoke her.

The light came on, and she blinked into the brightness, momentarily unsure of where she was. Someone was standing over her.

"Jon?" she murmured. Then saw the man's face.

It was Mamba.

He stood, staring down at her lovely body. He was wearing a bathrobe, which he pulled undone and shrugged off onto the floor. He was naked beneath, his cock large and uncircumcised, hanging down beneath a thick dark bush of pubic hair. Even as she watched, it began to swell as he took in her nudity.

He moved forward, climbing onto the bed and straddling her body, his large balls feeling cool against her skin. He sat on her stomach, his hands reaching for her breasts and kneading them. Charlie said nothing, staring into his face, watching the way his eyes roved over her body as he caressed her softness, his cock stiffening as he did so.

He slid himself up her body, over her breasts. Instinctively she raised her head, opening her mouth and taking his penis

75

inside. By now it was semi-erect, and she sucked hard at it, feeling it swell and stiffen as she did so. In no time it was rock-hard and she was working her head back and forth, sucking at it as he rammed his hips down against her.

He grabbed hold of the back of her head, fucking her face with relish, his heavy balls slapping against her chin. Charlie was almost gagging now, but she knew she must give the bikers' leader what he wanted, clamping her lips about his engorged shaft and sucking as hard as she was able.

He came suddenly, filling her mouth with hot glutinous spunk which she struggled to gulp down as spurt after spurt gushed into her throat. His seed was copious, some of it leaking from the sides of her lips, but still she sucked and swallowed until the twitching of his cock began to slow, and she felt the last few drops escape from him.

When, at last, he was done, he withdrew from her mouth, climbing off her and reaching for his bath robe. She watched him as he pulled it on, his still erect cock making it bulge out at the front.

He paused for a moment, staring down at her. Then he gave a nod and a grunt of approval and turned to go. Charlie heard the key turn in the lock outside. Then there was a click and the room was plunged into darkness once more.

Chapter 8

Charlie clung hard to Zep's body as his motorcycle hurtled down the motorway. The sheer exhilaration of the ride was overwhelming as he sped through the traffic, dropping the machine low into corners and twisting the throttle wide open as they straightened up. She stared about her at the other bikes. There were twenty or thirty of them, zooming along in a makeshift convoy, weaving in and out of one another, formatting together and then splitting up again in a random series of moves as they carved their way through the traffic.

They had been on the move since soon after dawn. Charlie had been woken by Zep just as the sky was beginning to lighten through her cell window. This time she was allowed to perform her ablutions on her own, and on returning to her cell had found some clothes waiting for her. It was a pair of denim shorts, as inadequate as the ones they had given her the day before, and a short white shirt that tied beneath her breasts, leaving a wide expanse of cleavage uncovered. For her feet there were a pair of high-heeled sandals.

Zep took her down to the room she had been in the night before. Next to it was a kitchen, where she could already smell food being prepared. A small stout biker with a long beard seemed to be in charge, and he immediately gave Charlie the task of laying the tables in the room. Charlie set about the job without complaint, glad to be busy. It was the first demand that had been made of her that wasn't of a sexual nature, and it was a relief to be doing the work of a normal woman.

She was surprised at how organised the group was. It was clear that each biker had his or her job, and before long the entire gang were seated at the tables whilst great plates of bacon, egg and sausages were laid out in a buffet.

Charlie ate hungrily, seated next to Zep, then joined three other gang members at the washing up. In no time the place was restored to order and the bikers were packing their bags for the journey. Most of the gang seemed to have slept the night at the clubhouse, and it was a huge convoy of bikes that pulled out of the car park. All through the town they picked up more bikers until at last they reached the open highway and headed south.

And now, after two hours of fast riding, they were nearing the coast. Despite herself, Charlie found herself enjoying the feel of the powerful machine between her legs and the smell of Zep's leathers. She thought back to her normal day. By now she would be hanging her washing on the line and preparing to visit the local supermarket. To be here, on the open highway with this band of adventurers was light years from that. She thought of the night before, and the taste of Mamba's spunk, and a shiver ran through her, a shiver of fear.

They were approaching the port now, and Zep throttled back, falling into line with the rest of the gang. Ahead was the ferry terminal, and they drew to a halt at the barrier.

Half an hour later they were leaning against the rail of the ferry watching the port disappear behind them. Zep passed Charlie a beer and she sipped at it. All around were bikers. At least two more gangs had joined the ferry with them, and now, wherever she looked, Charlie saw leather-clad figures, most of them swigging from cans.

The journey went quickly, much of the time spent drinking and chatting. A number of the bikers from the other gangs took an interest in the beautiful and sexily-clad young apprentice, and Charlie found herself the centre of attention amongst the men, with more than one of them running a hand over her behind or taking the opportunity to squeeze her breasts through the thin material of her blouse, actions that she dared not protest about.

They rode on down the highway for another two hours, then swung off onto smaller, winding roads. As far as Charlie could see in each direction there seemed to be bikers, with all manner of logos on the back of their leathers.

All at once Zep slowed and, peering round him, Charlie saw that the bikes ahead were pulling off the road onto what appeared to be a track through a forest. Soon Zep was heading down the track behind them, the trees rushing past the bike like a green screen. Then they burst into a clearing and Charlie gasped at the sight that met her eyes.

She had never seen so many bikes, parked in gleaming lines, beyond them all manner of tents and bivouacs. Zep and his companions raised a fist in the air as they raced across toward them.

They drew their bikes into a circle and cut their engines, dismounting together. At once they set about pitching camp. Charlie was made to work extremely hard, ordered this way and that by the bikers, but she was a good and obedient worker and soon they had put up a number of tents and thrown their sleeping bags inside. Then Zep took Charlie's arm and led her into the crowd.

A makeshift stage had been set up, and a band was playing, their heavy metal music amplified to an almost painful volume, thanks to a generator and a bank of speakers. Most of the bikers were gathered round the stage, dancing or just listening. Zep passed Charlie a beer and they settled down on the grass. It was a warm, sunny evening and Charlie was feeling almost mellow as she sipped at her drink and watched the sea of bikers pass by.

It was almost an hour later when the band put down their instruments and a middle-aged biker stepped onto the stage. He drew a faint cheer from the crowd, who clearly knew him. He cracked a few jokes, then held up his hands for silence.

"Right," he shouted. "Time for a spot of proper entertainment. I can see we have a number of ladies here who'll fit the bill nicely."

Zep laughed, and turned to Charlie.

"Fancy upholding the honour of the Spirits?" he asked.

"I beg your pardon, Sir?"

"You're about to represent us up on the stage. Just listen."

Charlie stared at Zep in puzzlement, then turned her attention back to the stage once more.

"That's right guys," the man was saying. "Time for the wet T-shirts."

A cheer went up from the watching bikers, and Charlie noticed some of the girl bikers around her being pulled to their feet by the men. She turned back to Zep, who was still smiling, then realised that they were surrounded by other members of the Spirits, who were all staring at her.

"Come on, my sexy little apprentice," said Zep, taking her by the arm. "You heard what old Ted said. You're about to enter your first wet T-shirt competition."

Chapter 9

Charlie scarcely knew what was happening as the men pulled her to her feet. There was a good deal of laughter all around as the Spirits gathered about her. Then she found herself facing Mamba himself.

"You know what's required of you?" he asked.

"No, Sir."

"It's not just a case of putting on a good show. With a body like yours you should be able to win easily, and that's what I expect of you."

All of a sudden something was thrust under her nose, and she looked up to see Zana holding out a small bundle.

"These should do," she said, grinning.

Charlie examined the garments. There was a small, white T-shirt and a pair of very brief panties.

"Put them on," ordered Zep. "Just fucking do as you're told for a change," he added roughly as she hesitated. She looked about her for some kind of changing facilities, but there were none. She stared round at the Spirits, who were watching her expectantly. She made as if to protest, then changed her mind. Her face glowing red, she reached down for the button on her shorts.

She gazed guiltily about her, but only the Spirits seemed to be watching, so she slid the shorts down over her hips and stepped out of them. Then she grabbed the pants and pulled them on quickly. They were very brief indeed, and made of a thin material through which the dark thatch that covered her pubis could clearly be seen. The rear of the panties was not much more than a string that tucked into the crack of her behind, so that her bottom cheeks were completely uncovered. She adjusted the skimpy garment as best she could, then reached for the knot beneath her breasts.

She pulled it undone and shrugged the shirt off. Once again, she was quick to grab the T-shirt, pulling it over her head and dragging it down to cover her top. It was small, so that her breasts pressed hard against the material, the nipples clearly outlined. It barely came down to her midriff, leaving her feeling very exposed indeed.

Zep inspected her carefully, smoothing down her hair and straightening the T-shirt. Then he nodded.

"You'll do fine," he said. "Now get up on that stage."

Charlie glanced across at the stage. There were two or three girls there already, all wearing white T-shirts like her own. Only too aware of the sight she made, she pushed her way through the crowd, trying to avoid the inevitable hands that groped her as she passed.

As she came closer to the other girls she saw that all, like her, were young and attractive, and all were eyeing one another with some suspicion. Her eyes dropped automatically to their breasts. There were some lovely specimens, but she felt certain that her own pair were a match for any of them.

All at once there was a disturbance behind her and another girl burst through the crowd to join them. She was blonde, her long, wavy tresses hanging to below her shoulders. She had a lovely curvaceous body and large firm breasts that pressed the material of her T-shirt out in front. There was no doubt that this would be the girl to beat.

A girl biker began organising them into a line. Charlie found herself at the back, behind the blonde girl whose name, she discovered was Anya. Then the man was back on the stage again, and the first of the girls was being called up.

She was tall and dark, her breasts small but shapely. She swaggered across the stage, to the cheers of the watching bikers. Then someone passed a bucket of water to Ted. As the girl turned toward him he swung the bucket back and hurled the water over her. Her shrieks were drowned by the roar of the crowd, and now Charlie realised just what the contest was about.

The water had soaked the T-shirt, rendering it immediately transparent. In a moment, from merely having the shape of her breasts on view, the girl was almost completely exposed, her large brown nipples contrasting with the pink of the rest of her skin. For a moment she covered herself with her hands, but the shouts of the onlookers persuaded her to drop her arms and reveal herself to those watching.

She continued to strut back and forth whilst Ted described her charms to the audience, then she was taken to the side of the stage and the second girl was summoned up to receive a soaking.

Charlie watched in nervous anticipation as the girls went up one by one onto the stage. Each one put on a brazen act before her audience, though Charlie suspected that most of them were as petrified as she was.

Eventually it came to Anya's turn, and a louder than usual shout went up from those watching as she climbed up onto the platform. Standing there, high and exposed above the onlookers, Charlie was able to get a good look at her rival, and was once again struck by the girl's beauty and the perfection of her figure. Anya looked more confident than any of the other girls had done as she placed her hands on her hips and grinned down at the watching men, before dropping into the rhythm of the music.

She took the bucket of water with barely a flinch, and Charlie looked on in admiration at the lovely breasts suddenly revealed beneath the thin material. Anya's bust was firm, projecting forward deliciously, the nipples hardened by the temperature of the water.

There was no doubt that Anya was a cut above the rest of the contestants as she swayed across the stage, every inch of her body conveying a sensuous message of arousal to those watching. Charlie glanced down at her own body, and blushed at how hard her own nipples were as the excitement within her increased with every moment.

All at once the music ceased and Anya made her way to the edge of the stage to join the others. Then Ted was beckoning to Charlie, and her stomach tightened into a knot as she gazed up at the empty stage.

"You're on," said a voice in her ear. She turned to see Zep standing beside her. Charlie's throat was dry, and she swallowed hard. Then, taking a deep breath, she stepped up onto the stage.

"Ah, a newcomer," said Ted. "Guys this is Charlie, the new apprentice with the Spirits. Come on then Charlie, show us what you can do."

Charlie dropped easily into a dance routine, her lithe young body swaying to the music. She had always been an expert dancer and something of an extrovert on the floor. Even so she had never appeared so scantily clad before, and her face glowed at the way her breasts bounced with every movement.

So absorbed was she with her dance that she had almost forgotten the contest. The audience hadn't, though, and she turned suddenly to be confronted by Ted holding the bucket. Her natural reaction was to flinch away, but she never got the opportunity as the bucketful was flung straight at her.

The water was so cold it almost stung, and Charlie gasped aloud as her T-shirt was drenched. She glanced down at herself. Like the other girls, she found her breasts almost totally visible through the thin, wet material, her nipples even harder now, projecting like firm knobs that almost seemed to invite a man's lips to close over them. She stood still for a moment, stunned by the sudden drenching, then the shouts of the crowd reached her ears and she remembered what was required of her.

She threw herself back into her dance, suddenly strangely excited by the cries from below and the way her body was so exposed. She was reminded of the way the Spirits had put her on display in the clubhouse, and of her naked ride about town. She knew her body excited men, and all at once the perverse thrill she always got from exhibiting herself came to the fore.

Charlie was almost lost in the music now, her slim, lovely young body swaying back and forth, thrusting her breasts forward, aware that the Spirits would be watching her and would be listening for the crowd's appreciation. When the music finally stopped it almost took her by surprise, and she staggered across to join the other girls as if in a trance.

Ted began speaking again, and she struggled to listen to what he was saying. Apparently the bikers were to vote for the best girl, and Ted called the first girl forward onto the stage once more.

He began pointing out the girl's obvious assets, much to the enjoyment of those watching. Then a vote was called and the attractive biker waved to the crowd in appreciation.

One by one the girls came forward, and the crowd indicated its preferences. When it was Anya's turn, Charlie noted, without surprise, the volume of the cheers the blonde girl received. There was little doubt in her mind who would be the winner of the contest, and a shiver ran through her as she anticipated the wrath of the Spirits.

Then Ted was calling to her, and she stepped forward nervously.

Charlie was astonished at her reception. Clearly the crowd had liked her more than she had anticipated. She moved up beside Ted, who placed an arm about her waist.

"And now for our new arrival," he said. "I'm sure that most of you were as impressed as I was by this gorgeous pair of tits." He ran his hand up her chest and cupped her breast, squeezing it and pressing it forward, much to the delight of those watching.

Charlie found herself spreading her legs slightly in an almost unconscious gesture which wasn't missed by the crowd.

"Right, time to vote," called Ted above the hubbub. "If Charlie was the girl you'd most like to fuck, raise your arms now."

Charlie was shocked by the way he had phrased the vote, but a strange thrill went through her as she surveyed the sea of arms raised in the air. There was something unexpectedly exciting about the thought of all those stiff cocks out there. She smiled as best she could and waved nervously out at the crowd as the hands were counted. Anya was bound to win though, she thought. She was glad to see the end of the ordeal, though fearful of the reaction of the gang at her failure. She was somewhat surprised and relieved, therefore, when Ted, at the same time as calling Anya back on stage, held her arm to prevent her from leaving.

"Well, ladies and gentlemen," he said, once Anya had joined the pair of them. "It seems it's too close to call. It looks like you're split on whether you'd prefer to get your dicks into this sexy little newcomer from the Spirits, or the gorgeous Anya."

Charlie stared at him in surprise, then once again out at the crowd of cheering bikers.

"So we'll have to have a play off," went on Ted. "To decide which of these two delicious little beauties you prefer. Let's have some more water."

At this point two bikers climbed on either side of the stage, each carrying a bucket. Ted made Charlie and Anya stand back to back, then jumped down from the stage. Charlie stared at the biker approaching her, his bucket held in both hands. Her instinct told her to shy away, but she knew the Spirits were watching, so she stood her ground.

The second bucket was even colder than the first, and Charlie spluttered as it struck her, her body thrust back against Anya's whose own reaction told Charlie that she had received her drenching simultaneously. Then the music started again, and the two girls dropped into the beat.

Charlie danced as sexily and as sensually as she could, weaving round Anya as she too displayed her body to the men in the most blatant manner. The hoots and catcalls from the audience were almost deafening as the two girls pranced about the stage, each trying to outdo the other in the way they presented their bodies to the onlookers. The dance seemed to go on and on, yet still the audience called for more. Then Charlie noticed that Anya had paused at the front of the stage.

A slow handclap began in the audience as Anya swayed back and forth. Charlie stopped her cavorting and stood, watching as her rival became the centre of attention. At first Charlie was unsure what was happening, then she saw Anya reach down for the hem of her T-shirt, and the young apprentice held her breath as she realised what the girl was doing.

Slowly Anya lifted her T-shirt until the soft pink orbs of the undersides of her breasts were revealed, bringing fresh whistles from those watching. Charlie looked on, rooted to the spot, then she heard her name called and turned to see Zep staring up at her.

He didn't speak. He didn't have to. The nod he gave her was sufficient. Charlie knew at once what was expected of her, and she knew too that she dare not disobey. She turned to look at Anya again. The girl was still teasing her audience, half uncovering her breasts, then letting the hem of the garment fall back. Charlie cast a final glance in the direction of Zep, then, her face bright red, she moved forward to stand beside Anya.

She half expected a hostile reaction from her rival, but Anya merely laughed and clapped when she too reached for the lower part of her T-shirt and began raising it. The two lovelies stood facing each other, lifting their shirts on one side, then the other, giving the onlookers tantalising glimpses of their areolae but never quite uncovering their breasts completely, bringing loud boos from the crowd whenever they covered themselves again, despite the inadequacy of the T-shirts.

All at once Anya caught Charlie's eye and winked at her. Then she gave a slight nod. Charlie recognised this as her cue. She glanced out at the sea of eyes before her, recognising the shamefulness of what she was about to do. Then, gripping the hem of her T-shirt once more, waited for Anya's signal.

The pair pulled the garments over their heads simultaneously, to the vocal delight of the crowd. Anya began swinging hers about her head and Charlie, her face scarlet, followed suit, hurling the sodden shirt into the audience at the same time as Anya did. The two beauties stood for a moment, bare breasted in front of the bikers, both soaking up the rapturous applause.

"Let's dance," mouthed Anya to Charlie.

Charlie stared at her in surprise. Wasn't what she had done enough? Then the other girl nodded to Ted.

At once the music began again, a hard-driven beaty number that had Anya moving at once. Charlie watched as the other girl's unrestrained breasts bounced delightfully to the beat. Then she looked down and caught Zep's eye and realised she was expected to follow suit.

She fell into the rhythm, only too aware that her breasts were similarly mobile as she boogied with her sexy partner. The pair danced like their lives depended on it, their hips thrusting back and forth, their shoulders shaking as they gave the onlookers the show they wanted. Then Anya moved close to Charlie, wrapping her arms about her.

Charlie did not resist, though she had never embraced a woman who was so scantily before. It felt oddly erotic to feel Anya's nipples pressed against her own, and her mind went back to the kisses of the girl bikers the night before in the clubhouse. Anya moved her lips close to Charlie's ear and spoke.

"Zep's watching you pretty closely. Is he your master?"

"Yes."

I think he wants you to win this. In fact you'll be thrashed if you don't."

Charlie looked at her in consternation.

"Oh no!"

The girl grinned "You can if you want, you know."

"How? Please tell me," pleaded Charlie.

"How do you think? Listen to what the guys are shouting."

Charlie gazed out over Anya's shoulder. At first the shouts just seemed a cacophony. Then she began to discern the words.

"Get 'em off! Get 'em off!"

She pulled back slightly and stared at Anya in amazement. "You mean..."

Anya nodded, then stepped away.

"Better do it, little sexy apprentice."

For a moment, Charlie was rooted to the spot, unable to fully grasp the import of what was being asked of her. She turned to face the crowd, her heart beating hard. She couldn't do it, could she? She couldn't strip totally naked in front of all these men. What would Jon say if he knew what she was doing, dancing on an open stage wearing only skimpy briefs in front of this crowd of strangers? Then once again she saw Zep's expression, and she knew she had to do it or she would be beaten.

As she stepped forward to the edge of the stage the crowd went silent. Anya had moved off to the side, so that Charlie was the sole object of attention. The scantily clad little apprentice felt the panic inside her rising as she contemplated what was being asked of her, but she forced it down again and reached a trembling hand for the waistband of her panties.

She hooked her thumbs inside the elastic and took a final glance out at her audience. Then, with a single movement she pulled them down, over her thighs and off. She stood for a second, staring out at the sea of hungry eyes. Then, as with her shirt, she swung the tiny garment about her head and flung it out into the crowd, placing her hands on her hips and standing with her legs apart.

The silence lasted a moment longer, then the loudest cheer yet went up. Charlie glanced down at herself, noting with dismay that her nipples were bullet-hard now, her dark pubic triangle contrasting with the paleness of her smooth skin. Despite her embarrassment, though, she knew the Spirits demanded a good show from their exhibitionist apprentice, so she threw back her hair and stood, head erect, her cheeks crimson as she showed her lovely young body to the crowd.

She wasn't sure how long she remained there, brazenly displaying herself, accepting the plaudits of the bikers, becoming more aroused by the second at the thought of all the men watching her. All at once, though, she became aware of someone standing close behind her, and of a pair of hands on her back. She glanced round to see Anya standing there, her fingers tracing the smooth curve of Charlie's flank.

The girl moved closer, so that Charlie could feel the hard flesh of her nipples against her back. Then the arms slid around her, pulling her close as Anya began to gently kiss her neck.

"No!" she exclaimed.

"Relax, little one. They want to see it, and I can tell you enjoy showing it."

"But I'm not..."

"Relax for fuck's sake. Let them know how turned on this is making you."

All at once, Charlie realised that the sensation of the girl's kisses was beginning to excite her to an extraordinary extent, and she leaned back against the girl biker. As she did so, Anya's hands slid up over her stomach and moved smoothly towards her breasts.

Charlie gave a little gasp as Anya's hands closed over her mammaries, squeezing the soft flesh in a smooth massaging movement. Her fingers sought out Charlie's nipples, rolling them between finger and thumb, sending tingles of excitement through the naked girl. For a moment Charlie forgot where she was, letting her head loll back onto Anya's shoulder, moaning slightly as the girl massaged her breasts. The sensation was wonderful, and Charlie felt a warm wetness seep into her thighs as she drank in the scent of her companion.

So lost was Charlie in her own arousal, that when Anya began sliding her right hand down over her ribcage and towards the top of her legs she responded by widening her stance in an unconscious acceptance of what was to come.

All at once Charlie noticed how silent it had become, and she opened her eyes. Below her was a sea of upturned faces, all watching intensely as Anya caressed her naked flesh. Charlie realised with a shock the exhibition she was making of herself, standing naked, her legs spread, her arousal obvious to all. For a second her natural inhibitions returned and she tried to wriggle free, but Anya held her fast, forcing her to remain in position.

"No, you mustn't," whispered the hapless apprentice as Anya's fingers continued their journey down over the softness of her belly. "Oh!"

The cry was audible to all as Anya's fingers found the wet little bud that was Charlie's clitoris. For a moment she tried to close her legs, but the sensation was too delicious and instead she sagged back into Anya's arms.

Anya took control now, her left hand continuing to massage Charlie's bare breasts whilst the fingers of her right ran up and down the girl's slit, sliding into her vagina and bringing new cries from the now hopelessly aroused girl.

Charlie found herself unable to stop pressing her hips forward against Anya's insistent probing fingers as the heat inside her increased. Once again she stared out at those watching. She should have been dying of shame, her display and arousal obvious to all, but all she could think of was the delicious feeling as the girl caressed her. Somewhere below a camera flashed and a shiver ran through her as she considered the image it captured, a beautiful naked youngster standing, legs spread wide apart, grinding her hips down on another girl's fingers, the wetness inside her plain for all to see.

She wondered who else would see the shot. She imagined a man holding the picture in his hand and masturbating, working his foreskin back and forth until a gob of spunk spurted from his cock onto her naked image. Then all of a sudden Charlie was coming, crying aloud with pleasure as Anya thrust her fingers hard into her hot sex. The orgasm was the most intense she had ever experienced, every nerve in her body alight with lust, jabbing her hips forward, the moisture inside her leaking out onto her thighs as she groaned with joy. Anya worked her fingers back and forth expertly, holding her at her peak for the longest possible time before finally taking her down the other side, supporting Charlie as she crumpled into her arms.

It was some time before Charlie regained her breath, and it was only then that she realised that the roaring sound in her ears was he cheering of the crowd. She glanced across at the mass of people, and a slight smile crossed her lips. Then her legs gave and she crumpled to the ground, totally exhausted by her performance.

Chapter 10

The next morning they were on the road again. Charlie took her customary seat behind Zep as the bike swept down the country roads, occasionally roaring through small villages where the local townsfolk would stop what they were doing and emerge to watch the convoy of bikers process past.

Charlie was exhausted, leaning against her master, almost falling asleep despite the exhilaration of the ride. After the contest the day before, the revelry had gone on long into the night. Charlie had descended from the stage to the congratulations of all the Spirits. She had hunted for her clothes, but in vain, and had been forced to accept a simple cloth wrapped about her waist and nothing to cover her breasts at all. During the dancing that night the men were constantly feeling her up, and later she lost even the cloth, so that she was obliged to spend the rest of the evening naked. She lost count of the number of men who fingered her sex that night, and she actually orgasmed twice on the dance floor, much to the amusement of those watching. Fortunately, though, Zep was never far away, and she knew nobody touched her without his permission.

Despite the fact that he treated her with feigned indifference, Zep's presence was somehow a source of comfort, and she had felt almost content spending the night with her wrists tied to the foot of his bed in his tent, unmolested by the other bikers. She had half expected him to want to fuck her, and his failure to do so caused mixed - on the one hand, her modesty made the thought of letting him take her so casually was abhorrent to her, but on the other she felt almost insulted by his failure to take advantage of her.

That morning they had had an early start, and their speeding machines had soon left France behind and crossed the border into Germany. A long run down the autobahn had brought them into thickly forested country, where they had left the busy highway and headed off into the countryside. Now Charlie sensed that they were nearing their destination as they turned down ever narrower lanes.

At last they turned off the main road altogether. Like the day before they took a track that ran through thick woods, taking them ever further from the roads, towns and houses. Charlie began to wonder what could possibly lie in this deserted area, but Zep clearly knew where he was going, and all at once the trees parted and they found themselves in the centre of a vast array of low wooden buildings.

The buildings were old, the paint peeling from the walls, the grass around them overgrown. It seemed to be some kind of abandoned military installation, and it reminded Charlie of a prisoner of war camp she had once seen in a film. In the centre was a wide square, where a number of motorcycles were already parked, and it was towards these that Zep headed, wheeling his machine round in the soft grass and kicking down the stand.

The bikers unloaded their machines, carrying their bags into one of the huts. Inside, the building was set out like a long dormitory and each biker chose a bed and began unpacking their things. Charlie had nothing of her own to unpack, but she set about emptying Zep's bags for him. She had been allocated a bed next to him, and was a little nervous to discover that she was the only female in the hut. There were a few pairs of shorts and a couple of small tops in Zep's bag that she assumed were for her, though he made her unload them into his own locker.

Once everything was stowed, they wandered outside, where a camp fire was burning and a number of bikers were gathered round it. Charlie was sent off to procure beers for Zep, Zana and two other bikers, and they settled down on the grass beside the fire.

Charlie found herself excluded from the conversation, which revolved around the merits of various motorcycles, and she soon started dozing off, relaxed by the warmth of the evening and rather exhausted by the journey. She wasn't certain how long she had slept, but she was aroused by the sound of raised voices. She opened her eyes to discover the tall, burly figure of Garth standing over her.

At first Charlie couldn't make out what was going on. All the bikers wore serious expressions, and Zep had risen to his feet and was confronting Garth.

"Why don't you just fuck off, Garth," he was shouting.

"Because I'm making a challenge," growled back the large biker. "You chicken or something?"

At this suggestion, Zep fairly bristled.

"I never chickened out in my life."

"Then take the challenge."

"Look, Garth," Zep replied quietly. "She was placed in my care, and that's an end to it."

"So you are chickening out."

"I told you, don't fucking call me chicken."

"You're chicken, Zep. You're too fucking chicken-shit scared to take me on, and if you're not fucking her you must be a fucking queer as well."

Zep's face reddened, and Charlie could see that he was extremely angry. When he spoke, his voice was low.

"All right," he said. "Have it your way. I'll take you on. Out the back in half an hour."

"Winner gets charge of the slut?"

"Winner gets Charlie."

Chapter 11

Charlie hadn't known quite what form Garth's challenge on Zep might take. She supposed it would be some kind of fight, possibly with weapons, and she was surprised to find how upset she was by such a prospect. The more she thought about it, the more she realised how strong her feelings were for the tall, quiet biker who had introduced her to the Spirits and had brought about her apprenticeship. Since that first encounter, when he had run her off the road on Jon's bike and had subsequently fucked her in the woods, she had had no intimate contact with him, yet simply being under his charge gave her an odd sense of security, and she doubted whether she could have undergone any of the ordeals set her by the Spirits were it not for his support.

What made things worse was the thought of Garth becoming her new master. The burly biker was the very opposite of Zep, with his uncouth aggressive manner, his arrogance and, worst of all, his obvious desire to unleash his cruelty on her.

As the time approached for the challenge, the bikers all began making their way toward the edge of the area of the hutted village. Zana and the rest of the Spirits were among the first to leave, and Charlie followed them at a discreet distance, suddenly rather lost without her master.

When she reached the place at which they were gathering, Charlie was surprised to find that it was a long track, either side of which the bikers were gathered. Clearly this was to be no ordinary fight. She found herself a vantage point on a small hillock set back from the track and settled down to watch.

Within ten minutes the track was lined with bikers on either side, and there was an atmosphere of anticipation as they waited for the action to begin. Charlie became more and more nervous as time passed, so that soon her stomach was like a tight knot.

The first sign that something was happening was the sound

of approaching motorcycles, and all eyes turned to the right as two riders suddenly came over a rise about half a mile away. Even Charlie's untutored ear could perceive that these were not the monstrous snarling machines that the bikers used for touring. The note of the engines was high and rasping, and the bikes snaked from side to side as they sped up the track.

Zep and Garth swung their machines round as they reached the centre of the track, sliding sideways and coming to a halt in a cloud of dust. The bikes were tall, with upswept exhausts that chattered loudly and emitted small puffs of blue smoke. The two sat side by side for a moment, revving their engines. Then they simultaneously cut their ignition, and the bikes fell silent.

For a few moments nothing happened, the two bikers sitting quietly whilst the dust drifted gently away. Then, from the crowd, a figure emerged, and Charlie's heart seemed to skip a beat as she recognised Mamba.

The bikers' leader stepped out in front of the protagonists and a hush descended over the crowd. Charlie found herself leaning forward to catch his words as he began to speak.

"Okay," he said. "I guess we all know Zep and Garth. Garth's issued the challenge, so he's going to tell us what it's all about."

Garth kicked down the side-stand on his bike and climbed off.

"Spirits have a new apprentice," he barked in his gruff voice. "Zep here got given her, but I reckon I could do a better job."

"What's your grounds?" asked Mamba.

"Bastard's too soft. Hasn't even fucked the bitch since he got her. Hasn't even thrashed her. Everyone knows an apprentice needs thrashing regular. Stands to reason he's not doing a proper job."

Charlie listened to his words. It was scarcely credible that he was discussing fucking and thrashing her in so casual a way. It was true that Zep had done neither, but after all she had been in his charge for less than two days. Just what would life be like under Garth's power?

Zep too had dismounted. "The girl was put in my charge," he said. "I'll do things the way I see fit. I don't need advice from

Garth."

"Where is she?" asked Mamba. "Bring her here."

There was a murmur of conversation as the bikers looked around them. Charlie shrank back, but already two of the Spirits had risen to their feet and were heading to where she was sitting. They pulled her to her feet and, taking an arm each, frogmarched her through the onlookers and out to stand beside Mamba.

"This is the cause of the trouble, then," said Mamba, somewhat contemptuously, eyeing the youngster up and down. "Tell me young lady, are you content with your master?"

Charlie looked at Zep, who stared at her without expression. She wanted to protest about the whole concept of having a master, and to beg for freedom, but she knew this was neither the time nor the place.

"Yes Sir," she said quietly.

"And I'm happy with him too," said Mamba. "So what's your game, Garth? Don't you respect the leader's decision?"

"I issued a challenge," said Garth, somewhat sulkily. "And the bastard accepted."

"You accepted then?" asked Mamba, turning to Zep.

"Yes."

"But only because Garth accused him of being chicken," burst out Charlie.

"Quiet!" thundered Zep. "Don't you know better than to speak only when spoken to? Especially to the gang leader."

"Don't worry, Mamba," said Garth, smirking. "When she's in my charge she'll learn how to behave."

Charlie hung her head, her face scarlet. She cursed herself for speaking out of turn. All she had done was support Garth's case and incur Zep's wrath.

"Is what she says true?" asked Mamba.

"True or not, Garth issued a challenge and I accepted," said Zep.

"So you're not going to withdraw?"

"No."

"So be it." Mamba turned to the watching bikers. "The challenge, then, is for possession of this apprentice."

A murmur of approval went up as he turned and went back to the crowd line. Charlie lingered a little longer, staring at Zep, but he said nothing.

"Give us a kiss for luck, darling."

Garth grabbed Charlie and pulled her to him, Placing his mouth over hers as he mauled at her breasts. For a second Charlie's instincts took over and she tried to push him off, slapping his face. He was too strong for her, though, grabbing her arm.

"Is this the way you train your apprentice, Zep?" he roared. "Rest assured, young lady, once this contest is done I'll thrash your arse for that. Now come here."

This time the thought of the damage already done to Zep's reputation brought Charlie to her senses, and she relaxed, allowing him to press his tongue into her mouth and offering no resistance as he squeezed her.

He kissed her long and hard, his bristles stinging her cheek, Then he broke away, pushing her aside.

"There'll be more of that when you're in my charge," he said. Then he turned to Zep. "Ready?"

Zep nodded.

Charlie turned and made to push her way through the crowd once more, but a hand was held up in front of her. It was Mamba.

"Stay!" he ordered. "You are the prize."

Charlie took her place beside him and turned to watch the action. A biker had stepped out to where the two protagonists were standing. He was carrying two poles, each more than ten feet long, with a circular padded disc on the end about a foot across. He handed one each to Zep and Garth. The two bikers examined the poles, then mounted their machines and kicked them into life.

So it was to be a joust, just as in the tales of mediaeval knights. The two men would attempt to unseat one another using the poles.

The more she thought about it, the more apt the comparison became. After all the ancient knights had fought for a maiden's honour by riding their steeds at one another. She was hardly a maiden, and it was her body that they were fighting for, yet still the similarities were there. In fact she almost expected one of the bikers to come and ask for her handkerchief as her favour. Instead they wheeled their bikes round and headed off to opposite ends of the track, where they turned to face one another.

Once again a silence had descended upon the onlookers, as all gazed expectantly one way or the other, waiting for the contest to begin. In that moment the whole thing seemed almost unreal to Charlie, the crowd, the track, the two bikers, their lances held high in the air. It was as if she was dreaming it all. Then the scratching buzz of the two-stroke machines suddenly sliced through the silence and the two men were racing down the track toward one another.

To Charlie it seemed that they must collide as they approached one another at breakneck speed. They crossed just in front of where she was standing, and the crowd roared as Zep's lance caught Garth a glancing blow. The challenger's machine wobbled dangerously, and it seemed to the watching girl that he must fall off. Somehow, though, he managed to wrestle the machine back under control, and she gave a sigh of disappointment as he headed back to the opposite end and turned once more to face Zep.

The two bikers paused for a moment, then they were hurtling toward one another once more, their lances forward, each man's eyes fixed on his opponent.

Charlie scarcely dared look as they crossed, but a smart jink to the right at the last second by Garth meant that no contact was made, and once again they sped off to opposite ends of the track.

They turned for a third time and began bearing down on each another. This time they seemed to Charlie to be going faster than ever, and she clenched her fists with anxiety as they neared one another. Then, all of a sudden, the note of Zep's engine died. Charlie watched in horror as the nose of his machine dipped, the power suddenly gone. In what was obviously an instinctive reaction, Zep glanced down at his machine.

That was his undoing. Garth was coming down the track flat out, his lance levelled, and by the time Zep looked up it was too late. The lance caught Zep full in the chest, lifting him bodily from his machine and hurling him into the dirt, where he rolled over before coming to rest on his back. There was a shout from the crowd and Charlie ran forward to where the biker was sprawled on the ground. She crouched down over him anxiously, and gave a gasp of relief as he opened his eyes.

"Are you all right?" she asked, anxiously.

He gazed blearily up at her. There was a cut across his forehead and his nose was bleeding.

"What?"

"Are you okay?"

He shook his head and raised himself on one elbow. Then, to Charlie's relief, he dragged himself to his feet. He looked a trifle unsteady, and his leathers were badly scuffed, but there didn't appear to be any bones broken. She went to place an arm about him to help him to the side when she felt a hand on her shoulder. She turned to see Garth grinning down at her.

"Leave him. He'll survive. You've got to come with me."

Charlie took a last, despairing glance at Zep, then followed Garth over to where Mamba was standing.

"She's mine now," he said to the bikers' leader.

Mamba nodded. "She's yours."

Garth looked round in triumph at the other bikers.

"Now you'll see how an apprentice should be treated," he said. "You all saw the bitch strike me before the contest. Well, she's about to get it back ten times over. Down in the square in fifteen minutes."

A general murmur of assent came up from the crowd as he spoke, then they began to move off. Garth turned to Charlie.

"Go to my locker and look inside, bitch. You'll find a whip in there and a bag with some rope. Bring them down to the tree at the meeting place. And get a fucking move on!"

Chapter 12

Charlie's heart was beating fast as she rummaged through the mess that was Garth's locker. It bore no resemblance to Zep's. The clothes were simply flung in with the rest of his things, and many of the garments seemed to be long overdue a wash. Delving through the piles of dirty clothes, pornographic magazines, and weapons of all sorts, she finally found the whip tucked at the back. It was made of fine leather, long and thin and extremely flexible. She ran her fingers down its length, shivering slightly as she did so.

She searched further and found a bag full of lengths of rope. It was a coarse hempen rope in strands of between three and six feet. In addition there was a mallet and some metal staves that resembled tent pegs. Charlie pulled the bag from the locker and closed the door. Then, her stomach full of butterflies, she began to make her way to the meeting area.

Once again a large crowd met her eyes as she walked down the slope to where the campfire still smouldered. There was a real buzz in the air, and all eyes turned towards her as she came into view. She searched around for Zep, but he was nowhere to be seen. Garth was there, though, standing by a sturdy tree in the centre of the area, his arms folded as he watched her approach.

She stopped in front of Garth and held out the whip and the bag of rope, which he took from her without speaking. He quickly checked the contents of the bag and nodded.

"At least you can get something right," he said. "Now, stand over there by the tree. And stand like a good apprentice should, hands behind your head and legs apart."

Charlie moved across to the spot he had indicated, and took up the stance. All around more bikers were arriving, squatting down on the grass to watch what was to happen. Charlie knew she was the centre of attention, as she had been on the stage the day before. On that occasion, though, the bikers had been intent on pleasure. This time she knew that Garth had punishment on

99

his mind.

She stood for about ten minutes, feeling very lonely and isolated from the crowd that surrounded her. It was almost as if the
anticipation was worse than the punishment itself, and she
guessed that that was precisely why Garth was making her wait.
She determined not to show herself to be intimidated by his tac-
tics, though, holding her head high and staring out into the middle
distance. Meanwhile still more bikers were arriving until she
was sure that nearly all the occupants of the camp were gathered
round waiting to see what was to follow. The one person she
couldn't see was Zep.

At last Garth moved across to where Charlie was standing.
He stood close to her, looking her up and down.

"Thought you could get away with slapping me, eh?" he said
quietly. "Well, you're about to learn who's boss. Understand?"

"Yes Sir."

"Hold out your arms."

Slowly Charlie stretched out her arms in front of her, and
Garth began wrapping the rope about her wrists. He tied it tight,
knotting it so that the rough cord bit into her tender flesh. He
secured a length to both wrists, then threw the ends up over a
branch that ran out parallel from the trunk of the tree above her
head. The branch was at such a height that Charlie could barely
reach it, even standing on tiptoe. He tied her arms about three
feet apart, leaving her hardly able to move.

He hadn't finished yet. From the bag he produced the mallet
and stakes and drove two of the stakes into the ground on either
side of where she stood, at a similar distance apart to the bonds
on her arms. Then he took hold of her ankles and, hauling them
apart, began to secure them to the stakes.

By the time he had finished, Charlie was totally helpless.
Her feet barely touched the ground. Her body was spread-eagled
and held in the most excruciating tension, her wrists and ankles
burning with the pressure of the ropes. It was the most extraordinary experience to be thus totally at Garth's mercy, yet at the
same time there was something strangely erotic about her situation. The notion of her subservience to the bikers had been some-

thing that had been a turn-on to her since she had joined the gang. This bondage took her one step further towards servitude, and once again she wondered as she felt her masochistic tendencies come to the fore.

What happened next took her totally by surprise. All at once Garth stepped forward and, taking hold of the neck of her blouse in both hands, ripped it open. Buttons flew in all directions as he rent the garment apart, tearing the material from her shoulders until he held no more than two useless rags in his hands and Charlie was naked to the waist. The blood ran to her face as she stood facing the crowd, quite unable to cover herself, her plump, delicious breasts on display to all.

Garth reached out and cupped a breast, squeezing it from underneath and pressing the nipple upward. To Charlie's embarrassment she felt the brown flesh harden at once into a solid knob and she avoided his eyes as he grinned at her.

"Still feeling tough?" he asked, flicking at her rubbery teats, clearly enjoying her discomfort.

Charlie said nothing.

His hand dropped to her shorts, and he ran his fingers down between her legs, pressing the thin material against her sex. Charlie gritted her teeth, trying hard not to display any emotions as he rubbed her in her most sensitive spot, his fingers pressing insistently up into her crotch, making her body writhe slightly as he felt her up.

He reached for her fly, and Charlie opened her mouth to protest, but thought better of it. No objection by her would stop Garth, and to do so would simply give him satisfaction.

He pulled down the zip, so that she knew the dark curls of her pubic bush would be showing. Then he grasped hold and, as with the blouse, ripped her shorts apart in a single movement.

A murmur went up from the crowd as Charlie's last vestige of modesty was removed. She watched them as they craned forward, anxious for a look at the gorgeous young apprentice strung up naked before them. A lot of them had already seen her nude the day before, but most had not, and there was no doubt that she was the centre of attention. She glanced down at herself.

Her nipples were harder than ever, pointing upwards and outwards from the firm globes of her breasts. Her belly was flattened by the tension in which her body was being held, the paleness of her skin contrasting with the darkness of her pubic triangle, beneath which she knew they could see the open lips of her sex. Once again a flush of shame coloured her face, yet at the same time the thrill of arousal coursed through her. There was something totally sexual about her situation which she was quite unable to deny. Something which, despite herself, brought a warmth and a wetness to her crotch that she feared might soon become visible to the onlookers.

Garth was in front of her again now, and this time he was holding the whip in his hand. Charlie watched fearfully as he flexed it, his eyes burning into hers.

"Now, my little beauty," he said. "How does it feel to be in the power of a real man?"

Once again Charlie remained silent. The proximity of this powerful man with his male smell was having a totally unexpected effect on her and, despite her dislike for the uncouth biker, she felt her body respond to his closeness in a totally physical way that shocked her with its intensity.

Garth seemed to sense her arousal, as he gave another grin.

"All in good time," he murmured. "First of all, there's a little score to settle. Ten strokes I think."

The sound of the words sent a shiver down Charlie's spine. Ten strokes of the whip! And on her bare backside in front of all these people! She could scarcely credit what was happening to her.

He ran his fingers over the soft swell of her behind, squeezing the flesh.

"Yes," he mused. "A few stripes across your lovely rear will look very pretty indeed."

He moved round behind her and tapped her with the end of the whip. Then he drew it back.

Swish! Whack!

He swung the whip down with all his force, delivering a stinging blow that rocked Charlie forward. The pain was excruciat-

102

ing and she bit her lip to suppress a cry as he drew the weapon back again.

Swish! Whack!

The whip bit into Charlie's backside with a crack that echoed back from the walls of the huts. She could scarcely believe the agony she was in already, yet there were still eight blows to come.

Swish! Whack!

This time the whip struck her across the back of the legs, slicing into the tender flesh there and leaving a mark that darkened to blood red.

Swish! Whack!

Swish! Whack!

Garth beat her with an enthusiasm that matched the savagery of his assault, each blow painting a fresh stripe across her tender behind and sending new shocks of pain through her helpless body.

Swish! Whack!

Swish! Whack!

Charlie was twisting and turning in her bonds now, in a vain effort to avoid the whip as it slashed down relentlessly. A sheen of sweat had broken out on her naked body. Small puffs of spray rose every time the leather struck her. She knew there were only three more strokes to come, yet she doubted her ability to withstand even one more.

Swish! Whack!

This time she screamed as the pain assailed her body. He drew back his arm again.

Swish! Whack!

Another scream rent the air. Tears were coursing down Charlie's cheeks, her body bouncing like a marionette as her fruitless struggles continued.

Swish! Whack!

The final blow fell with undiminished force, slicing into her bright red behind and rocking her forward once more, her breasts shaking as great sobs wracked her young body.

Then he was standing in front of her again, tucking the whip into his belt. Charlie wanted desperately to conceal how much the whipping had hurt, but she couldn't hide the tears that streamed down her face as she hung, naked and helpless before him.

He took hold of her chin, gazing deep into her eyes whilst his other hand slid down between her legs and penetrated her sex. Despite her agony she gave a gasp at the intimacy of his touch. She knew she was wet down there, and that he would be able to feel her arousal. Amazingly the whipping had done nothing to dampen her ardour. If anything she was even more turned on than she had been before. Once again she wondered at the extraordinary way her body responded to this cruel treatment.

He pulled her face up to his, his fingers delving deep inside her.

"Now I'm going to fuck you, little apprentice," he said.

The sound of the words sent a shiver through her and she almost came then and there, the bondage, exposure and the pain of the whipping combining to bring her to a state of high excitement.

He used a knife to cut her down, leaving the ropes hanging where they were, as silent witnesses to the punishment that just taken place. Charlie stood, rubbing the deep red rope marks about her wrists and staring down without hope at the tattered remains of her clothes.

"Go to my hut and wait on my bed," he ordered. "And make sure your legs are spread."

Charlie looked about her. He had spoken the words loudly, so that all those watching had heard him. She felt the colour rise in her cheeks once more as she stared at their faces. Some were grinning broadly, others had intensely excited expressions on their faces. Many of the men's crotches were bulging. She turned away from Garth and began making her way through the crowds, trying not to meet the gazes of the men and women as she headed toward Garth's hut. The whole situation was at once mortifying and extremely arousing to the young beauty, walking stark naked through this crowd of fully-clad strangers, on her way to be fucked by a man she barely knew.

It was a relief to her when she finally broke free of the on-lookers, though she knew all eyes were on her red-striped back-side as she walked up the track. The hut was on the far side of the camp, and she passed a number of other bikers before she finally found herself at the door.

She went inside. As with all the huts, this was like a long dormitory, with beds lining each side. There were a few bikers inside, sitting on the beds or chatting together. They looked up with interest as the naked girl entered, some of them wolf whis-tling at the sight she made.

Charlie made her way to Garth's bed. She paused beside it, aware once again of being the centre of attention. Then she low-ered herself down onto her back and slowly spread her legs.

Some of the young men made their way down the room to get a better look at the young beauty, lying back on Garth's bed clearly waiting to be taken by her master.

"Shit, what a beauty."

"Look at those gorgeous tits."

Charlie lay, gazing up at the ceiling, trying not to listen to the men's crude remarks. She knew she made quite a sight, her lovely breasts standing up firmly, the hard nipples pointing slightly to the side with her prone position, her open thighs per-fectly displaying her slit and the wetness within. Even without this evidence, the shortness of her breath was enough to betray how totally aroused she was as she lay, awaiting the ravishment Garth had promised.

It was nearly ten minutes before he finally entered, the door crashing back as he strode inside. During that ten minutes Charlie had been obliged to endure the mocking comments of the others almost continually, as they sat and studied her body, so that it was almost a relief when she saw the burly figure of Garth framed in the doorway.

The other bikers melted away as he approached, though they stayed close. Charlie wondered if Garth would object to their presence, but he said nothing. Clearly he didn't care who was there. To Charlie, the idea of being watched sent confused mes-sages to her brain. On the one hand, to be asked to perform such a totally personal act in public was completely outrageous, yet the thought of being watched brought her exhibitionist tendencies to the fore once again, and she felt a fresh surge of wetness inside her as she contemplated the act.

Garth did not stand on ceremony. Moving to the side of the bed he stood, looking down at her whilst he slowly unbuckled his pants. Charlie was becoming more aroused by the second now. Garth was not exactly the sexual partner she would have chosen, but somehow that seemed to add to the thrill she was getting from the situation. This would be raw, uncomplicated sex, free of emotions, just a man getting his relief in a lovely young woman completely in his power.

Garth's cock sprang up from his fly, thick and hard. Charlie stared at his long pink rod, reached out a hand and wrapped it about his shaft, feeling the heat of his arousal and the pulsing as the blood coursed through the engorged knob.

"Suck me," he ordered.

Charlie propped herself up on one elbow and leaned towards his groin, her breasts seeming to swell as she allowed them to fall forward. She studied his knob for a moment, noting how the foreskin barely covered the erect glans, leaving the purple end, with its small slit, visible to her. She extended her tongue and licked at the hard, shiny helmet, tasting the saltiness of his arousal. Then she opened her mouth and took him right in, her lips closing about his shaft as she began to suck him.

Now it was Garth's turn to gasp as the naked girl manipulated his penis in her mouth, allowing her tongue to dart back and forth over the sensitive tip whilst her hand worked slowly up and down his shaft. For the first time in her life, Charlie realised what intense pleasure could be gained from sucking a man's cock. Previously she had thought of it as nothing more than a means of arousing her partner, but here, in this room, with the eyes of the other bikers upon her, it suddenly became as pleasurable as the actual act of coitus.

Garth thrust his hips against her face with vigour, clutching her hair and pulling her head down against his groin, pressing his cock deep into her throat so she was almost gagging. Still she sucked at his thick organ, wanking him hard as she did so, sensing his pleasure increase with every stroke.

All at once he withdrew, staring down at her, his glistening cock twitching.

"Get up on all fours," he ordered tersely. "Press your tits down and show me your arse."

Charlie obeyed at once, scrambling up onto her hands and knees on the bed and positioning herself as instructed, her pert backside, criss-crossed with he stripes of the whip, thrust high in the air, her legs spread as wide as she was able. She was almost panting with lust now, careless of the exhibition she was making as she pressed her behind back at him, willing him to penetrate her.

Garth climbed onto the bed behind her, his cock jutting conspicuously from his fly. Charlie strained round to watch him as he took his stiff shaft in his hand and guided it toward her love hole, grabbing her thigh with his other hand in order to steady himself.

He penetrated her in a single movement, bringing a cry from her lips as she felt herself filled and stretched by his organ. He took her carelessly, ramming himself inside her until she could feel the coarse mat of his pubic hair pressed against the tender flesh of her behind, then beginning at once to fuck her with vigour.

His movements took on a regular rhythm, shaking her small body as he screwed her hard. Charlie stole a glance at the other men in the room. All had their eyes fixed on her, seeing the way her breasts swayed back and forth with every thrust of his hips.

Garth's thrusts were becoming more urgent now, and she could sense the passion in him building. The prospect of being filled by his spunk spurred Charlie on to new heights of lust and she knew that she too was approaching her climax. She clung hard to the blanket on which she was perched, biting her lip as her arousal threatened to overwhelm her.

He came with a grunt, suddenly squirting his hot semen into her vagina. Spurt after spurt shot from his cock deep inside her. Charlie cried aloud at the exquisite sensation of having her cunt filled by him. Then she too was coming, her body writhing back and forth as her entire body trembled with sheer delight. It was an orgasm like none she had ever known before. Somehow the rough treatment, the bondage and beating, and the sheer publicness of her ravishing all combined to bring a shuddering, screaming climax that totally overwhelmed her.

He continued his onslaught, emptying his balls into her vagina, his hands gripping her hips as he pulled her back into his groin. Charlie squeezed the muscles of her sex about his organ, milking him of every last drop of his semen, loving the way it filled her so.

Then he was done, pushing her away so that she flopped forward onto the bed, gasping for breath. She lay there as she felt him climb from the bed, her eyes closed, her breathing coming in rasping sighs. When she finally opened them again he was gone, and she was alone with the other bikers once more, her cunt leaking his spunk, her body the picture of ravishment.

Slowly she rolled onto her back and climbed to her feet. There was a man standing in front of her and she glanced into his eyes. Then she gave a little cry of surprise and dismay.

It was Zep. And he had witnessed the whole thing.

Chapter 13

Charlie sipped at her beer and gazed around at the throng of bikers gathered about the camp fire. This was by far the biggest crowd there had been since the expedition had begun. Bikers had been arriving in a steady stream all day, and now every inch of space around the huts was jammed with motorcycles. Men and women of all nationalities sat together and drank together, their different logos making flashes of colour wherever she looked.

At her side sat Garth, his arm about one of the girl bikers as he swigged at his beer. Charlie was glad that he had turned his attention to another woman. She was called Michelle. She had arrived with one of the other gangs that evening. She was French, and was clearly an old friend of Garth's. The pair of them had been snogging and feeling one another up all evening, leaving Charlie to sit quietly, her only duties to see to it that the pair of them were kept supplied with food and drink.

Across the other side of the fire she could see Zep, sitting with some other bikers. They were holding an animated conversation, but he was making little effort to join in, and she could tell he was far from happy. He hadn't said a word when he had encountered her in the dormitory earlier. He had brought her few clothes from his locker, and had simply dropped her tops and shorts onto the bed beside her and turned and walked away. She had wanted to call after him, but, in the state she was in, with Garth's spunk still leaking from her sex, she had felt too embarrassed and had simply let him go.

She wondered about his feelings for her. In the short duration of her apprenticeship to him he had shown no real outwards sign of affection, yet she had sensed a warmth when he was close and had always felt safe in his company. That was much more than she could say for Garth who, when he wasn't displaying some form of cruelty, was simply indifferent to her.

She felt a dig in her ribs from his shoe, and looked up.

"Get some more fucking beers," he said.

Charlie rose to her feet. She was wearing a shirt that he had given her, with nothing underneath. He had insisted that the bottom buttons be undone so that her crotch was barely covered. Now, as she stood in front of him, she pushed the material down in an attempt to preserve her modesty.

"Stop trying to cover yourself," he said, "or I'll make you take the fucking thing off.".

Charlie turned away and began to make her way towards the great ice buckets that were filled with cans of beer. She was glad to get away from the pair of them, and lingered a while after picking up two cans.

"Hello, little slave."

She turned to find herself facing Zana, who was standing next to her, smiling. The greeting took her by surprise. It was the first really friendly greeting she had heard all day.

"Hello," she said, suddenly embarrassed by the girl's familiarity and by her own inadequate dress.

"That was quite a thrashing Garth gave you," the biker girl went on. "You took it bloody well. Most apprentices would have been wiped out by the first three strokes. He's a bloody animal, that Garth. I suppose he fucked you afterwards?"

Charlie blushed. "Is Zep all right do you think, Mistress?"

Immediately Charlie bit her tongue. Not only was she speaking out of turn, but she was betraying her feelings toward the biker, feelings she hadn't fully admitted to herself yet.

Zana looked a her closely. "You really like him, don't you? Even a little slut like you can care for a man."

Charlie dropped her eyes. "I was just worried," she said. "He came off that bike very hard."

"He'll survive. It's a pity he had to lose you, though. He'd have done a much better job than Garth. Oh yes, you were much safer with Zep. Garth is too unpredictable. I bet he tries something reckless against the Easterns."

"Against the what?"

"The Easterns. Didn't anyone explain?"

"No, Mistress."

"The Easterns are the biker gangs from Eastern Europe. The Russians, the Poles, the Hungarians. All the guys from behind the old Iron Curtain. Their camp is on the other side of the woods. We've been at war with them for years."

"Will there be fighting then?"

"There sometimes is, although it's not as bad as it used to be. They don't generally come after us nowadays. The only fights happen if we meet them by chance. The real problem is the idiots who go out looking for trouble. Idiots like Garth."

"What happens?"

"They try to infiltrate their camp and come away with a trophy. A biker's colours or something like that. Sometimes there can be some pretty nasty fights."

"What, people get hurt, Mistress?" asked Charlie in alarm.

"Wait a minute. Are those beers for Garth and his floozy?"

"I beg your pardon?" Charlie was momentarily confused by

the sudden change of subject.

"The beers. Are they for Garth and that French slut, Michelle?"

"Yes, Mistress."

"Well I suggest you get a move on before he gives you another thrashing. He's looking this way."

Charlie glanced across and saw that Garth was, indeed, staring in her direction. She turned back to Zana but the girl was already chatting to someone else. Clutching the two beer cans she hurried back toward her master.

She arrived to find Garth deep in conversation with two other bikers who wore the same colours as the French girl. Charlie handed the beers to Garth and Michelle, then settled down beside them.

"I tell you we should strike early this year," Garth was saying. "Before they're ready for us."

"I'm not so sure," replied one of his companions. "They're certain to have the place well guarded."

"But if we can get away with a set of colours on the first night, it'll be a real victory."

"Or a real disaster."

The conversation went on, the plotters becoming more and more involved in what they were discussing. Charlie's mind began to wander as she gazed round at the crowds of bikers gathered about the fire. Despite her new master's indifference to her she felt strangely excited to be where she was. She found it an unexpected thrill to be amongst these rough young people and there was a perverse kick in being part of their lives. Even the cruelty and the subservience they demanded from her were extraordinarily exciting. She had never known such arousal as that afternoon's whipping had brought her, and the sudden realisation of her own masochistic tendencies was a real eye-opener to her. The memory of her day-to-day existence back at home seemed a distant one to her now.

"You! I'm talking to you!"

Suddenly Charlie felt a boot against her thigh and she realised with a shock that Garth had been addressing her. She sprang to her feet, ready to fetch more beers, but he shook his head.

"Stay there!" he ordered, then turned to his companions. "What do you think?" he asked. "She should provide a good enough diversion."

"Not bad," agreed one of the men. "She might do it."

"Of course she will. Undo that shirt."

"What -"

"The shirt. Undo the buttons and show Marc here what you've got to offer."

Charlie glanced down at the young Frenchman, who was watching her with some interest, then around at the other bikers sitting close, some of whom had heard Garth's order and were staring in her direction.

"Get a move on," barked Garth. "Otherwise I'll take the shirt off you, and you won't get it back until half this crowd has fucked you."

Charlie knew there was no arguing with her master. Slowly, her eyes cast down, she reached for the buttons at the neck of the shirt and began undoing them. She avoided the gazes of those looking as she did so, keeping her eyes fixed on the ground as, one by one, the buttons came unfastened. When she reached the last one she stopped, her hands holding the garment closed.

"Open up and show yourself," said Garth.

Slowly, reluctantly, Charlie pulled the shirt open, revealing her naked charms beneath. She shrugged the shirt back so that her shoulders were uncovered, then stood, her eyes still cast down, her breasts and sex displayed to those around her.

The biker called Marc gave a low whistle. "Not bad," he said appreciatively.

"I'll let you fuck her sometime," said Garth. "Meanwhile, she'll be ideal for our purposes, don't you think?"

"I guess you're right," said the Frenchman. "Those tits are exquisite."

Charlie said nothing, still slightly shocked by the casual way in which Garth had offered her favours to the French biker without any thought to her own consent. She glanced down at herself, noting the way her teats had swelled into hard protrusions.

She wondered if the wetness inside her was visible to those watching.

"You agree my plan's a good one?" said Garth to the Frenchman.

"With her, I guess it could work," Marc replied. "Have you checked it with Mamba?"

"No need," Garth replied. "Once he sees the enemy's colours, he'll know I was right."

"Even so, shouldn't you tell him?"

"Hell no. Besides," he lowered his voice. "If you ask me, Mamba's getting a bit soft. This might show him that he's not the only guy capable of running the Spirits."

"You mean you might make a challenge?"

"Anything's possible. Meanwhile we're agreed? We do it tonight?"

"Agreed."

"Right young lady," said Garth. "Go and wait by my bike. We've got a little exercise planned, and you're going to play a crucial part in it."

Chapter 14

Charlie clung to Garth's waist as the motorcycle sped through the forest, bumping over the roots and potholes that littered the narrow track. She gazed round him, trying to pick out any landmarks on the route, but in the pitch darkness it was impossible. She wondered how the biker could possibly see his way with no lights showing on his machine. All she could see ahead of them were vague shapes, yet he was able to follow every twist and turn of the tortured path they were riding down. She glanced back at the other machines. Marc and Michelle seemed quite able to match Garth's pace, their own bikes staying close behind as they plunged ever deeper into the woods.

They had been on the track for at least twenty minutes now, and Charlie had lost all sense of direction. She wouldn't have been able to find her way back in daylight, let alone in the darkness in which they were travelling. Yet Garth showed no sign of hesitation, steering the motorcycle effortlessly between the trees.

All at once the engines of all three machine cut simultaneously, and they were engulfed in a silence broken only by the crunch of the wheels as they continued to coast on. They covered another hundred yards before Garth swung his machine to one side and drew to a halt in a small clearing.

The other bikers followed, pulling up beside them and kicking down their stands. To Charlie it seemed quite eerie to be surrounded only by the sounds of the night after the roar of the motorcycle engines. The wind swished in the trees and somewhere an owl hooted. She shivered, suddenly missing the noise and comfort of the camp fire.

"Right," said Garth in a low voice. "Follow me."

He climbed from the motorcycle and headed off into the woods. Charlie followed as close as she was able, dodging the low branches. She was still wearing only the shirt, and she was concerned lest she scratch her legs as she weaved through the trees with Marc and Michelle close behind.

They walked for another ten minutes before Garth signalled for them to halt. He placed a finger to his lips as they gathered found him.

"The Easterns camp is about two hundred yards away," he said in a low voice. "They're bound to have guards posted, so don't say a word."

Charlie glanced in the direction he was indicating, but could see nothing. She wondered how it was that Garth knew these woods so well. It must have taken many hours of reconnoitring to have such a thorough knowledge.

"Right," he was saying. "There's just the three of us, so we're not going to be too ambitious. All we want is to get an Eastern's colours. That'll do for a first night raid."

Charlie opened her mouth to remind him that there were, in fact, four of them, but she closed it again when she realised that, to Garth, she didn't count. After all, she was only an apprentice.

"So what's the plan, lover-boy?" asked Michelle.

114

"It's simple," said Garth. "My plan means that we not only divert their attention, but we get them to take off their colours as well, so they'll be easy to snatch."

"How?" asked Marc.

"With this pretty little piece of bait here," said Garth, indicating Charlie.

"M-me?" gasped Charlie.

"That's right darling," said Garth. "You're going to wander up to the guards and pretend to be lost. They won't be able to resist that lovely little body of yours, and once you've got them out of their clothes, we'll move in."

"Oh but -"

"Quiet!" rasped Garth. "There's nothing to discuss here. You'll just do as you're told."

"So we wait until the guards are fucking her, then move in," said Michelle. "Clever."

Garth grinned, his teeth showing white in the darkness. "And simple," he said. "The best plans are always the simplest. Come on."

He grabbed Charlie by the hand and pulled her along behind him. She tried to hang back but he was too strong for her. Reluctantly she followed him, aware that further resistance would result in another whipping.

They climbed a small rise, coming to a halt at the top. Then Charlie saw the Easterns camp for the first time. It was very similar to their own, consisting of a group of huts and tents set about a clearing. In the middle of the clearing a fire was burning. It was about a quarter of a mile from where they were standing, and Charlie could make out the dark shapes of figures moving back and forth in front of it. The sound of music wafted through the night air from the camp, a harsh, beaty sound not unlike that which had been playing at their own.

Garth pulled her close to him.

"The guards are stationed just on the edge of the camp," he whispered. "Look, by that tree."

He pointed down and Charlie strained her eyes. There, about twenty yards out from the nearest hut, she could just make out a

115

pair of silhouettes standing together in the darkness. As she watched, a match flared, momentarily illuminating the face of a man.

"Now listen," hissed Garth. "You're lost in the woods, understand. You need directions. Those bastards are bound to try it on with you."

"I - but -"

"Is that clear?" The menace in Garth's voice was unmistakable.

"Yes Sir."

"You're to make sure they get their jackets off when they fuck you."

"F-fuck me?"

"Of course, what do you think you're here for? While you're being raped we'll move in. Once I've grabbed the jacket, you follow me. And don't hang around. Get it?"

"But what if -"

"What if nothing! Get going! NOW!"

Charlie stared round at the three bikers. They were all watching her expectantly, waiting for her to go down the slope and get herself raped. Well, she was a biker's apprentice now, and was obliged to do as she was told. There was no doubting that they were serious, and not going would be considerably worse than going.

Slowly she turned and began to make her way down the slope, making as little noise as possible, although the music was loud enough to cover her steps as she came closer to the camp.

As she approached, the figures of the guards became clearer and she knew that they must see her soon. For the first time it crossed her mind that, since there were two of them, they might both demand to have her. She glanced down at herself and shivered. She felt very inadequately dressed in just the shirt, and reflected that even a simple pair of knickers would have made a difference. But it was too late to be concerned about such things now as, even as the thought crossed her mind, one of the guards suddenly looked in her direction.

He shouted something in a foreign language as his companion jumped to his feet. Charlie continued to walk towards them, though her footsteps faltered slightly as he barked out the words again.

"I don't understand you," she said as the men walked out to meet her, each holding what appeared to be a baseball bat.

The first of the guards grabbed her arm, twisting it behind her and making her cry out with pain.

"Stop it, you're hurting me," she complained.

The man spoke to her again, but she didn't understand a word.

"Don't you speak English?" she asked.

"You English?"

It was the second man who said these words. He had been slower in reaching her, but now, as his companion pinned her arms behind her, he stood facing her.

"Yes," she replied. "English. Please tell your friend to take his hands off me."

"What you doing here?"

"I'm lost. I was camping with some friends on the edge of the forest. I went for a walk and got lost. Then I heard the music, so I followed the sound."

"Where is your bike?"

"Bike? I haven't got a bike. I was walking."

"You are with the Western bikers?"

"I don't know what you're talking about. I tell you I was camping. Now please ask your friend to let me go."

The man spoke a few words to his companion, who was holding both Charlie's arms, trapping them behind her back. He turned back to Charlie.

"I must search you."

"What for? What are you looking for?"

"Stand still."

He reached for the buttons at her neck.

"No!" Charlie struggled hard to free herself, but without success.

"Stand still," ordered the man. "I am going to check you for weapons."

"But where could I be hiding weapons?"

117

"You be quiet while I search."

He began undoing the buttons. Charlie continued to struggle as she eyed the man in front of her. He was a big man, with long dark hair. It was difficult to tell the colour of his eyes in the darkness, but his stare was captivating, the eyes appearing to gleam beneath thick black eyebrows. His mouth was wide, the lips thin, so that what should have been a handsome face was marred by an underlying cruelty that made her shiver. He was well-built, though, his chest broad and muscular, his hips slim. His hands were big and strong, and she knew he was capable of ripping the shirt apart should he so wish.

He flicked the buttons undone easily. Charlie had given up the struggle now and she stood, staring defiantly into his face as he unfastened the last of them. The shirt opened, and the man feasted his eyes on Charlie's breasts and belly. Her flesh glowed pale in the moonlight and she knew she made a delicious sight, her young breasts firm, the dark nipples hard.

"You see?" she said quietly. "Now please do me up again."

He smiled. "All in good time. Now tell me what you are doing here."

"I already told you. I'm camping on the edge of the wood. I got lost."

"Do you always wear so little?"

"I didn't expect to meet anybody."

"We can't afford to take chances," he said. "I am called Zenski. I am the leader of the Diablos."

"Who?"

"We are bikers. We're are camping here. You are trespassing."

"I'm sorry. Please let me go and I'll leave you alone."

"But you said you were lost."

"I'll be all right. I'll find my way on my own."

"In this wood you could be wandering for days. Better you stay with us for a while. Then maybe I'll show you the way."

"Stay with you?"

He reached out and ran his hand over her breast. Charlie tried to draw back, but the man behind was holding her fast.

"Please!" she cried. "You can't do that.

"You're in my territory now," he said. "Here I can do what I like."

He caressed her nipple, his touch surprisingly gentle, and she felt the hard brown flesh stiffen even more, much to her embarrassment.

"You're not prejudiced against bikers, little English girl?" he asked?"

He reached down and ran a hand up the inside of her thigh. She tried to close her legs, but still he forced it upward until it was against her slit.

"Don't fight it, English girl," he said. "Share that lovely body with us. Give us pleasure and we will give you pleasure. Then we will help you to find your camp."

At once the man behind her released her arms. Charlie's instinct was to cover herself with her hands, but she fought it. Instead she let them dangle by her side as the two men eyed her.

"Take off the shirt," said Zenski.

Charlie hesitated for a second, then shrugged it off her shoulders and let it fall to the ground. In doing this she knew was tacitly surrendering to the two men. Now she stood, alone and naked before them, aware that three more pairs of eyes were watching her from the woods.

Zenski put an arm about her, pressing her naked body against his. Charlie's nipples chafed against the denim of his jacket as he placed his lips over hers and pushed his tongue into her mouth, the intimacy of the kiss taking her breath away.

For a few moments Charlie simply melted into his arms, pressing her body against his as his tongue explored her mouth. His proximity was a total aphrodisiac to the lascivious youngster and she felt the juices within her begin to flow as her arousal increased with every second.

He broke the kiss, staring into her face as his hand slid up her inner thigh once more. This time Charlie allowed him the access he was seeking, even widening her stance slightly to allow him to slip a finger into her.

"Oh!" she exclaimed aloud as he touched her in the most

intimate place. He ran his finger around her clitoris and she felt it swell and harden under his touch. Then he slipped his index finger into her vagina and she moaned aloud at the sudden shock of pleasure that coursed through her young body, making her shiver with suppressed excitement.

"That's better," he murmured. "You really want it now, don't you?"

Charlie didn't answer, simply nuzzling closer into his neck and pressing her hips down onto his fingers.

So turned on was she that she almost forgot why she was there. It was only the feel of his embroidered jacket under her fingers that reminded her of her goal. She must get the jacket off him in order for the plan to work. She slid her fingers under it and ran her hand up the front of his shirt, pushing the jacket back off his shoulders.

"You're one horny chick," he said, and, to her relief, allowed her to drop the jacket to the ground.

As he continued to finger her she undid the buttons of his shirt. His chest was thick with black, wiry hair and she ran her fingers through it, feeling the solid strength of his pectorals. She slid her hand lower, over the flat muscles of his stomach, then down the waistband of his jeans. He wore briefs, and already they were bulging as she cupped her hand about the front of them. She could feel his cock, alive and twitching, and she began to caress it through the thin nylon.

"Don't fucking tease it," he growled. "Get it out and suck it."

At once Charlie withdrew her hand and began undoing his belt, whilst all the time he continued to thrust his fingers into her hot, wet vagina. She was gasping now, afraid that she might come such was the strength of her arousal. She concentrated on what she was doing, sliding down his zipper and delving into his briefs, freeing his rampant organ, which immediately sprang to attention, standing proud from his groin, thick and pale, its circumcised tip swollen.

He pulled his fingers from inside her.

"Suck me."

Charlie dropped to her knees and wrapped a hand about his shaft. His balls had tightened into a pliant sac tucked just beneath the base of his organ and she caressed them gently. Then she opened her mouth and took him between her lips, shivering as the taste and scent of his maleness filled her senses.

She began to suck, her face moving back and forth, allowing the shiny helmet to slide over her flicking tongue. As she did so, he seemed to swell even more, and he began to moan softly, his hips jabbing against her as he fucked her face with enthusiasm.

All at once she felt a body press against her from behind and she remembered the second guard. His flesh felt warm and alive, and she could tell that he was naked, his stiff member pressing into her back. He knelt behind her, his hands coming round her body and caressing her breasts, taking them in his hands and kneading them in a way that sent new thrills coursing through her. Charlie continued fellating Zenski with enthusiasm, working her hand up and down his shaft as she did so whilst revelling in the touch of his companion.

Suddenly he pulled his erection from her mouth. Charlie gazed up at him, a questioning look on her face.

"Get on your hands and knees," he ordered.

Charlie did as she was told, turning to face Zenski's companion. He was a small, wiry man with a painfully thin body and a long, slender cock that bobbed up and down as he watched her. He sat back onto his ankles, then indicated his stiff erection.

Charlie understood at once, leaning forward and tasting her second cock in as many minutes, taking him deep into the warmth of her mouth and sucking hard at him. As she did so she threw a glance towards the dark edge of the woods where the three bikers were concealed. She had expected that they would have attacked by now, but they were clearly going to allow her to go a lot further before they made their move.

Something brushed against Charlie's backside. Something hard and wet that pressed forward insistently, sliding down the crack of her behind, over her anus and on towards the centre of her desires. There was no resistance when he slipped his cock into her. She was so turned on that her sex was running with juices and his organ was well lubricated as he rammed it home, filling her with his meaty manhood.

He began to fuck her hard, jamming his hips against her backside as he pumped back and forth inside her. It was all Charlie could do to keep her balance, her breasts swinging to and fro, her mouth filled with rampant cock, her whole body totally aroused. Once again the danger of her situation and the mission she was on were pushed to the back of her mind as she lost herself in the sheer pleasure of the double-fucking.

The two men took her dispassionately, ramming their cocks into her without thought for her own desires, using her to satisfy their basic carnal desires. Charlie was no more than a receptacle for their spunk, but one that was alive and helpless. As her body was thrown back and forth between them, she revelled in the way she was able to allow herself to be used in such a way.

When the first jet of spunk was unleashed into her mouth it took her quite by surprise, the hot fluid splashing against the back of her throat and almost making her gag. In a second, though, she was back in command, sucking hard at him, swallowing down his seed, her arousal suddenly increased by the taste of his orgasm.

Moments later she felt Zenski's grip on her thighs tighten and his thrusts suddenly increase in intensity. Then he too was coming, filling her with a second helping of creamy sperm, his cock seeming to leap inside her, bringing on a shattering orgasm inside her that shook her entire body. Charlie struggled to maintain her balance, revelling in the sensation of spurt after spurt of come jetting deep into her vagina whilst she slurped the last vestiges from the cock in her mouth. Then, when both men had finally shot their loads, she collapsed onto the ground, her chest heaving.

The attack, when it came, took Charlie almost as unawares as her two lovers. One moment she had been stretched out, naked and fulfilled, gazing up at the two men, the next dark figures were emerging from the darkness and running down the slope.

Zenski reacted first, leaping to his feet and facing Garth and Marc as they rushed toward him. The pair hesitated when only about five yards from him, and Charlie thought for a second that the attack had failed. Then, without warning, Michelle ran in from the side, snatching up Zenski's colours and racing back toward the woods. Immediately her two companions followed. Zenski bellowed with rage and began to pursue them, along with his companion, but both were struggling to pull up their jeans and were quite unable to match the pace of the Western bikers as they tore back into the trees.

Charlie was alone now. Deserted, with the two enemy bikers between her and her friends. She gave a cry of anger and dismay. There had never even been a provision in the plan to allow her to escape. They had got what they wanted and simply abandoned her to find her own way back to the camp.

Almost at once she heard voices behind her and swung round to see that the figures that had been gathered round the campfire were heading in her direction, attracted by Zenski's cries. She stared about her, searching for her shirt, but it was nowhere to be seen. The figures were coming closer now, and the distant roar of motorcycle engines told her that her companions were gone. With a cry of despair she began to run in the direction of the sound, only to remember that her flight was taking her directly into the hands of Zenski. She paused for a moment, looking right and left, then headed off to her left, plunging into the trees even as the Eastern bikers emerged from the camp behind her.

Chapter 15

Charlie ran as fast as she was able, dodging between the trees, trying desperately not to scratch her bare flesh on the bushes and low-hanging branches as she raced along. Behind her she could still hear the shouts of the bikers and, far in the distance, the roar of the three bikes that had brought her to this place. She had lost all sense of direction now and was simply intent on putting as much distance as she was able between herself and the Easterns camp. She was convinced that they were still hot on her tail as she leapt across fallen tree stumps and splashed through shallow river beds in a blind, panic-stricken flight from the enemy camp.

She had no idea how much ground she had covered. It was impossible to tell in the darkness of the thick forest. But at last she could run no more and she came to a halt, resting her lovely young body against a tree, gasping to regain her breath. She stood there for some time, her chest heaving. Then, when at last she had regained some of her senses, she stopped and listened hard.

All about her was silence. Even the wind seemed to have paused in the trees. The sound of the motorcycles had long since died away and, if she was still being chased, her pursuers were far behind her. She leaned back against the tree, waiting for the pounding of her heart to subside and trying to get her thoughts in order. It was a further ten minutes before she quite felt herself again.

She glanced about herself. All around her were thick trees. There was no clue as to where she was or which direction was back to the camp. She was quite alone and totally lost. Worse than that, she was stark naked. She looked down at herself, noting the swell of her bare breasts and the contrast of her pubic triangle with the flesh of her belly. Down the inside of her thighs she could feel Zenski's spunk still trickling from her vagina.

She picked some leaves from a tree and tried to find a way to weave them together to make some kind of crude apron, but it was impossible. She was destined to remain naked until she found something to wear, and there was nothing in this wood.

She began to walk, taking her direction by the light of the stars just visible through the trees. She picked her way gingerly around the bushes and through the trees, hoping against hope that she would come across something recognisable. She paused at a small stream, wading in and using the cold water to wash the remnants of Zenski's seed from inside her.

Progress was slow, but she kept doggedly on in the same direction, using the paths made by small animals where she was able and avoiding the thick bushes that threatened to scratch her delicate skin.

Then, all at once, she came across a track. It was about two yards wide, running straight through the wood, quite clearly a man-made feature. She gave a little gasp of relief. If it was a track, then it must lead somewhere. The question was, which way to turn?

In the end, her instinct told her to turn right, and she set off at a much faster pace, her young breasts bouncing as she strode, naked and alone, through the dark, forbidding wood.

She walked for about half an hour. The further she went, the less confident she became in her decision. The wood simply seemed to go on and on, and she feared she might be going ever deeper into it, making it less likely with every step that she would ever find a way out.

Just as she was beginning to wonder whether she should turn around and try the other direction, she fancied she saw something through the trees far ahead. She squinted forward. She could have sworn she had glimpsed a light, but now it seemed as dark as ever. She went on, keeping her eyes fixed on the spot. Then she saw it again, the faintest glimmer that disappeared almost immediately.

Spurred on, she increased her pace. The path led directly toward the light and, as she approached, its light became brighter until she knew it was no more than a hundred yards or so away. Then she came round a copse of trees and she saw it properly for the first time.

The light she had seen was by the front door of a large house, two stories tall and built of stone, nestling amongst the trees. Even through the darkness Charlie could see that the house was somewhat dilapidated, with shutters hanging askew and cracked windows. An ancient pick-up truck was drawn up outside and a driveway snaked away from where she was standing and in between the trees.

Now that she had found evidence of other people in the wood,

Charlie's footsteps began to falter. The closer she came to the house, the more aware she was of the awkwardness of her position. Here she was, lost and naked, standing outside a strange and rather forbidding building. She knew she had to knock on the door, but she feared what the occupants might think of her and her predicament. She felt her face glow as she considered the sight she must make.

And yet there was something oddly erotic about her situation. She knew she was beautiful, and that most men would find her irresistible. As she glanced down at her alluring curves once more, she felt a familiar surge of excitement at the idea of revealing her body to yet another stranger. She ran her hands over her breasts, shivering slightly as she realised how hard her nipples had become. She toyed with them, loving the thrill that they transmitted to her sex as she squeezed the hard flesh between finger and thumb.

She stopped in the light from the house, staring at the front door, wondering who was behind it. At the same time her fingers slid down between her legs and sought out her clitoris. She gave an audible gasp as she found the swollen bud of flesh and began gently to rub it.

All at once she was very turned on indeed, shivers of pleasure coursing through her body as she gently masturbated. She spread her legs wider, allowing her fingers to slide into her hot slit, moaning quietly as her passion increased, her other hand still kneading her breasts. She closed her eyes, remembering how she had abandoned herself to the Eastern bikers and imagining what the house's occupants might do when they laid eyes on the naked beauty at their door.

She began frigging herself hard, her legs spread, her knees bent as she thrust her fingers into her vagina. She was extremely wet now, her love juices leaking out onto her hand, her breath coming in hoarse grunts as she worked herself.

"Was tunen sie?"

Charlie gave a start as the voice rang out, the tones harsh and guttural. She snatched her fingers from her sex and slapped her hand over her pubic mound whilst hugging her other arm to her breasts.

"Warum sind sie hier?"

All at once the men emerged from the shadows beside the house. There were two of them, one in his early forties, with a grey goatee beard, the other much younger, a slim, gangly man of about twenty. Charlie's face flushed red as she realised that they must have been standing there all along, and had seen her approach and, worse still, had probably been watching her masturbate. She stared at them in alarm, trying desperately to hide her nakedness with her hands.

The older man shouted something else at her, and she shook her head.

"I don't speak German," she said.

The men stopped just in front of her, their faces dark.

"You are English?"

"Yes."

"You are with those damned motorcycle people?"

Charlie's heart sank at the tone of his voice. "Yes."

"Every year they come with their damned machines making noise and disruption. Now their bloody sluts are trespassing on my land."

"I'm sorry. I just needed some help."

"You'll get no help here. Get off my land."

"But you must help. I'm lost and I've got no clothes."

"That is not my problem. Maybe you like to be naked. You were playing with yourself, weren't you? Fucking whore!"

Charlie's colour deepened.

"I lost my clothes," she mumbled.

"Is that any reason to frig yourself? Depraved bitch."

"I'm sorry. I don't know what came over me. Couldn't I just come inside?" she pleaded.

"This is a working house. We don't take guests."

"I could work."

"What could you do?"

"Anything you asked." The words were already out of Charlie's mouth before she realised the possible interpretation he might put on them.

"Anything, eh? Maybe you could be of use. It's a long time since we've used our little playroom. We used to have to get female prisoners from the local gaol who wanted to shorten their sentences, but maybe you'd be a good substitute."

"P-playroom?" Charlie suddenly felt very vulnerable. It hadn't been a good idea coming to the house, she realised that now.

"It... It doesn't matter," she stammered. Still clutching her breasts and sex she turned and began walking quickly away.

"Not so fast, little English whore."

All at once Charlie felt her arms pulled back behind her It was the younger of the pair who had caught her. She gave an exclamation of shock and dismay as he dragged her elbows back, forcing her to reveal her naked charms once more.

"Stop it, you're hurting me," she complained

"Bring her into the light," said the older man.

"No! Let me go!"

But he was too strong, and Charlie was dragged across until she was in the beam of the bright light.

"Please let go," she pleaded. "It hurts."

"Of course it hurts," said the older man. "Promise to stay where you are and you'll be released."

Charlie looked from one man to the other. What she wanted more than anything else was to run, but she daren't. She took a deep breath.

"I promise not to run away," she said quietly.

"And you'll do as you're told?"

She hung her head, staring down at her naked body. "Yes."

The young man held her for a moment longer, then let go. Charlie went to cover herself again, but the bearded man barked out an order.

"Put your hands behind you. Lean back against that post."

"I beg your pardon?"

"You heard me. Do it!"

Charlie glanced back and saw that there was a low concrete post behind her. Slowly she placed her hands on it and leaned back.

"Press your body forward. Spread your legs and show us what you've got."

"Please..."

"Do it!"

Charlie wished desperately that she had some clothes on. Even a pair of panties would have been better than nothing. Her face scarlet, she widened her stance.

"Wider. Show me that cunt you were playing with, slut."

Avoiding their gazes, Charlie spread her legs wide, planting her legs about three feet apart. Then she pressed her upper body backwards and thrust her hips forward, giving them the clearest view possible of her breasts and sex.

"That's better. Now, I'll ask you some questions, and you must answer me truthfully. If I think you're lying, your punishment will be worse. Do you understand?"

"P-punishment?"

"Of course. Now listen carefully and remember to hold nothing back."

"Yes Sir."

"Have you been fucked today?"

"What?"

"The question was clear enough. Have you been fucked today?"

"I... I..."

"Well?"

Charlie closed her eyes.

"Yes."

"Look me in the eyes and say it."

She looked at him.

"Yes."

"How many times?"

"Twice."

"By different men? Answer truthfully!"

"Yes..."

"And what else? Are you holding something back? Tell me the shameful truth."

"And... and I sucked off a third."

129

"Christ what a wanton this is. And now she flaunts her tits and cunt like that. Just look at yourself."

Charlie gazed down at her body again. Her lovely, firm young breasts were thrust upwards, her nipples stiff. Her thighs were open wide, and she knew the men could see the wetness of her sex and the way her cunt muscles were convulsing as her perverse nature responded to their gazes.

"Tell me," said the man. "Do you walk around like that in front of other men?"

"Sometimes they make me," she whispered.

"They?"

"The bikers."

"And you obey them?"

"Yes Sir"

Tell me, have you been doing it today?"

"I..."

"Speak up. How many men have seen you naked today?"

"I don't know."

"Five? Ten?"

"Maybe fifty or sixty."

"Slut."

Charlie stared down at the ground and said nothing.

"You know I don't approve of all these motorcyclists coming here every year and disrupting our peace," he said. "Now you come here, stark naked and obviously horny as hell and expect my sympathy."

"I'm sorry..."

"All right then, get inside, slut. We'll ask the others what to do with you."

Charlie wasn't sure whether to be relieved or not by the words. She felt very exposed and vulnerable, standing here stark naked in the open with these two men, yet the man's harsh words and unfriendly attitude made her wary of entering his house. In the end, though, she really had no choice, since he just opened the door and, taking her by the shoulders, pushed her roughly inside.

She found herself in a long, dimly-lit passageway. Instinctively her hands went to cover herself again. She stood, nervously watching as the two men entered and closed the door. Her trepidation increased when the older man turned the key in the lock, then slipped it into his pocket. Whatever lay in store for her in this strange, dark house, there was no way out now.

"Through there," ordered the man. He indicated a door about halfway down the corridor.

Charlie went up to the door. It was closed. Reluctantly she dropped her hand momentarily from her breasts and turned the handle, clasping them once more before nudging the door open and stepping inside.

It was a large room, obviously a sitting-room, though the furniture was old and the carpets threadbare. On one wall was a cabinet containing a large collection of guns, but otherwise there was no kind of ornament. At first Charlie had thought the room empty. Then she saw, sitting in a corner on a small sofa, two young women. Both looked up in surprise as she entered, then collapsed into giggles at the sight of the naked youngster, trying desperately to retain her modesty with her hands. At once Charlie regretted her decision to enter. She wished she was back outside in the wood, away from the frightening men and the scorn and ridicule her nudity was arousing in these two girls. She turned to flee, but the men were blocking the door.

A short conversation ensued, none of which Charlie could understand. The two girls were clearly highly amused by their visitor, and fired questions at the man. As they talked, Charlie examined the pair.

Both were in their mid-twenties, slim and quite attractive to look at, though with the same hard, stern faces as the older man. They bore a striking resemblance to the young man, and Charlie concluded that they were his sisters, and that the older man was their father. Her guess was confirmed when the man spoke again.

"I am Herr Garten," he announced, somewhat formally. "Fortunately for you I studied in England and speak your language well, as do the rest of my family. These are my daughters, Anna and Trudi and my son, Miko. In my house you will obey our orders. Do you understand?"

Charlie looked about at the four. "Mrs Garten?" she asked.

"Mrs Garten has been dead many years. There are just the four of us. It is not important. What is important is your obedience."

"Yes Sir."

One of the girls rose to her feet and skipped across to where Charlie was standing.

"Where are her clothes?"

"She was naked when we found her, Anna. And masturbating."

"Masturbating?" The girl's eyes brightened. "With her fingers?"

"That is right."

Anna turned to Charlie. "Show us."

Charlie's eyes widened, and she turned to Herr Garten.

"Obedience," he said.

"But I can't..."

"Anna told you to show us what you were doing. Now show!"

His voice brooked no argument, yet still Charlie found herself rooted to the spot. Trudi was on her feet now, and all were staring at her. She looked about her, vainly searching for a way out of her predicament, but there was none. Slowly. Without uncovering her sex, she began to move the hand that covered it.

"Open your legs," ordered Herr Garten. "Use your finger. Let us see the extent of your depravity."

Slowly Charlie moved her legs open. Just a few inches at first, but then Herr Garten kicked her ankle until they were at least two feet apart. She continued to move her hand in small circles, still effectively covering herself. Then she caught the glint in the man's eye, and knew she must obey.

She moved her hand up, stroking her pubic hairs and uncovering the pink slit of her sex. Then, her face glowing, she extended her middle finger and used it to tease her clitoris out from between the folds of flesh. It was wet, glistening in the light of the room, and she ran her finger over it, shivering at the delicious sensation it gave her. As she did so, the two girls collapsed into another fit of giggles, and her face glowed even redder at the display she was making of herself.

Despite her embarrassment, as Charlie began to rub harder she felt her arousal return in a rush and, almost unconsciously, she began to toy with her breasts, dropping her arm from them so that they came into full view of those watching, the nipples hardening and protruding as she ran her palms over them.

Charlie's control slipped quickly away, and she began masturbating vigorously, her hips beginning to jab forward, her breathing coming in short gasps as she plunged her now dripping fingers into her hot, pulsating vagina. She looked up at the four watchers. The two girls were grinning broadly, hugging one another as they watched the display. Miko was wide-eyed, his crotch bulging. Their father, meanwhile, looked on with feigned indifference. Charlie knew she should be deeply ashamed by the exhibition she was making of herself, but once again the effect of displaying her gorgeous young body was turning her on tremendously, the fact of being watched simply increasing the excitement she was feeling.

She came with a gasp, her hips thrusting forward, her breasts shaking up and down as she rammed her fingers hard into herself, crying aloud as the relief of orgasm overcame her. The climax was a long and noisy one as she lost herself in the lascivious pleasure of self abuse, continuing to slide her fingers vigorously in and out, draining every last ounce of pleasure from herself until, with a heave of her shoulders, she was done and she stood, legs spread, arms by her side, gazing shamefacedly at the floor

There was silence for a few moments, then Trudi stepped forward.

"You were right, Father, she is a slut," she grinned. "Can Anna and I take her to the playroom?"

"Of course," smiled her father. "But don't wear her out. Your brother and I will want to use her later."

Chapter 16

Charlie stood, quite unable to move, forced to stare at her reflection in the mirror opposite. In the brightness of the spotlights that were playing on her not a single inch of flesh was concealed, and she shuddered as she contemplated the sight she made.

The room they had taken Charlie to was called the playroom, but it was like no playroom she had ever seen before. It more closely resembled a dungeon. The walls were of bare brick, with signs of mould and green slime the only decoration. One wall was hung with gleaming chains and manacles, whilst the others held cupboards and cabinets that simply bulged with instruments of torture. There were racks of whips and canes of all shapes and sizes, leather harnesses and wicked looking spikes. There were clamps and screws, cuffs, thongs and ropes, and there were other instruments, the purpose of which Charlie could only guess at.

Charlie herself was completely immobilised, standing in the centre of a large wooden frame, her wrists and ankles chained to its corners so that she was spread-eagled and helpless, her breasts stretched almost oval by the tension in her lovely young body. She had been like this for more than half an hour, her muscles aching, quite unable to move.

The two girls had shackled her, giggling and chattering as they immobilised their naked captive, paying no heed to her anguished cries as they had pulled the chains tight. Then, when they had her where they wanted her, they had switched on the infernal spotlights, bathing her in bright light so that she was the centre of attention, like some lovely living ornament displayed for the pleasure of those watching, her open sex and firm breasts presented for all to see.

The pair had stayed for a while, admiring their captive, running their fingers over her smooth bare flesh, squeezing her nipples and laughing as they hardened, watching the passion on Charlie's face as they fingered her sex. Charlie had tried her best to keep in control, but the sensation of small hands probing at her vagina was almost more than she could take. She bit her lip to avoid moaning with pleasure as they toyed with her, cursing the recalcitrance of her body as it responded to them, her sex muscles clamping about their fingers in a way that had delighted her two young captors. Then they had gone out, and left her to contemplate her fate, staring at her image so beautifully spread before her in the mirror.

At last she heard the sound of footsteps outside the door, and her stomach knotted as she realised that the girls were returning. She feared that they might bring the men with them, but was relieved to see that it was only the sisters who entered, closing the door behind them.

They stood, regarding their captive with obvious glee. Charlie couldn't understand what they were saying, but she knew they were talking about her, and the way they pointed and prodded at her unprotected flesh gave her some idea as to what they were discussing.

Suddenly Trudi said something to Anna, and the girl gave a little squeal of delight. She ran across to a cabinet at the side of the room and opened a drawer. She pulled out two gleaming objects and hurried across to where her sister was standing, handing one to her. Charlie squinted down at their hands as they held out the devices to her. They were clamps, the jaws lined with tiny needle-like teeth and held shut by strong springs. Attached to each was a long, fine chain that gleamed in the spotlight. As Charlie watched, the two young women worked the jaws back and forth, giggling as the clamps snapped shut.

The pair moved forward, and each began to caress one of Charlie's breasts, pressing the firm flesh with her hand, taking the nipple between finger and thumb and rubbing back and forth in a way that sent spasms of pleasure through the captive's body despite her trepidation about what was to come.

The red-faced Charlie glanced down at herself, watching how her teats hardened and projected under the ministrations of the two grinning girls. She felt ashamed and humiliated at the way her body was reacting to their touch, but she couldn't suppress a groan of passion as they teased the hard brown flesh to erection.

By the time they had finished, Charlie's teats had swelled to twice their size, projecting upwards and outwards in a way that made the two girls squeal with laughter.

It was then that they held up the clamps once more.

All at once, Charlie realised what they were for, and she gave a cry of protest as they squeezed the jaws open. She struggled with her bonds, trying to draw away from the evil sisters, but she was held fast. Each girl held a thick nipple between the teeth of her clamp. then allowed it to close over the tender young flesh.

The teeth were curved back slightly, and they sank into Charlie's nipples, stinging horribly as the jaws clamped tight shut, bringing tears of pain to the captive's eyes as those sensitive spots that had previously been bringing her such pleasure suddenly brought an agonising pain to both her breasts.

The girls let go of the clamps, clearly delighted with the way they squeezed Charlie's nipples, and with the expression of pain that distorted her young face as the teeth had their effect. Charlie had never known such agony, and she wondered at the fiendish nature of anyone who could invent such devices.

But the sisters weren't finished yet. Even as the tears rolled down Charlie's cheeks they took hold of a chain each and began to pull, causing the curved teeth to bite even deeper into Charlie's flesh and bringing fresh gasps of agony from her.

The girls tugged at the clamps, each pull bringing a new cry of pain from their helpless captive. They experimented with the chains, one tugging, then the other, then both together. Charlie's cries for mercy went unheeded as they played their fiendish game. Then Anna said something to her sister that brought new peals of laughter and caused Charlie's heart to sink once again.

They stopped pulling and turned their attention to two chains that hung down from the ceiling about seven or eight feet in front of Charlie. On the end of each of these chains was a hook, and the girls threaded these through the ends of the chains attached to the clamps. Then Anna went to the wall and began to turn a handle.

At once the chains began to wind in, taking up the slack. Charlie watched in incredulous dismay as they tightened and began to pull at her breasts. Anna went on turning the handle, making the chains tighter and tighter, each pull causing the teeth to dig deeper into the hapless girl's nipples. Only when they were so tight that Charlie felt sure the flesh must tear did the girl stop and return to stand by her friend, admiring their captive.

Charlie could scarcely bring herself to look in the mirror. Her breasts were stretched to an almost conical shape, the nipples pulled upwards and elongated by the tension in the chains. The pain was like that of a thousand wasp stings, the agony clearly showing on her face, much to the delight of her captors.

No sooner had they satisfied themselves with the position of the clamps, however, than the two girls were rummaging in another of the cabinets. Charlie blinked through her tears as she tried to focus on the new object they produced. Then her jaw dropped as she recognised what they were holding. It was a phallus, a model of an erect penis precise in every detail, the rounded knob and bulging veins lovingly recreated. But this was no ordinary dildo. It was mounted on a stout pole about three feet long. The girls held it up to Charlie's face, so that she could smell the rubber from which the imitation cock was formed. They ran it down her body, over the stretched flesh of her breasts, across her belly and through her pubic hair, laughing at the way Charlie's sex lips twitched as they slid it over the hard bud of her clitoris.

They began to rub it back and forth over her open slit. Charlie watched it in the mirror, the pain from her nipples momentarily forgotten as she saw her juices coat the surface, making it glisten with moisture under the spotlights. She could scarcely believe that she was still wet down there after the treatment she had received, yet, if anything, the ministrations of the girls was turning her on even more. Even the agony of the clamps was somehow adding to her arousal so that she found herself shaking with desire, her sex lips contracting as if trying to devour the dildo.

Charlie's state was not lost on the two sisters, who rubbed all the harder with the rubbery object, pressing it hard up into her slit and laughing aloud at the way it made Charlie moan with desire. Despite herself, Charlie wanted to be penetrated now, and she found herself thrusting her pubis forward in a lewd dance of lust that she was powerless to control.

All at once the two girls drew the phallus away from her burning sex, only to lower the other end of the pole so that the false penis was pointing upwards. Charlie watched them, her heart beating fast as she realised what was about to happen. They moved the thick object up, so that the tip was resting against the very entrance to her vagina. Then they began to push.

Charlie cried aloud as she felt herself penetrated by the dildo, her hips squirming from side to side. She bit her lip to suppress her own moans as, twisting and pushing, the two girls pressed the makeshift cock deep into her vagina, filling and stretching her in the most delicious way imaginable. They forced it all the way in, until only the pole on which it was mounted was visible and Charlie felt totally filled. Then Trudi dropped to her knees and, for the first time, Charlie noticed the recess set in the floor in front of where she stood.

Trudi pressed hard on the pole, forcing it even further inside Charlie, stretching her vagina so that she felt sure that something must give. Then the base of the pole slipped into the small hole where it fitted snugly.

Charlie was dumbfounded by the ingeniousness of the device, forced deep into her, the base slotted into the recess in the floor so that it was held in position by the tension of her chains. She had never in her wildest dreams imagined a more terrible, yet at the same time more exquisite bondage. She was naked and immobile, her limbs spread wide, her breasts stretched and elongated by the excruciating clamps, her cunt filled with the imitation cock so that the slightest movement brought a new spasm of pleasure coursing through her.

The girls stood back, content for the moment to enjoy their young captive's discomfort, watching as she writhed back and forth, the expression on her face alternating between one of agony and ecstasy with each passing moment. Then they turned and crossed to one of the cabinets, and Charlie's heart sank still further as she saw what they took from it.

Each girl held a long leather belt in her hand. Anna's was thin, no more than an inch wide, the leather shiny and new. Trudi's was a good two inches across, but no less flexible, making a cracking sound as the girl brought it down against the palm of her hand. Each was about three feet long, and Charlie shivered as they approached her.

Anna moved round behind her, running her fingers over Charlie's pert behind.

"You have been punished today, yes?"

"Yes," mumbled Charlie through gritted teeth.

"But not with a belt, I think," said Trudi, a smile playing about her lips.

"No. It was a whip."

"Have you ever been beaten with a belt?"

Charlie shook her head.

"Good. It will be a new experience."

Trudi nodded to Anna, who moved back from the captive slightly. Charlie watched nervously as the pair of them drew back their arms.

Thwack!

Anna's belt descended onto the soft, tender flesh of Charlie's behind , the thin leather biting into her and stinging terribly.

Thwack!

Barely had Charlie the chance to react to the first blow than Trudi brought her belt down across her belly, cracking into the skin just above her pubic triangle and making a loud smacking sound.

Thwack!

Once again Anna lashed Charlie's behind. Then:

Thwack!

Trudi's whip cut into her belly once again.

Thwack!

Thwack!

Thwack!

Thwack!

Charlie barely had time to think as the blows crashed down alternately on her front and back, each one shaking her young body back and forth as red stripes began to adorn her pale flesh.

Thwack!

Thwack!

Thwack!

Thwack!

The strokes fell relentlessly, so that poor Charlie could barely distinguish one from the other, such was the excruciating agony they were inflicting on her.

Thwack!

Thwack!

Thwack!

Thwack!

The blows began moving up her body, striking her back and her rib cage alternately, then higher still, the thin belt falling on her shoulder blades whilst the thicker was angled up, laying angry red stripes across the underside of Charlie's breasts and causing the clamps to tug even more at her swollen nipples.

Thwack!

Thwack!

Thwack!

Thwack!

Each of Anna's blows rocked her forward, and each of Trudi's rocked her back, and the result was that the dildo was thrusting in and out of her sex every time the belts fell. All at once Charlie realised the effect they were having, and with it came the shocked realisation that a climax was beginning to build within her. Despite the stiffness of her limbs, the excruciating pain of the nipple clamps and the stinging blows of the two belts, her body was responding in a totally perverse manner, the wetness inside her flowing anew as she felt a fresh wave of passion sweep through her.

Thwack!

Thwack!

Thwack!

Thwack!

The blows continued to fall. But now the pain was almost eclipsed by the pleasure as the thick phallus plunged relentlessly into Charlie's vagina with a force that no lover could ever achieve, making her moan with passion, her arousal increasing by the second.

Thwack!

Thwack!

Thwack!

Thwack!

The two sisters seemed to sense their naked captive's excitement, and began to beat her even harder, the cruel leather leaving stripe after stripe across her young flesh. Barely an inch of her back, belly and breasts was free of the marks of the belts as they laid into her with gusto, the cracks of leather on flesh ringing about the room

Thwack!

Thwack!

Thwack!

Thwack!

"Ahhh!" Charlie came with a piercing scream, her hips thrusting forward against the dildo as she abandoned herself to her shameful desires, her face contorted with lust and agony, in stark contrast to the laughter of her two tormentors who continued to lay into her with gusto, concentrating on her breasts and backside as they enjoyed the sight of their captive's orgasm.

They beat her until her hips ceased to jab forward and the cries from her lips had died to low moans. Only then did they stop, standing back to gaze at their helpless prisoner. Charlie, her body weakened by the sheer passion of the orgasm, gazed up at her reflection once more. Her trim little body was a mass of red stripes, her breasts swollen and inflamed, her flesh bathed in sweat. Down the inside of her thighs ran a silver trickle of moisture that had leaked past the grotesque dildo that still stretched her vagina, bearing witness to how the object had turned her on.

Trudi stepped forward, running her hands down Charlie's stomach, grinning at the way the youngster flinched at the stinging pain.

"That should teach you to come onto our land flaunting yourself," she said. "Now I think Father and Miko want their fun, so we won't need this any more."

So saying she took hold of the pole to which the dildo was attached, pulling it from its recess, then slipping it out of Charlie's vagina. It was wet and shiny with her juices, some of which ran all the way down the pole, and the girl held it under Charlie's nose so that she could smell her own arousal on it. Then she tossed it aside, and her sister moved forward.

Charlie could barely respond, but gave a gasp as Anna released the chains on the nipple clamps, giving her at least some relief from the dreadful pain they were bringing her.

Trudi pushed something out from the corner of the room. It resembled a hurdle such as an athlete would vault in a running race, although the top was made of a thick plank of wood covered in black leather. Trudi manoeuvred it until it was just in front of Charlie and adjusted the height so that the bar rested against her pubis. Then there was a clatter, and Charlie realised that they were slackening the chains that held her arms above her.

As the tension came out of her body, Charlie slumped forward, but Trudi was there to catch her. She undid the cuffs at Charlie's wrists and for a second the hapless girl thought her ordeal was over. Then she felt herself being dragged forward over the hurdle, her hands pulled down and affixed to a new set of manacles attached to the floor. Then, to make matters worse, Trudi pulled down the chains on the nipple clamps and these too were affixed to rings in the floor, bringing back the dreadful agony of the teeth with a vengeance.

Charlie's new position was, if anything, even more uncomfortable than before, her backside thrust high in the air, her legs still spread wide, her lovely young breasts pulled taut by the chains.

Trudi picked up her belt, and Charlie flinched as she anticipated another beating on her bare behind, but the girl just laughed, tossing the object behind. Then the door opened and the two men entered.

Charlie raised her head and watched as the pair sauntered in. They were both wearing bathrobes now, and both paused to admire the job the two girls had done with their young visitor.

"Very nice," murmured Herr Garten. "Did the little slut come?"

"Of course," said Trudi. "Now she is prepared to give you pleasure."

Herr Garten smiled at his offspring. "Well done girls," he said.

The pair curtsied and went to the door, taking one final look at their prisoner before leaving. Then Charlie was alone with the two men.

She had no illusions. Here she was, a beautiful young girl, stripped completely naked, bound and helpless, her sex perfectly presented. She knew that she should protest. Rail against the indignity of her situation, against the cruel clamps that bit into her flesh and the chains that bound her in this undignified manner. But what good would that do? If anything, she suspected it would increase the satisfaction of her captors. So she remained silent, her heart beating hard as she anticipated what was to come.

Herr Garten moved to stand just in front of her. He let his bathrobe fall to the ground. Beneath it he was naked, his long, thick cock jutting up just in front of her face. He said nothing, simply thrusting his hips forward, but Charlie knew what was required of her.

She opened her mouth and took him inside, tasting his arousal as her tongue delved under his foreskin, seeking out the smooth, bulbous knob of his glans. He pressed himself deep into her mouth, his stiff erection sliding almost to the back of her throat, so that it was all she could do to prevent herself gagging. Charlie began to suck at him, the pain once again put to the back of her mind as she savoured the sensation of having a man fill her mouth with his manhood for the second time that evening. It seemed as if her entire life was being taken over by sensual experiences, whether it be the pain and humiliation inflicted on her by the bikers and the two strange sisters, or the pleasure which these men took and gave in her lovely, naked body. Since choosing to join the bikers she seemed to have foregone all choices as to what she did and with whom. She was entirely a slave to others' whims now, whether voluntarily as with the bikers, or reluctantly, as now, entirely at the mercy of Herr Garten and his cruel family's perversions.

Miko stood and watched as she fellated his father, his own erection obvious beneath his loose-fitting gown. Charlie had no doubts that he would soon be using her body too, and she wondered what his intentions were. She didn't have to wait long, as Herr Garten pulled his knob from between her lips and indicated to his son to take his place.

Charlie sucked the younger man's cock just as she had his father's. It was shorter and thicker than the older man's, jutting up from a mass of thick black pubic hair, the large balls slapping against her chin as he fucked her face. She concentrated hard on pleasuring him, the saliva escaping from the sides of her mouth and dribbling down her neck with every thrust of his powerful hips.

All at once she felt hands on her behind. Hands that squeezed the flesh and stretched the cheeks apart. She wanted to turn round and see what the older man was doing, but Miko's thrusts prevented her. She shivered as she felt his fingers run down the crack of her behind, probing at the tight hole of her anus which she knew was perfectly displayed by the way she was positioned. She felt a sudden chill of wetness, and guessed that a blob of his saliva had been deposited in her nether crevice. Then, with a shock, she felt the smooth, wet tip of his cock press against her behind, and she understood what he was doing.

He was going to bugger her! The realisation came to her with a shock. He was pressing his heavy organ against her behind with the intention of penetrating her rear. And there was nothing she could do to stop him.

Charlie could scarcely believe it. Her backside was virgin. No man had ever taken her there. But now she was helpless to prevent it, trapped and bound in such a position that he could take her at will. Her body tensed as he began to press his glans relentlessly against her anus, twisting back and forth as he tried to force himself into her tight rear hole. Charlie knew that there was no point in resisting, and she began trying to relax her sphincter, overcoming her natural urge to tighten the muscles as he pressed relentlessly against her.

Then, with a final shove, he was in her, pressing his thick organ into her back passage. Charlie would have cried aloud but for the meaty mouthful of cock that prevented her. It was the most extraordinary sensation, a mix of pain and pleasure as he forced himself deep into her rectum, pressing on until she felt the flesh of his stomach against her bottom. There he stopped, clearly savouring the feel of the tightness of her behind whilst she writhed her hips back and forth, quite overcome by what was happening to her.

He began to move, his heavy cock sliding back and forth inside her rear passage. It was like nothing Charlie had ever experienced before, her rear feeling stretched to the limit. Then he slid a hand round her body and sought out her hard, wet clitoris with his fingers and she gave a gasp of delight.

At once the sheer sensual pleasure returned to Charlie in a rush. As he expertly manipulated her love bud she felt the wetness inside her increase once again, and she sucked all the harder at Miko's cock, sensing the excitement that was building within him.

The two men fucked their young captive with vigour, Herr Garten shaking her body back and forth as he thrust into her backside, each thrust placing new tension on her nipples, alternately stretching and slackening the flesh of her breasts, the needles in the jaws still stinging her dreadfully. But Charlie was oblivious to the agony, savouring her bondage and the two cocks that violated her so freely, her entire being concentrated on the pleasuring of the two men.

Miko came first, his firm young cock delivering spurt after spurt of thick, creamy come into Charlie's mouth. For a second she choked, pulling back and letting his semen splash over her face. Then she had him between her lips once more and was gulping down his seed with relish.

Almost at once his father gave a grunt and she felt her rectum being filled with spunk for the first time. The sensation was extraordinarily erotic as his hot seed pumped into her back passage, his cock seeming to swell and contract inside her with every spurt.

Charlie's own orgasm suddenly shook her naked frame, her body shuddering with pleasure as she climaxed once again, the taste and feel of the men's spunk bringing yet another peak of pleasure to the wanton youngster.

The men continued to thrust their hips back and forth until their orgasms were spent. Only then did they withdraw, leaving Charlie limp and exhausted as she hung in her bondage, spunk trickling down her neck and onto the stretched flesh of her breasts. As the men pulled on their gowns the two sisters entered once more, and Charlie noticed that Trudi was carrying something. It was a long, black strap-on dildo, and she held it up for the captive to see, a wicked grin on her face.

Charlie gave a sigh. Clearly the evening was far from over.

Chapter 17

Charlie lay, stretched out across the bare mattress, trying to find comfort in the minute amount of movement she had been allowed. Her wrists were shackled to the top of the bed, her ankles chained to each corner so that her naked body was, once again, quite helpless. As she stared up at the ubiquitous mirror on the ceiling she asked herself for the umpteenth time why she had strayed into this cottage and placed herself at the hands of this extraordinary family.

She studied her body. The marks made by the straps on the first evening had almost completely faded, although she knew that her backside still carried the unmistakable stripes of the numerous canings she had received there since entering this place.

She had been in the cottage three days now, Three days in which she had suffered almost constant bondage and pain, her lovely young body stretched, clamped, beaten, pinched, and maltreated in numerous other ways by the dreadful sisters, who revelled in bringing her to orgasm in the most fiendish ways imaginable, much to the enjoyment of the men.

They too had taken full advantage of their submissive young captive, fucking her mouth, breasts, sex and backside at every opportunity so that even now she could see the spunk stains in her hair and on her breasts and feel it seeping from her rectum and vagina as she lay on the bed.

And yet Charlie couldn't deny that, in spite of the pain and the degradation the foursome had heaped upon her, she had never felt more alive, and had seldom been far from an orgasm at any time during her visit. Even now her nipples, swollen by repeated application of the clamps, were stiff with excitement as she recalled the screwing she had received not half an hour earlier, Miko shooting his load into her cunt whilst his father had come between her breasts, spattering her face with hot spunk.

Charlie's reveries were interrupted by a sound and she turned to see the doorhandle move. Instantly she felt her sex muscles contract as she contemplated what might be in store for her.

The four occupants of the house entered. All four were dressed as they had been when she had arrived, and they gathered in front of her, gazing down at her body.

Herr Garten said something to the others in German, then turned to her.

"You have indeed proved a most diverting plaything young lady," he said. "I have never come across a girl with such an appetite for the more extreme sexual practices. But we must return to our work, so it is time for you to leave."

Charlie could scarcely believe what she was hearing. They were going to free her at last. She had entertained visions of being held as their naked captive indefinitely, a prospect that had both thrilled and appalled her. But now it seemed her captivity was over. But what would they do with her? Simply send her back into the woods to find her own way?

Herr Garten seemed to read the question in her eyes. He laughed.

"We have contacted the bikers," he said. "They will be here in half an hour to collect you. Meanwhile you had better get washed and ready to go."

The two sisters moved forward, Trudi undoing the shackles at Charlie's feet whilst Anna freed her hands. They helped her to her feet and led her through to a large bathroom. Hitherto Charlie had been forced to wash in an old zinc tub in front of the fire, so the foam bath filled with perfumed salts was a luxury and she sank into it, feeling the pain in her breasts and behind fade to a dull throb as the water lapped about her.

She lay back as the two sisters washed her, their hands gliding over her skin, removing the sweat and spunk from every crevice. They shampooed her hair, then combed it out over the edge of the bath. Then they lifted her out and dried her with thick, warm towels, dabbing the moisture from her body in the most sensuous way, making her moan with the pleasure of it.

When she was finally clean and dry, they led her, still naked, out to where the men were waiting. The pair stood, hands on hips, eyeing Charlie, who, despite the total intimacy of the previous days, found herself blushing under their gaze.

"Well done girls," said Herr Garten approvingly. "I think she's in a fit state to be released now. They should be here at any moment."

Even as he spoke, Charlie heard the roar of powerful motorcycle engines in the distance, and she felt her stomach tighten into a knot as she thought of rejoining the bikers and falling once more under the spell of Garth and his friends. She wondered what they had thought about her absence, and whether they had been looking for her. Then she glanced down at her body, and her discomfort increased as she thought of how they might react to finding her naked.

"Have you any clothes I could wear?" she asked timidly.

Herr Garten smiled and shook his head. "No. We like you as you are, little wanton rose," he said. "Besides, I'm sure the bikers will appreciate it."

The sound of the bikes was very loud indeed by now, and Charlie knew that, at any moment, they would arrive outside the house. She moved to the window and stared out onto the drive. As she did so the first of the machines came into view, kicking up a cloud of dust behind it as it roared up the track. Close behind were more, about ten Charlie estimated, all holding close formation behind the lead machine.

Charlie squinted at the rider at the front. She had fully expected it to be Garth, but, as it came closer, she realised that the features were not those of the burly biker in whose care she had been placed. Then her hand flew to her mouth as she suddenly recognised the man's face.

It was Zenski!

Charlie turned, wide-eyed to Herr Garten.

"It's the wrong ones!" she said.

"What's the matter?"

"It's the wrong gang. Those are the Easterners. They're the enemy. They're the ones who were chasing me."

Herr Garten shrugged. "What difference does it make? They're all bikers. Noisy scum polluting the atmosphere of my wood."

"But you can't let them get hold of me. I came with the Westerners."

"They're the worst," said Miko. "At least the Easterners speak our language."

"You mustn't hand me to them," she said desperately.

"Well they're here now," said Herr Garten.

"Why not let her out the back?" suggested Trudi suddenly. "She can get away into the wood."

"I suppose we could try it," replied Herr Garten. "After all, there's not much else we can do."

"Yes, that's a good idea," put in Anna. "Let her out the back."

Herr Garten hesitated, then nodded. "All right then," he said. "Follow me."

He led Charlie through to the back of the house. Even as he did so, a loud knock sounded at the front door, making Charlie's heart pound harder as she hurried along. They came to a stout door held closed by heavy bolts. Herr Garten began to draw them across.

"Couldn't I have something to wear?" asked Charlie quietly, but the question met with no response.

The door creaked open, and Charlie gazed out. She was confronted by a wide area of open land, the edge of the wood being nearly two hundred yards away. She turned to her hosts.

"But they might see me running across there," she said.

Herr Garten smiled. "That's a risk you will have to take," he said. "Unless you prefer to go out the front door." Even as he spoke the banging on the front door sounded through the house once more.

All at once Charlie realised that it was a set-up. They had known all along to which set of bikers she belonged. It was simply another example of their perverse sense of fun. Now they proposed to release her naked into the wood with the bikers in hot pursuit. Yet another little game to amuse them. She stared round at them, then down at her nude, defenceless body. She knew she had little chance of getting away from these strong young men on motorcycles, and she knew too that, once they had caught her, they would have no hesitation in taking advantage of her.

Herr Garten spoke again. "Well, little biker slut, what are you going to do? They'll stop knocking at the front soon and come round the back, you know."

Charlie looked round at her captors, then at the open door. There was no choice, and she knew it. Taking a deep breath she turned her back on her erstwhile jailers and threw herself through the door.

Chapter 18

Charlie hit the ground running, scarcely daring to glance behind her as she dashed as fast as she was able toward the relative sanctuary of the wood. It seemed an almost impossible distance away as she raced across the open area, her bare feet slapping against the dry ground, her breasts bouncing with every step. All the time she listened hard for any sound of pursuit, but none came.

She came closer and closer to the trees. Only fifty yards

now, then forty, thirty. She began to believe that maybe her get-away had been clean.

Then, with less than twenty yards to go, she heard a sudden outraged cry behind her. She threw a glance over her shoulder. The bikers had moved round to the side of the house and were standing, staring at her and shaking their fists. Even as she watched they turned and ran back toward where their motor-cycles were parked.

Charlie put on a final, desperate spurt of speed and plunged into the wood, dodging between the trees, leaping over small bushes and tree stumps in a frantic effort to get as far as she was able from the house and the bikers. Behind her she heard the sound of the motorcycle engines coming to life once more, spur-ring her to run even faster.

The wood was thick, and amongst the trees there was no space to ride one of the heavy machines used by the bikers. It was, however, criss-crossed by paths, many of which were wide enough to accommodate a skilful rider. She knew she must get as deep as possible into the trees before the bikers could reach her.

She raced on, closing her mind to the sound of the cycles behind her. She had lost all sense of direction now, her instincts simply telling her to put as much space as possible between her-self and her pursuers. She ran for a full ten minutes, then could go no further, collapsing against a tree, the breath rasping in her throat as she fought for air.

When at last her breathing had become more shallow she turned her attention once more to her predicament. It seemed that she was even more precariously placed than before now, the relief at having escaped from Herr Garten's dreadful family as nothing compared to her dread of falling into the hands of the rival biker gang.

She gazed down at herself. Her nakedness made her doubly vulnerable, her breasts and sex blatantly on display. She knew that, if she was caught, they would rape her, and probably worse.

She strained her ears, listening hard for her pursuers. In the distance she could still hear the roar of the motorcycles, though they didn't seem to be coming any closer. For the moment, at least, she was out of their clutches, though she knew she must keep moving in order to stay free.

She set off again, picking her way between the trees. She could see the sun through the branches, and used it to navigate by. She still had no idea where she was going, but at least she was sure that she was heading in a straight line, so must eventually reach the edge of the wood.

She walked on for some time. It was a pleasantly warm day, and the going was not difficult, but still she remained alert to the sounds around her. Every now and then she would hear the distant note of a motorcycle engine and would stop and listen hard. But they always seemed a long way distant.

As the sun rose higher in the sky, navigation became more difficult, and eventually she came to a halt, her sense of direction beginning to fail her. She resolved to rest where she was, and move on later in the day, when once again she could use the position of the sun to guide her. She found a small, grassy clearing surrounded by closely planted trees and settled down, enjoying the softness of the grass and the feel of the sun's rays on her skin. In a short time she had fallen asleep.

She wasn't certain what had woken her. She had been dreaming of the bikers' camp, where she was stretched out on Zep's bed whilst he fucked her with some energy. She opened her eyes with a shock, and for a second struggled to remember where she was. Then she saw her nakedness and remembered her predicament, and her heart sank once more.

It was then that she heard the voice. It was close by, not much more than fifty yards away and she realised at once that that was what had woken her. She froze, her heart hammering in her chest, listening hard. For a moment there was nothing, then she heard it again, seeming even closer this time. It was speaking in a foreign tongue that she guessed to be German.

Charlie slowly rose to her feet, pressing her body back against a tree, then peered round in the direction from which the voices were coming. She could see nothing through the thick woods, but comforted herself with the thought that this meant that her pursuers couldn't see her either. She knew, however, that she would have difficulty remaining concealed for long. The pale colour of her naked flesh would be only too visible against the greens and browns of the wood.

She remained where she was for some minutes, listening to the voices. They were moving through the trees at a slow pace, getting closer all the time. Reluctant as she was to leave the relative shelter of the spot she was in, Charlie knew that she must move on soon, or be discovered.

Slowly she slipped further round the tree, then set off as quietly as she was able away from the direction from which the voices were coming. Leaving her hiding place made her feel more exposed than ever, and she was acutely aware of her nakedness and vulnerability as she crept down a narrow game path, staying as close to the trees as she was able.

She moved swiftly, all the time listening hard for the voices. There was no doubt that they were receding as she moved along, and she began to feel more confident as she stepped out through the wood once more, certain that she was leaving her pursuers behind her.

By the time she saw the bikes it was too late. She stumbled into the clearing and drew up short at the sight of the three motorcycles parked there. Then there was a shout, and a hand clamped itself on her arm. She swung round to find herself staring into the face of a biker, his face wreathed in a grin as he ran his eyes up and down her lovely young body.

"Let go of me!" she pleaded, struggling to free herself from his grip. But he simply held her all the tighter, his muscular frame more than a match for the slim, petite little beauty.

He shouted again, and this time there was a reply from the direction in which the voices had been coming. Charlie's heart sank as she heard the other bikers making their way towards the clearing. There would be no escape now.

The other men were with them in no time. There were two of them, one tall and slim with short blond hair, the other shorter, his head shaven, his ears and eyebrows studded with piercing rings. Charlie's captor had her arms pinned behind her, and he turned her to face the men as they approached, much to their obvious delight.

Charlie was helpless and she knew it. To these men a young female captive was no more than one of the spoils of war, and was required to submit or be taken by force. And to make matters worse she was already stark naked, as if tacitly offering herself to them. She looked from one to the other of them and down at their crotches, then she lowered her eyes, ashamed of what was about to happen.

The three men seemed in no hurry, though, obviously enjoying the embarrassment of their naked captive. The two new arrivals stood and admired her body, passing what were obviously lewd remarks to one another and laughing at Charlie's discomfort. One of them came forward and began slapping her breasts, grinning at the way they shook. He tweaked the brown knobs of flesh between his fingers, making the youngster cry out with pain.

Charlie hated the way they were treating her, and hated herself still more for the perverse way she responded to them. She was afraid, too, that more men would emerge from the bush. At the moment there seemed to be just the three of them, and she guessed that the party that had been pursuing her had split up, and that this was just one section.

The man who was holding her said something to his two companions, and Charlie watched in trepidation as they crossed to their bikes, returning with large hunting knives and lengths of rope. Struggling and screaming she was dragged backwards and pressed down onto her back on the grass. Her hands were roughly seized and pulled over her head and the ropes were wrapped about her wrists.

Ignoring her pleas for mercy, they tied her hands on either side of a sapling, then took hold of her legs and dragged her forward until her arms were pulled taut. More rope was attached to her ankles and her legs secured to two more sturdy young trees about three feet apart. Then they stood back, obviously delighted with their handiwork.

Charlie was trapped and totally vulnerable, her thighs spread wide, her naked body completely at the power of her captors. She stared down at herself, only too aware of the sight she must make, her firm breasts standing up from her chest, the nipples hard and protruding, her bare sex lips gaping so that she could feel the cool air on the moist flesh within.

"You Diablo whore now," said the first of her captors, grinning. "Now you get Eastern cock in you."

His voice was harsh, with a strong German accent, and he grinned as she protested, writhing about on the ground at his feet.

He unzipped his jeans, and Charlie watched as he eased his cock from his fly. It was long and hard, the end circumcised. Despite herself, a spasm of desire ran through Charlie's small frame as he knelt down between her thighs.

He reached out and slid a finger into her slit. At once Charlie's body was shaken by a trembling orgasm, her cries ringing out as she pressed her hips up against his hand. It took her totally by surprise, and was so violent that it was impossible to conceal the perverse passion it engendered in her.

The men shouted with laughter at the hapless youngster's lasciviousness. Charlie closed her eyes, deeply ashamed of her arousal. She tugged hard at her bonds in a futile attempt to free herself. Then she felt a hard, stiff cock nuzzling at the entrance to her vagina.

He slid in easily, her wetness saw to that. His cock was big, and it filled her totally so that she moaned with pleasure as he began to thrust.

He fucked her without finesse, grunting his enjoyment as he thrust his cock into her vagina, running is hands over her bare breasts. For her part Charlie was unable to suppress the passion within her, and her cunt muscled tightened about his rod as she felt her own hips begin to press upwards against his own in a manner that was quite beyond her control.

He came suddenly, his cock pumping gobs of semen deep inside her sex and triggering a second orgasm in her, one which made her thrash about beneath him, her shouts of release echoing back from the trees as if mocking her wantonness. Then he was pulling out and her second captor was allowed to enjoy the spoils of their lovely young captive.

Both the others took her quickly, their cocks filling her burning sex with still more spunk and making her come twice more, much to their delight. Barely had the last of the three withdrawn than Charlie heard the sound of a motorcycle approaching.

Once again she tried to struggle, devastated at the thought of being found in this state, her naked body tethered and helpless, the evidence of her ravishment plain to see as it leaked onto her open thighs.

But there was to be no escape, and seconds later the bike burst into the open clearing and headed toward her. For a second she feared it would run over her but the wheel stopped just short of her face. She squinted up at the rider as he dismounted. Then she felt a sensation of dread in the pit of her stomach.

It was Zenski.

Chapter 19

Charlie stood alone in the tent, her heart hammering, her body trembling. She tried to move, but the fiendish bondage that had been inflicted on her made even the slightest movement an ordeal.

Her hands were locked together behind her, the thick leather bands about her wrists attached by shiny steel rings. About her neck was a heavy black collar, and this was joined by a short chain at the back to her wristbands, dragging her arms up and back in a most awkward manner.

Worse still was the way they had shackled her legs. The same kind of leather bands that immobilised her hands had also been strapped about her ankles. Then the two men in whose care she had been placed had produced a heavy wooden pole about three feet long with metal rings at each end. Ignoring her protests they had spread her legs apart and, to Charlie's horror, the rings had been attached to her ankle bands, forcing her legs wide in a way that exposed her crotch perfectly.

Once she was immobile, her captors had stood back to admire her, their faces wreathed in grins. One of them had produced a piece of card and, using a marker pen, had written the word 'SLUT' on it in large capitals. This he had attached to a piece of string and hung about her neck so that it rested just above her bare breasts. Finally came the blindfold, wrapped about her head and plunging her into complete darkness.

Once the bondage was complete they had felt her up, bringing small whimpers from her as they fingered her crotch. Then they had left her, alone and disoriented in the tent, unable to see and barely able to walk, waiting in nervous anticipation to find out what they had in store for her.

It was half an hour before they back came for her. She heard their footsteps, then laughter as they saw her predicament. A hand stroked her breast, then a finger slipped into her vagina. Charlie wanted to draw back, but she had no idea what was behind her and she was afraid of falling. So she stood and let them caress her.

Now she heard another man enter. He barked an order and the fingers left her. Charlie could feel the muscles of her sex convulsing as they slid out of her, and she knew this betrayal of her arousal would not be lost on her captors.

She felt another metal chain being attached to the front of her collar. Then came a sharp tug.

"Come!"

Walking was painfully difficult for the naked young captive with her legs forced so wide. Her gait was awkward and uncomfortable as she struggled to keep up with the biker, fearing that at any moment she might fall. As they progressed she could hear a hubbub of people talking and laughing and she realised with horror that she was being taken towards the source of the sound. She tried to pull back, but succeeded only in getting a hard whack on her behind from one of her captors.

She hobbled on, the sound coming closer all the time. All at once she bumped into something wooden.

"Steps," said a voice tersely.

If walking had been difficult, climbing the steps was well nigh impossible. She made it to the top, though, and found herself on what seemed to be a stage. With a sudden pang of dread she realised that she was about to be put on display, her naked body cruelly chained, her legs spread wide, the placard declaring her a slut visible for all to see. The laughing, chattering bikers were very close to her now, and she guessed that she must be hidden from their view by some sort of curtain. She tried to draw back, horrified by the prospect of being seen like this, but to no avail.

At that moment she felt a hand grasp the pole that was spreading her thighs. There was the sound of a click, and she realised that it had been locked in place, attached somehow to a ring set in the floor of the stage. Her heart sank. There was no escape now. At any moment her charms would be displayed to all and sundry.

The crowd went suddenly silent, and she heard someone talking. There were shouts back from the floor, followed by laughter. Then she heard the sound of the curtain being drawn aside.

At once a great cheer went up and she knew she was exposed. Her face glowed scarlet as she heard the shrieks of laughter and the loud catcalls from the audience. Something struck her on the breast, an empty beer can she guessed, and the jeering rang in her ears.

Suddenly the blindfold was pulled from her head, and Charlie blinked out at the crowd, her vision temporarily blurred by the pressure from the cloth. She found herself staring down at a sea of grinning faces. The stage was positioned in a clear space in the middle of the huts and tents and she was standing at the front, about four feet above the ground, with bright lights playing on her body. In front and slightly to the side of her was a full length mirror, though where they could have got it from she couldn't think. It's purpose was clear, though. To allow her to see herself as they saw her and to realise the full humiliation of her position.

They left her standing there for more than an hour whilst the festivities continued below. The bikers came to the edge of the stage in groups to laugh and jeer at her, occasionally throwing their empty cans at her. Charlie remained silent, her face bright red as she stood and stared out at them.

Something else was starting to happen to Charlie as she stood alone on that stage, though. It was something she knew was inevitable given her situation and her perverse nature, and she feared it more than anything they could do to her. Although she felt ashamed and humiliated at her treatment, she simply couldn't suppress the effect her situation was having on her young body. The more they stared at her nakedness, the more aroused she became, her sex getting hotter and hotter as the wetness seeped into it. She glanced down at herself and saw that her nipples were stiff and hard, protruding from her soft, round breasts as if begging to be sucked. Then her eyes caught the writing on the sign about her neck and she bit her lip. Perhaps it was true. Perhaps she was a slut. Everyone seemed to tell her she was. All she knew was that the desires inside her couldn't be suppressed, and that the cruel things men did to her brought her a pleasure that was impossible to describe, or to understand.

All at once she realised that Zenski was mounting the stage at the side. She glanced in the mirror and shuddered at the sight she made. She watched him as he walked across to her.

"So little English beauty that was lost in the woods," he said. "Don't you regret the way you tricked me now?"

Charlie said nothing.

He reached out and took her breast in his hand, squeezing it.

"Your nipple is hard," he commented. "And I see the wetness in your cunt. You are excited I think?"

Still she remained silent.

"Now I must see to your punishment. You made me look a fool in front of these men and women. Now I am returning the compliment. We'll see how you like some stripes across your behind."

"No, please," begged Charlie. But even as she spoke she saw a biker mount the stage carrying a long, thin cane. Zenski took it from him and flexed in his hands. It was very supple indeed, and it bent as he swished it through the air.

He stretched out his arm and ran the wood over Charlie's distended nipples. She gave a little shiver as he did so, and he grinned.

"Even this arouses you. You are a puzzle to me, little beauty. You are so sweet and innocent with those lovely big eyes, and you talk like a virgin nun. Yet you fuck like a bitch on heat at the slightest opportunity. I can see that this bondage turns you on, doesn't it?"

Charlie turned her face away, but he grabbed hold of her chin, forcing her to look him in the eyes.

"Answer me. You are turned on by this, eh?."

Charlie's colour deepened.

He grinned. "Little wanton slut," he said. "It is a long time since the Diablo's had their own whore in the gang. You will fit the bill nicely. You can forget those Spirit trash. They stole my colours, so we will have you in return."

Charlie's eyes widened. "How long are you going to keep me here?" she asked.

"For as long as I like. Maybe forever. You belong to us now."

"But you must let me go back to them," she pleaded. "They'll be leaving soon and I have to get back to England. My husband..."

"A husband? And he lets his wife go about seducing bikers for fun?"

"He doesn't know I'm here."

"Then he'll wonder why you don't return," said Zenski. He felt for her clitoris, bringing a moan from his captive. "I can feel that cunt of yours move," he mused. "It is hungry to devour some spunk I think. Well tonight it will get Diablo spunk, and much of it."

Charlie looked at him, a shiver running through her. She had known all along they would fuck her, but to have it told to her so clearly brought a fresh rush of wetness flowing inside her.

"But first I have to thrash you."

Zenski barked an order, and the biker who had brought up the cane approached Charlie. He undid the chain at the back of her collar, the one that was attached to her wrists. Then he pulled down another chain that was suspended from a beam that ran across the stage above her head. This he joined to Charlie's chain, then began pulling the other end.

Charlie's wrists were drawn up behind her, forcing her to bend forward as the strain in her arms became almost unbearable. He continued to pull until she felt sure her arms would break. Then he secured the chain.

All eyes were on Charlie now, and she raised her head and looked at her reflection in the mirror. She was bent forward, her hands dragged up behind her, her lovely breasts dangling. Her backside was presented perfectly for the beating that was to come, the skin drawn tight across her pert young cheeks.

Zenski tapped her rear with the cane, then pulled back his arm.

Swish! Whack!

The cane came down with incredible force, cutting into the flesh of poor Charlie's behind, the pain like the stinging of a thousand wasps.

Swish! Whack!

Down came the cane again, bringing a scream of pain from the anguished youngster as it whacked down on her naked flesh.

Swish! Whack!

Swish! Whack!

Tears poured down Charlie's face as the beating continued. The cane was fearfully painful, much more so than either the whip or the belts that had been used on her before. And Zenski was showing her no mercy, his ears deaf to her cries as he wielded the weapon.

Swish! Whack!

Swish! Whack!

Each blow found a new and virgin area on Charlie's pale behind and laid a dark, angry stripe across it, forming a crisscross pattern that positively glowed.

Swish! Whack!

Swish! Whack!

Then, as suddenly and unexpectedly as before, Charlie felt

her arousal return. It shocked her that this humiliating treatment and pain could have such an effect on her, but there was no denying it, and she gasped with passion, her hips beginning to pump back and forth as her cunt burned to be penetrated.

Swish! Whack!

Swish! Whack!

Swish! Whack!

Swish! Whack!

The blows rained down relentlessly, each one bringing new pain and passion simultaneously to the young masochist as she writhed about in her chains, her backside on fire.

Swish! Whack!

Swish! Whack!

Swish! Whack!

Swish! Whack!

Zenski beat her with unrelenting force. Her body was shiny with sweat now, drops of it falling from her face and breasts onto the stage, forming dark pools beneath her.

Swish! Whack!

Swish! Whack!

Swish! Whack!

Swish! Whack!

And then at last he stopped, his chest heaving with exertion, and stepped back.

The other biker moved forward, slackening the chain that had held the sobbing girl bent over and refastening her hands to her collar. Charlie swayed slightly as she tried to retain her balance, the pain in her backside excruciating. But along with the pain came the arousal, and at that moment her mind was filled with the heat in her sex, and the overwhelming desire for a orgasm, her hips thrusting in sharp jabs now, to the delight of those watching.

Zenski must have sensed her desires, for he moved close to her and placed the cane on her inner thigh, watching her face as he moved it higher.

"Oh!"

Charlie exclaimed aloud as she felt the hard wood against

her solid little clitoris. He held it there and she pressed down against it, moving her hips back and forth so that it sawed deliciously against her tingling love bud.

Charlie looked up at the crowd. They could see she was masturbating, and she felt her cheeks glow with shame. But she was too far gone now, and there was no way to stop herself. The desires inside her were too great.

She came with a scream, and the crowd cheered in delight as they watched her writhe back and forth, the release of her orgasm making her shudder as she pleasured herself on the cane. Zenski continued to saw it to and fro, wringing more cries from her as her body shook with desire. It was fully two minutes before she was finally spent, her breasts rising and falling, her face as red as her backside as the shamefulness of her behaviour came home to her.

Zenski shook his head, then turned to the crowd.

"The punishment is over," he announced. "What shall I do with her?"

"Give her to us," came the cry.

Charlie looked at Zenski in amazement. Surely he couldn't be contemplating sending her down there? But even as she watched he was bending down and releasing the chain that was attached to her hobble.

"Please," she pleaded. "Can't I have my arms free at least?"

He shook his head.

"But I've got nothing to protect myself with."

He grinned again. "That's how they want you.

Then he took hold of her arm and, dragging her forward, pitched her off the end of the stage.

Charlie landed in a sea of arms that grabbed at her, pinching and pressing her bare flesh. A finger slid into her vagina and she gasped as they groped for her breasts. Then she was on the grass, lying on her back, her arms pinned behind her.

She looked up, her eyes wide with panic, as a burly young biker was kneeling down between her legs and reaching for his fly. A cheer went up from those watching as his cock sprang free. Charlie eyed it. It was stiff as a pole and he took the shaft in his hand, grinning down a the helpless young girl.

He leaned forward and, despite herself, Charlie gave a moan of desire as she felt his erection pressing against her vagina. He slipped in effortlessly, her lubrication allowing him an easy penetration, the muscles in her sex tightening about his rod as if trying to draw him deeper inside her. He gave a grin of triumph as he saw the desire on the naked girl's face. Then he began to fuck her.

The biker began laughing aloud as he took her, ramming his stiff cock into her and fucking her hard. She made to cry out in protest, but at that moment another erection appeared in front of her face and, before she knew what was happening, her lips were forced apart and the stiff cock was pressed into her mouth, obliging her to suck hard at it whilst hands from unseen men mauled her defenceless breasts.

The man who was fucking her gave a shout of triumph, and she felt her vagina filled with his sperm, the hot fluid jetting from his cock deep into her. He went on thrusting until she had taken all he had to offer, then he rolled aside and another man was on her at once, forcing the walls of her sex apart as he rammed his erect penis into her without a thought for consent. Charlie barely had time to take in this new penetration, though because all at once her mouth was filling with spunk as the man she was fellating came suddenly.

Almost before she had gulped down his semen another cock had taken its place in her mouth, and Charlie was sucking again. This time as the man in her cunt came she came too, her cries muffled by the mouthful of stiff erection.

They continued to fuck her mouth and cunt simultaneously one after another until she lost count of the number of orgasms she had had. Then they laid her out over a table and beat her belly and breasts with their belts, laying red weals across her pale young skin and bringing her to a new level of excitement before they were on her again, pumping yet more spunk into her tired young body.

Charlie lost all sense of time. She had no idea how many men fucked her that night, or how many times she had gulped down the contents of one of the biker's balls. All she knew was the terrible passion inside her as orgasm after orgasm shook her small body.

At last, though, it was over and Charlie lay slumped across one of the tables, her naked body covered in red weals, her breasts and belly streaked with sperm, more of which was matted in her hair and leaked from her now swollen vagina. She barely noticed as someone lifted her and carried her across to one of the huts where he laid her on a bare mattress, chaining the pole between her legs to the end of the bed.

Within seconds Charlie was asleep, her tired and abused young body entirely drained of all energy.

Chapter 19

Charlie lay back on the grass, every fibre of her alive with arousal as the biker thrust into her sex, his grunts of enjoyment bringing her to new highs as she writhed beneath him. He stared into her eyes, making her close hers in embarrassment as she felt her sex muscles caress his rampant cock.

Charlie was quite naked, her legs spread by the now familiar hobble, her hands trapped behind her by the straps that were now a constant reminder of her slavery. As such she was quite incapable of rebuffing the man who was screwing her.

He came, and went on ramming his cock into her until his semen stopped flowing, then he abruptly withdrew and was gone, leaving the naked beauty alone in the warmth of the afternoon.

She glanced about her. There was nobody around apart from the two guards, who had been standing at a distance watching her get fucked. She wondered why they insisted on guarding her so closely. After all, the pole that held her legs apart was attached to a tree by a strong chain, allowing her no more than a few yards of freedom in either direction and ensuring that any man who wished to take her could have her without difficulty.

Charlie sighed. She had been with the Diablos for ten days

now, and at no time had she been allowed any clothes at all. In fact she had only been freed of her handcuffs for long enough to bathe and the pole between her legs was a permanent fixture, ensuring that she was prepared to be fucked at any time. When Zenski had told her she was to be the gang whore he hadn't been joking. At all hours of the day he would allow men to take her in any position they liked. At first she had protested, but it had been of no use. The men enjoyed taking her against her will and would taunt her with her nudity and helplessness before ramming their cocks into her.

The whole thing was controlled by Zenski. Men could only take her with his permission, a favour he appeared to bestow quite freely. For Charlie it was a bittersweet experience. Much as she hated the way the gang treated her as no more than a chattel, her body never failed to respond to their ministrations and, despite her shame, she found herself having multiple orgasms whenever she was fucked.

The evenings were the worst time for Charlie. She would be placed on display on the stage whilst the Diablos ate their dinner, then would be made to perform for them. Sometimes they would hand her a dildo and make her bring herself off with it whilst they laughed and cheered. On other occasions they would make her dance with them, an almost impossible task with her legs spread by the pole. As they danced, they would grope her pretty young body.

Then there were the raffles, where she would be made to choose raffle tickets, pulling them from the bag with her mouth. This was a devious idea thought up by Zenski. The first number she chose would define what was to befall her. Sometimes it was a caning, sometimes a whipping. Sometimes she would have to bend over whilst a plug was inserted in her anus, or bear the pain of nipple clamps biting into her tender flesh. The second number would indicate which biker was to inflict the humiliation. She never knew from one night to the next who was to be her torturer, but whoever it was, they showed no mercy.

The third number was the worst of all, though. It indicated which orifice she was to use to satisfy her torturer once he had finished with her. If it was her vagina she at least knew that she herself would also enjoy an orgasm. Her mouth simply meant swallowing more spunk, but her backside was the one she liked least, straining to relax her sphincter whilst the man enjoyed the tightness of her rear hole, spurting his hot come into her rectum whilst his friends watched.

But what depressed Charlie most was the permanence of her enslavement. If they had made her a sex slave for a limited period she would have been able to cope, and would have accepted the fact. But the knowledge that Zenski had no intention of returning her to the Spirits was an awful thought for her to come to terms with. Despite her fear of the British bikers, at least she knew that they would eventually take her home. Here, with the Eastern bikers, her situation seemed hopeless.

All at once a shadow fell across Charlie's face and she looked up to see that a biker was standing over her, his cock jutting from his pants. With a sigh she lay back and watched as he dropped to his knees between her legs and guided his erection toward her open sex. With a single motion he penetrated her, stretching the walls of her sex with his rampant organ. Then he began to thrust, staring down in contempt at Charlie, who was already gasping with arousal, her breasts shaking back and forth as he took her. She wondered for the umpteenth time at the recalcitrance of her body, and the way it responded to this kind of treatment. Already the muscles inside her sex were contracting about the thick rod that was invading her and she began emitting little cries of pleasure as he rammed into her harder, his hips jerking back and forth.

He came without a sound, suddenly flooding her already sopping vagina with yet another helping of semen and triggering a gasping orgasm in the wanton young captive.

He pulled out, and she expected him to wander off. Instead he took her arm and pulled her roughly to her feet. He undid the chain that attached her to the tree then pushed her forward.

"Come on, whore," he grunted. "You're wanted."

Charlie was surprised and confused by the move. Although she had no clock or watch she was certain it was too early for the evening's entertainment. Nevertheless she knew better than to question her captors and she followed the man into one of the huts, her gait, as always, made extremely awkward by the pole that kept her legs held stretched apart.

The man took her into a bathroom, then undid her wrists. Charlie stretched her arms up, enjoying the luxury of the freedom. She wanted to cover herself with her hands, but knew that would simply be met with a slap on her breasts or behind.

"Get in the shower and wash all that spunk out of you," barked the man. "Make yourself look presentable."

Charlie obeyed at once, shivering as the cold water flowed over her naked flesh, making her nipples tighten into hard, brown nuts.

She washed herself thoroughly, then shampooed her hair. She sat on the bathroom stool drying it whilst the man watched, his eyes constantly straying to the open slit of her sex so perfectly displayed by her bondage.

When she had finished he pulled her to her feet and fastened her wrists behind her once more. Then he inspected her, letting his hands stray over her bare flesh in a way that made Charlie gasp with the sensation.

"Hmm, you'll do," he grunted. "Now outside, quick."

Charlie followed him out into the afternoon sunshine once more. But this time they headed, not for the square but toward the camp entrance. It was the first time since she had arrived that Charlie had been allowed beyond the bounds of the camp, and she glanced about her guiltily, afraid that some passer-by might see her.

They walked for about ten minutes, the naked captive finding herself exhausted as she struggled along in her bondage, her firm young breasts bouncing with every step. The man led her down a narrow path that suddenly opened into a small country road. At once Charlie tried to hold back, fearful that she might be seen, but she succeeded only in receiving a smart slap on the backside from her captor. Then, to her dismay, she realised that they weren't alone. Parked about fifty yards up the road was a white van.

Once again Charlie's footsteps faltered, and once again she was rewarded by a stinging slap on the behind. She struggled on up the road, her face glowing red as she considered the sight she must make, walking naked on a public road, her arms pinned behind her, her breasts thrust forward, her legs spread wide.

There were two men in the cab of the van, and they were laughing and pointing at the girl as she approached them. As she came close the doors of the van opened and the pair climbed out. They were both very young, no more than seventeen, she estimated, one with long, dark hair tied back in a pony-tail, the other a skinhead, a spider's web tattooed on his neck. They were not bikers, their casual clothing that of workers. They both wore broad grins as they saw the way Charlie was blushing.

The pair went round the back of the van and opened the doors. Inside it was empty. They grasped Charlie on either side and hoisted her into the back of the vehicle. Charlie stared at them fearfully, wondering what could possibly be in store for her.

There was a chain hanging from a bracket in the centre of the van's roof and Charlie was made to stand beneath it. One of the men unfastened her wrists and pulled her arms above her head. Then there was a click and they were fastened once again, this time held fast to the chain in the roof. The youth paused for a moment, his hand cupping Charlie's breast and she felt the nipple harden at once. He pointed to it and said something to his companion, who laughed aloud. Then they both jumped down and slammed the doors with a bang, plunging Charlie into virtual darkness. A few moments later she heard the doors close, then the engine started and the van lurched forward, carrying the naked young biker slave to yet another unknown destination.

Chapter 21

The van drove for about half an hour, bumping and swerving as it went along so that it was all its naked captive could do to keep her balance as she hung in her chains. They seemed to be taking small winding roads and Charlie guessed that they were not covering any great distance.

All at once they swung left and she heard the crunch of gravel under the wheels. They trundled on for a few more yards before the vehicle lurched to a halt and the engine died. There was silence for a moment, then Charlie heard the front doors open and close. A few seconds later the van was flooded with light as the pair swung open the rear doors once more.

The tattooed youth hopped up into the vehicle and undid Charlie's hands, pinning them behind her once more. Then he shoved her forward.

Charlie jumped down, almost losing her balance as she landed, but just managing to remain upright. The gravel felt hot and hard under her feet and she winced in pain, but the young men were unmoved, prodding her in the back and indicating that she was to walk on.

Charlie followed the track, taking the opportunity to survey her situation. The van was parked in a small driveway close to the road. Once again no concession had been offered to Charlie's modesty so that, had anyone been passing, she would have been in full view from the road. Ahead of them was a double-storey building which they were obviously approaching from the rear. There was a single green door, outside which were stacked crates and beer barrels, suggesting to Charlie that the place was some kind of hostelry, though why she should have been brought there she couldn't imagine. As they came closer the door opened and a grim-faced woman appeared in the doorway. She was about forty years old, austerely dressed with her hair held up in a bun. She stared disdainfully at the naked youngster through winged glasses.

"Where are her clothes?" she barked at one of Charlie's adolescent companions. Her voice held no accent, so that Charlie realised with a start that she was English. Somehow that seemed to make her own situation even more shameful and she hung her head, unable to meet her fellow country woman's eyes.

"Well?"

"She was like this, Madam Leticia," stammered one of the boys, clearly intimidated by the imposing woman.

"What she came all this way showing everything?"

"Yes Madam."

The woman tut-tutted.

"You should be ashamed of yourself," she said to Charlie. "Get inside before someone sees you like that."

Charlie wanted to protest. To point out that she had no choice but to be naked in front of these two young men. But she guessed her words would fall on deaf ears, and besides, she too was anxious to get into a less exposed situation.

She made her way through the door and into a narrow passageway.

"Take her through to the room at the end," said the woman. "Secure her there. Hurry up now."

The boys took their young charge down the passage and opened a door at the end. The room was brightly lit and almost completely devoid of furniture, the walls painted plain white and the floor bare. In the centre of the room was a single wooden post with a shiny ring set in the top. Charlie was taken to this and made to stand with her back to it whilst the cuffs at her wrist were secured to it. Once she was in place, the two young men took the opportunity to feel her up, groping at her open crotch and squeezing her breasts, taking advantage of the fact that they were out of the woman's sight.

At last she heard the woman approaching again and they sprang away, leaving Charlie to retain her composure as best she could before the woman re-entered.

She eyed Charlie.

"What are you two grinning about? Get about your chores. The place wants tidying up for tonight's show, so get on with it."

The pair scuttled away, and the woman turned back to Charlie.

"So you're Zenski's latest find," she said. "Not bad I suppose, though the proof of your real worth will come this evening. How did you get mixed up with Zenski's lot?"

"It wasn't my fault," said Charlie.

The woman raised an eyebrow. "You're English?"

"Yes."

"All the more reason why you shouldn't be mixing with those louts."

"I didn't," Charlie protested. "They captured me."

"Captured you? What were you doing here in the first place?"

"I was with some other bikers."

"So you are one of them. Well if you're going to hang about with that scum, you deserve all you get. Anyhow, that's none of my business. I've just got to make sure you put on a good show tonight."

"Show?"

"Certainly. There'll be a lot of rich and important people here this evening, so you'd better not let me down."

"But I don't understand."

"You will. Meanwhile just keep quiet. You'll be called for later."

Chapter 22

It was some time later that the two boys returned to collect Charlie. By that time her limbs were aching from her bondage, and she was glad to be able to move again. The pair led her down a corridor and into a bathroom where, to Charlie's relief, they freed her wrists and ankles. It was the first time she had been able to close her legs since she had been captured, and she stretched herself luxuriously.

They made her shower and dry herself. Then she was ordered to sit on a table, her legs spread, whilst one of them shaved the hair from about her sex lips. For Charlie it was an extraordinary experience, feeling the cool of the razor glide over her skin so close to her most sensitive place, and she fought to control her emotions as the young man's fingers ran over her open slit. Afterwards he trimmed her pubic bush, cutting the hairs very short and shaping it into a neat triangle.

Once they were finished, Charlie was led to a mirror. She

knew that this was a prelude to exhibiting her once more, and she eyed her body critically. Her pubic hair was now so thin that the whiteness of her mound showed through, and her bare sex lips were even more prominent than before, so that she knew men would see them and want to fuck her all the more. She ran her eyes over the rest of her body. If anything her treatment of the past two weeks had improved her looks. Her muscles were toned and firm and the sun had lightly tanned her all over, so that she knew she would make a delicious sight to anyone who saw her.

They secured her wrists and elbows with cuffs, forcing her arms back behind her and thrusting her pretty young breasts forward. The pair took their opportunity to feel them, clearly delighted at the way her nipples hardened under their touch. Then they led her out and down yet another passage. Ahead Charlie could hear music and chatter, and she knew that yet another ordeal was about to begin for her.

They stopped her at the end of the passage and one of them knocked on a door. It opened, and there stood the woman they had called Madam Leticia. She eyed Charlie up and down, then nodded.

"You'll do," she said.

"For what?" asked Charlie.

"You'll see soon enough. Now keep quiet. There are some important people in there, and they haven't come to hear you talk."

Charlie fell silent. It was clear to her that she was to be the centre of attention tonight, though there had never been much doubt in her mind about that. Now it was with a mixture of dread and excitement that she waited to find out what new indignity they could possibly be planning for her.

Suddenly she heard the voices next door go silent. Then the door was opened. Beyond it she could discern little. One of the boys gave her a shove.

"Inside," he ordered.

Charlie stepped forward hesitantly. The room was dimly lit. It was some kind of night club, the floor set about with tables each of which had a burning candle in the centre. The club was full, the tables occupied by both men and women. As Charlie's eyes became accustomed to the light, she saw that they were wearing evening dress, the men with black bow ties, the women in long, elegant dresses. The sight of these smartly clad people made her feel even more conspicuous in her nudity, and she tried to avoid the gazes of the patrons and to close her ears to the murmurs of approval as she passed the tables.

There was a stage at one end, and it was toward this that she was heading. Charlie guessed that Madam Leticia had been told by the bikers of her exhibitionist tendencies and how she was affected by the eyes of others on her naked body, and now they were clearly exploiting that area of her nature. She tried not to think of how many people were watching as she stepped onto the stage, but already their eyes were having an effect on her and she felt the wetness inside her increase as the youngsters made her turn to face the crowd.

She stopped, placing her legs apart, a shiver running through her as she contemplated the sight she must make. She was standing at the edge of the stage, about three feet above the floor. To her right was an oddly shaped couch, placed sideways, its surface sloping down toward the edge of the stage so that anyone lying on it would be clearly visible, even to those seated right at the front.

A strong spotlight was switched on, picking out the paleness of Charlie's young body. Then Madam Leticia appeared at her side.

The woman began to speak. Charlie didn't understand the language, but she was sure it wasn't German. It sounded as if was an Eastern European tongue, possibly Russian. The woman spoke at some length, her talk punctuated by murmurs of approval from the audience.

She turned to Charlie, still addressing the audience, and it was clear that she was indicating the young girl's charms. She took hold of Charlie's breasts and at once the nipples stiffened, a fact not lost on those watching. She turned Charlie round and pressed on her back, making her bend forward, then ran her hands over the soft globes of her behind, pulling the cheeks apart to show off her anus.

Charlie's face was scarlet as the woman demonstrated her naked charms to the roomful of strangers. Yet she couldn't deny her arousal at being displayed so blatantly, and when Madam Leticia turned her to face the front once more and ordered her to spread her legs and thrust her hips forward, she knew that the audience would be able to discern the sheen of wetness that coated her bare sex.

The woman eased Charlie's nether lips apart with her fingers, revealing the hard bud of her clitoris. Then she slid a finger into her vagina, bringing a stifled gasp from her as her sex tightened about the intruding digit. Madam Leticia worked the finger back and forth a few times, bringing little whimpers from her captive. Then she withdrew her finger and held it up to show those watching how wet it was. She reached out and placed it in front of Charlie's face.

"Clean it," she ordered.

Charlie protruded her tongue and ran it up and down the length of the finger, then took it into her mouth and sucked it, bringing another low hubbub of sound from below. The taste of her own juices sent a new spasm of pleasure through her, and for the umpteenth time she wondered at her lustful urges.

The woman stepped away and said something else, and the audience began to shout back. She replied and the dialogue went on for some minutes. Then she turned to Charlie once more.

"They want to see five," she said.

"I beg your pardon?"

"Five. I'm sure that from what I've heard you'll manage fine. Now make this good. These are important people and they'll expect to get their money's worth."

Charlie went to reply, but the woman had already left the stage. She stood, trembling slightly, not daring to move as she stared down at the onlookers.

There was a slight disturbance behind the curtain to her right, then it opened and a man emerged. It was one of the bikers, though she didn't know his name. He was wearing only a pair of boxer shorts and he moved to stand beside her. Then Madam Leticia was with her again.

"I don't want to see a soft cock on this stage," she said. She reached behind Charlie and undid the cuffs at her wrists and elbows. Then she nodded to the biker.

Charlie eyed him. He was tall and slim, with a broad chest. Clearly he had been chosen for his physique and looks. This to Charlie was something of a bonus, since she had had no choice of sexual partner since being captured and some of the bikers who had fucked her recently had been far from attractive specimens. She glanced down at his crotch and saw that it was already bulging. Then she looked out at the audience. An air of expectancy had descended over them, and she knew they were waiting for her to perform. For a moment she contemplated what she was about to do. Less than a month ago she had been a quiet, faithful housewife living in an English suburb. Now here she was, naked on a stage in a foreign country, about to perform the most intimate act a woman could perform, with an audience of strangers watching. And yet her prime emotion was excitement, and it was with genuine enthusiasm that she dropped to her knees before the man.

Her fingers were trembling as she reached for his shorts, though she couldn't quite understand why. After all, for the last few days she had been violated by more men than she cared to count. This was different, though. There was something slightly sinister about the well-heeled audience who were watching her so intently, an air of something about to happen that would affect her greatly.

Charlie ran her hand over the front of the man's shorts, feeling the swelling that had started inside. She moved closer, letting her nipples brush against his strong, hairy legs. Then she took hold of the waistband and pulled his shorts all the way down to his ankles and off. She stared at his cock. It was thick and heavy, already half erect, hanging in a long arc from his groin, his large balls dangling behind. She leaned forwards and, taking his shaft between her fingers, guided it into her mouth, closing her lips about the uncircumcised tip and beginning to suck at him, her other hand cupping his scrotum and feeling his balls move as he reacted.

She sucked harder, worming her tongue down under his fore-skin and seeking out the eye of his cock, feeling him swell inside her mouth as her ministrations took effect. She glanced to her right. She was kneeling sideways on to the stage so that all those present could see precisely what was happening. The audience were all watching with rapt attention, leaning forward in their seats as the naked young beauty fellated the man who acted as if he owned her.

Now she felt a hand on her shoulder and, letting the cock slip from her mouth, turned to see that another biker had come on stage and was standing behind her. He also was a fine specimen, with broad shoulders and a slim torso. His head was shaven, his arms tattooed. He wore a pair of briefs which swelled at the front in a way that drew Charlie's eyes to them. She turned back to the first man, who's erection glistened with her saliva. She ran her left hand up and down its length whilst at the same time reaching for the briefs of the new arrival, tugging them down to reveal his veined, circumcised tool.

She took the new arrival into her mouth, sucking hard at him whilst still masturbating the first, feeling his penis engorge itself with blood as it rose. Soon she had two stiff cocks at her disposal, and moved from one to another, endeavouring to keep both men aroused.

It was when the third man arrived and stood between the first two that she began to get an inkling of what was happening. She thought of Madam Leticia's words. 'I don't want to see a soft cock on this stage' she had said. At once Charlie turned to the new arrival, dragging his pants down and revealing a third cock. This was a magnificent specimen, like a great elephant's trunk that dangled from a thick bush of pubic hair and she set about fellating him without hesitation, her hands still working on the other two shafts.

She had barely got him hard, though, when two more figures stepped onto the stage. It was the two youngsters who had brought her to the club and they stood, grinning down at her, their briefs already threatening to split as their young cocks swelled in anticipation.

For the next ten minutes Charlie worked like a Trojan, holding at least one cock in her mouth whilst wanking hard at the others, moving from man to man, keeping an eye open for any signs of anyone going soft. She needn't have worried, though. Charlie's natural sexual talents ensured that all five of the men were clearly satisfied, and the lascivious youngster found herself more aroused by the second as she carried out her duties, her senses filled with the sight, scent and feel of the cocks she was ministering to.

All at once she heard a clap, and glanced sideways from the man she was sucking to see Madam Leticia on the stage once more. She barked an order, and Charlie found herself being pulled to her feet, strong hands clamping about her arms and dragging her across the stage toward the couch.

As they approached it the third man, the one with the largest cock, prostrated himself across it, facing the audience, his great erection standing up like a pole. At the same time, Charlie felt herself lifted bodily from the ground, her legs dragged apart. She cast an eye across the audience, all of whom were watching with silent attention as she was taken closer to the prone biker. She was to be publicly fucked!

They held her over the man's groin and began to lower her. When the rock-hard tip of his penis touched her open slit she gave a gasp, almost coming then and there, such was her state of arousal. They pushed her downwards, so that his meaty rod pressed hard against the entrance to her vagina. Then he was inside her, his massive organ stretching the walls of her tight passage as he slid ever deeper into her.

For a moment Charlie was uncertain whether she could accommodate his entire length, and she bit her lip as he forced himself ever deeper. Then she felt his thick, wiry pubic hair against her inner thighs, and she knew he was all the way in.

Charlie was moaning with passion now, and began to move her body up and down at once, hungry to feel his thrusts, But the hands were still holding her body, and she suddenly found herself being forced forward, so that she lay on top of the man, her pretty breasts pressed against his broad, hairy chest.

Then came another sensation. A finger was moving over her anus. With her legs spread wide she knew it was in full view of those watching, and now someone was rubbing something cold and slippery around her nether hole. She craned round to see the shaven-headed man spit on his fingers and rub her there once more. Then she felt hands pulling the cheeks of her backside apart and the stiff heat of an erection pressing against her there.

Charlie gasped as she realised what was happening. He was going to bugger her, whilst she still had a cock inside her vagina. She was about to be doubly penetrated. She stared out at those watching. Many of those at the back of the room were on their feet now, and her face glowed as she considered the spectacle she must make.

The man pressed harder, and Charlie closed her eyes, trying hard to relax and allow him the access he was demanding. For a second it seemed as if her backside was too tight for him, then she gave a little cry as she felt his knob penetrate her. He forced himself deeper, his cock filling her rectum as he drove it all the way in until he too was buried deep within the naked girl.

Charlie could scarcely believe what was happening to her. To have two thick erections inside her at once was the most extraordinary sensation, like nothing she had ever experienced. She lay across the chest of the man beneath her, struggling to calm her breathing as the second pressed down on her from behind, both their cocks throbbing with life. Then something touched her face, and she realised that they were not yet finished with her. There, right in front of her face, was the third man's cock, still wet with her saliva. He was pushing it against her mouth, and she knew at once what he wanted. She opened her lips and took his thick erection into her mouth.

Yet there were still two more stiff cocks on the stage with her, and all she had left were her hands. She thought again of Madam Leticia's words. 'They want to see five'. Five men. They were expecting her to satisfy five men simultaneously. Surely she couldn't do it? Yet what choice did she have? She was their slave, and must do whatever they asked. Already the two young men had positioned themselves on either side of her, and she reached out with trembling hands, closing her fingers about their shafts.

For a moment all was still. Then Charlie began working the two youngsters' foreskins back and forth. At once the other men began to fuck her with relish, the pair in her cunt and behind moving in unison as they slipped their cocks back and forth in her tight holes whilst the third rammed his erection deep into her mouth.

For Charlie the next few minutes were a confusion of pain, pleasure and exertion as three men pounded their stiff members into her small body whilst she wanked hard at the other two. She tried at first to move her own body in rhythm with her violators, but it simply wasn't possible. Instead she relaxed, surrendering her body to them, allowing them to shake her frame back and forth as she clutched at the other two shafts, concentrating on working them up and down. Behind her she could hear the murmur of the crowd as they witnessed this extraordinary quintuple ravishment of the lovely youngster. The thought of them watching brought a surge of excitement to the wanton youngster, and she tightened the muscles in her sphincter and sex whilst sucking all the harder at the man in her mouth , her hands flying back and forth.

Charlie was almost taken unawares when the man in her backside came. One moment his stomach had been slapping against the soft globes of her behind, the next he was pumping hot spunk deep into her rectum, his cock twitching violently as he shot his load into her behind. His orgasm went on and on, his stiff erection pumping spurt after spurt of his seed into her until there was no more, and his thrusts slowed to a stop.

He withdrew slowly, his cock sliding from her even whilst the two other men continued to pound against her body, She gave a little gasp of release as he finally withdrew from her aching backside, but her relief was short-lived. Almost at once the erection in her right hand was snatched from her, and moments later she felt it pressing insistently against her anus.

This time he slipped in more easily, though it was still painful for the tormented youngster. She barely had time to register it, however, when her mouth was being filled with spunk, making her gag as it shot to the back of her throat, the hot, sticky fluid spurting in copious amounts that she struggled to swallow.

The man took hold of her hair, holding her still as he rammed his hips against her face, his semen leaking from her mouth and dribbling down her chin. Charlie sucked as hard as she could, gulping it down hungrily, thrilled by the taste of the man's come, slurping every last drop from him.

The moment he withdrew, the second of her young captors took his place, a great grin on his face as he took hold of Charlie's head and rammed his erection into her mouth. Charlie accepted him without complaint, closing her lips about his swollen glans and starting to suck once more.

She was nearing exhaustion now, her backside raw, her jaws aching from sucking for so long. Yet there was no let-up from the three who were using her body, and she herself was tingling with arousal, the taste and smell of the spunk she had swallowed spurring her on.

The men fucking her backside and vagina came simultaneously, their cocks shooting yet more semen into her tired body. Moments later her mouth was filling up once again as the other youngster let go, and Charlie found all three orifices being filled with their seed. It was all too much for the lovely young girl, and with a muffled gasp she found herself coming too, her vagina convulsing as spasms of lust shook her. It was like nothing Charlie had ever experienced before, and she thrashed back and forth between the two men's bodies whilst keeping her mouth clamped about the shaft of the third, swallowing his semen as fast as he ejaculated it.

The three continued to thrust against her until they had spurted every drop of their seed into her. Only then did she feel the blessed relief of the young man behind her withdrawing from her backside. She let his companion's cock slip from her mouth, then felt her arms grasped and she was pulled from the stiff pole of the one beneath her. They dragged her round to face the audience. Charlie was exhausted, hardly able to stand, semen trickling from her anus and her sex, whilst more ran down her chin and onto her breast. She shook back her hair and gazed down at those watching, her chest rising and falling as she regained her breath. Then they led her off, her legs barely able to support her as she staggered from the stage.

Chapter 23

Charlie stood in the centre of the small cell, her hands behind her head, her legs spread, whilst the man examined her body. He was a thin-faced individual, with cruel eyes that seemed to bore into her naked flesh as he took in her lovely young form. In his hand he held a cane, and he used it to lift her breasts one after the other, running it over her nipples and nodding with satisfaction at the way they hardened.

It was more than an hour since her epic encounter on the stage. She had been taken from there back to the bathroom, where the two young men had watched her clean the spunk from her body. Then she had been led into this cell and allowed to lie down. Before long, though, a knock had sounded at the door and Madam Leticia had bustled in, ordering her to stand as she was now, then fussing round her to check that she was presentable. Only once she was satisfied did she show the first of the men into the room.

He was a short, fat man, his upper lip bathed in sweat, and he had positively panted at the sight of the naked beauty who awaited him. He had felt her all over, stroking her breasts and pressing his fingers into her sex and anus, making her bend forward and backward as he groped her body. The humiliating experience had lasted for almost ten minutes and, despite his appearance, Charlie had found herself close to orgasm on two occasions as he felt her in her most private places.

The second man had been no less demanding, making her take up any number of demeaning poses and grabbing and pinching her bare flesh. Now she was being examined by this third stranger, who used his stick to move her and bend her to the positions of his liking.

He made her turn and grasp the end of the bed, leaning forward and spreading her legs wide, pressing her backside back as if offering it to him. He moved the stick down, and a shudder ran through her as he ran the cane along the length of her slit, the rough surface scraping over her love bud and making her whimper with arousal.

He began to saw the stick back and forth, watching her reaction. Charlie tried to stay still, but her body refused to obey her, her hips thrusting down against the stick to increase the pleasure on her burning clitoris.

She came with a stifled moan, her sex lips closing about the shaft of the cane as her body shuddered with the force of the orgasm. The man held the stick where it was, allowing her to rub herself until her passion abated. Then she stopped, her face crimson.

Swish! Whack!

He brought the stick down hard across her behind with a suddenness that made her cry aloud at the stinging blow, which left a bright red stripe across her rear cheeks.

"Self control," he said quietly. "You'll be no good to me unless you learn to exercise self control."

Then he turned and left the room, leaving Charlie to puzzle over his words, and to contemplate the stinging pain in her bare behind.

She turned and took up her submissive stance again. A minute passed, then the door opened and another man entered. He was tall and well-built, his top hat pulled down low, so that the brim cast a shadow over his face. Charlie stood still, waiting for another inspection to begin.

"Hello Charlie."

He removed his hat, and Charlie's jaw dropped.

"Zep!"

It was indeed the biker. He had cut his hair short and, dressed in his evening finery, was barely recognisable as the rough biker she knew. Yet it was, indeed, Zep, and he smiled at her.

"So, I've found you at last."

"But how? What are you doing here? What's going on?"

He put his hand to his lips.

"Shh. They think I'm one of the traders."

"The traders?"

"That's right. That's what you're here for. Didn't you know?"

"What sort of traders?"

"Slave traders. They sell sex slaves to Eastern Europe and the Far East. There's a pretty rough crowd out there, and they're preparing to auction you."

"But what would they do with me?"

"There are plenty of rich men out there looking for pretty young things like you. And you'd be a good catch. They were very impressed with your little performance. Five at once! Even I've never seen a girl do that before."

Charlie dropped her eyes. "They made me do it," she said.

"You still came, though. You couldn't have faked that."

"I... I couldn't help it."

"I know. That's the point. You'd be just what they're looking for. Someone out there will pay good money for a submissive naked slave like you. It'd be public whippings and shows like today's all the time, as well as entertaining his guests."

"But wouldn't they ever free me?"

"What, and have you tell the world? No fear. Once they'd finished with you, in a few year's time, you'd be sent out on the plantations as a whore for the workers. You'd probably end up as a star in a snuff movie."

"A what?"

"Never mind. The fact is we've found you, and now I'm here. Look at me. I even got a haircut to convince these people I'm a trader. It wasn't easy."

She looked up into his handsome face. "It suits you."

He grinned and reached for her breasts, his fingers closing over the soft flesh.

"You can fuck me if you like," she said quietly.

"There isn't time. There'll be someone else in here in a

minute. You'll just have to curb those desires of yours."

Charlie blushed, ashamed at her wantonness in making the offer.

"You will help me escape?"

"Of course. We're pretty sure when they'll be shipping you out. For the time being, though, I'll have to leave you. Just be ready when it happens."

He kissed her on the lips. Then he was gone. She wanted to call after him, to ask him more questions, but she daren't. She knew now that she loved Zep truly, and would do whatever he asked of her.

Chapter 24

It was two days later when they came to take Charlie away. She was lying in her cell, her wrists and ankles chained to the hard bed when she heard the sound of the men approaching, and she knew her time had come.

It had been a fraught two days. Half a dozen more men had come to visit her that afternoon after Zep had left. They had inspected her in the most intimate manner possible. One had been in military uniform and had laid six stripes across her behind with a swagger stick. Another had simply bent her forward over the bed and fucked her from behind. A third had made her bring herself to orgasm with a bottle whilst he watched.

Then had come the auction, with Charlie back in her cuffs and hobble, standing, her legs forced wide apart, whilst Madam Leticia ran the proceedings. The bidding had gone on for fully ten minutes, though Charlie had had no idea what amounts were involved. The final winner was the man with the cane, and once Charlie had been taken back to her cell he had visited once more to take another look at his acquisition, obliging the young slave to suck him off before pronouncing himself satisfied.

The remainder of her stay at Madam Leticia's had been spent in her cell, the only breaks coming when the two youths, who were her jailers, took her out for her ablutions. This was usually done under the strict supervision of Madam Leticia. On the second afternoon, however, the woman had been absent and the pair had laid Charlie out on the cold floor of the bathroom, taking it in turns to fuck her whilst the other kept watch. Then they had made her bathe to remove all traces of the ravishment and had taken her back to her cell, both grinning with contentment.

Now though, as the heavy footsteps approached the cell, Charlie guessed that the time had come to move her. She watched as the door was unbolted, then swung open to reveal the cold, unsympathetic face of Madam Leticia.

"Here's the slut," she said. "I'll be glad to be rid of her. She's a bad influence on my two lads."

She stepped aside, and, to Charlie's surprise, she found herself staring into the eyes of Zenski.

"All set to go, little hot one?" he said. "We have an escort for you just to ensure your safety."

The two youths appeared and released her from the bed, pinning her hands behind her. Then they led her from the cell and out into the sunlight. There was parked the van in which she had been brought to Madam Leticia's, beside which were about a dozen motorcycles, their riders watching the naked youngster with interest as she was led across to the vehicle. The sight of them caused a pang of dismay to Charlie. She hadn't expected an escort. The point was, would the Spirits expect it? If not, her rescue seemed a forlorn hope.

The boys took her into the van and secured her to the ceiling as before. As they closed the doors she heard a roar of motorcycle engines, then the van jolted into motion and they were off.

The first twenty minutes of the journey were anguish to Charlie. She could hear the Diablos' bikes on either side of her, holding station beside the van. She knew there were more in front and behind. Would the Spirits come in force, she wondered. Would they come at all? What if they'd got it wrong, and they weren't even aware that Charlie was being shipped away? What if she really did end up a helpless slave in a foreign country?

When the attack came, it took Charlie by surprise as much as the Diablos. She discovered afterwards that the Spirits had stretched a rope across the road, pulling it up at the last moment and thus taking out the first four bikers. Just around the corner they had blocked the road with a series of logs, causing the van to slew sideways as it screeched to a stop and putting paid to another of the Eastern bikers. All Charlie heard was the crashing of expensive metal as the bikers came off, followed by a sickening lurch, leading her to believe for a second that the van may overturn.

Immediately the air was filled with the sound of engines and the shouts of the bikers as the ambush got under way. The Spirits had ridden out of the forest armed with staves and the Diablos were taken off guard, so that initially they were in confusion. Charlie listened in consternation as the noise continued, wishing desperately that she could see what was going on outside.

Then she heard something crash against the doors of the van and they flew open. There, holding a small axe, stood Zep. Charlie gave a cry of delight at the sight of her rescuer, who leapt up into the van. Two more quick blows dislodged her chain from the roof of the van, though her hands were still secured in front of her, then he led her out of the vehicle onto the road.

All about her the fight was still going on, bikers setting about one another with fists and sticks. Zep was leading her through the battle when he was confronted by one of the Diablos. The man stood in front of him, a bike chain dangling from his fist, a look of determination on his face.

"Get off the road," said Zep to Charlie.

The naked girl scuttled to the side and watched as the Diablo swung at Zep and he parried the blow with his arm, grabbing the other biker's wrist as he did so.. The chain fell to the ground and the pair began trading punches. Charlie wished that there was something she could do to help, but with her hands tied she knew she would be more of a hindrance, so she simply stood back out the way.

The two Diablos who snatched her took her completely by surprise. She was later to learn that they had been riding some way back from the van, and had held back when they saw the ambush begin. Now they suddenly emerged from the trees, their engines roaring, and, before she had a chance to register what was happening to her, Charlie felt strong arms grab her. She screamed and tried to pull away, but the man was too strong,, forcing her down over the tank of the motorcycle and holding her there. Then the machine was accelerating away down a track that ran through the wood, with Charlie trying her best not to fall off as it skidded between the trees.

The machine bumped and bucked as it made its way along the narrow path, driving the breath from Charlie's lungs. She was completely dazed by the suddenness of the snatch, her head held down so that all she could see was the grass and trees just in front of her eyes as they sped along. She couldn't believe her misfortune. Just a moment ago she had been close to rescue, and now here she was, once more being carried off by the Diablos, their naked captive.

They rode on and on down the rough track. The ride seemed interminable to the shocked girl, her ears filled with the roar of the engines of the two machines as they sped in single file through the wood. It was all she could do to keep from falling off as the machine bucked and skidded along, the cold, hard fuel tank driving the breath from her lungs with every bump. Then, suddenly, there was a screech of brakes and the machine she was on slid sideways to a halt. As it did so she found herself staring down a steep bank to a wide, fast-flowing river.

A hand grabbed her hair and pulled her to her feet, and at last she was able to get a look at her captors. Her jaw dropped as she gazed at the face of the man on whose bike she had been travelling.

It was Zenski.

"Fucking bitch," he snarled. "That deal was worth a lot of money to me, and now you've fucked it up."

The other biker shouted something urgently to Zenski, pointing back down the track. Zenski paused and listened. Far away was the sound of motorcycle engines.

Charlie realised at once that the Diablos were trapped. They had obviously been taking a blind route through the forest, and now they could ride no further, the river completely blocking their path. It could only be a matter of time before the Spirits found them. There was nowhere for them to go, apart from a game track that ran off to their left, a track far too narrow to manoeuvre their heavy motorcycles along.

Zenski barked something to his companion and the pair pushed their motorcycles into the bushes as far as they were able, dropping them onto their stands. They picked up some branches and stacked them against the machines in an attempt to camouflage them. Then Zenski grabbed Charlie's arm and dragged her down the game path with the other biker following.

The path was narrow and winding, and progress was slow, with Charlie doing her best to hold back and to avoid scratching her bare flesh on the branches that stuck out on either side. Occasionally the following biker would whack her behind to make her move faster, and all the time they could hear the Spirits' motorcycles drawing closer.

"This is hopeless," she said to Zenski. "I'm just holding you back. Why not leave me and get away on your own? You could travel much faster."

Zenski swore, but then the other biker began to speak, and Charlie knew he was agreeing with her. Clearly he considered his own safely more important than keeping their hostage.

The two argued for some time, then Zenski came to a halt.

"It seems that Ivan here wishes to abandon you too," he said. He ran his eyes over his lovely young captive. "You have been the cause of much trouble to me, little biker's whore," he said. "And I foresee more to come. But getting caught by the Spirits will not improve my situation."

"Then you'll go on without me?"

"Even if we stop here, they'll be some time finding us. There are many tracks in this wood. But you're right. With the river there the only way back is the way we came, and that will require some stealth. With you along, I doubt it will be possible."

Charlie's heart raced. She was to be free after all! Then she realised that Zenski was still speaking.

"However," he said. "We still have a little time, and I think I shall leave you with a lesson about tampering with the Diablos."

He barked an order to his companion, who grinned and nodded.

At once they grabbed hold of Charlie's arms and dragged her across to a stout tree that stood close by. Grabbing her wrists, Zenski undid the chains and wrapped her arms about the trunk, securing them on the other side. At the same time, Ivan wrapped a rope about one of her ankles and, dragging it round the trunk, tied her other ankle in the same way. Charlie found herself pressed hard against the trunk, the bark hard and rough against her bare skin.

Zenski took another length of rope and, looping it through the chains that held Charlie's wrists, tossed the other end over a high branch, dragging her arms upwards so that she was pushed harder against the trunk, her bare nipples chafing against the wood.

Charlie was helpless now, her entire rear exposed from her neck to her ankles. She glanced round fearfully at her captors, and her stomach knotted as she saw Zenski unwrapping a whip from his belt. It was a leather whip, about seven feet long, with a thick handle, the lash tapering to the thickness of a piece of string. At the end was a tight knot, and as Zenski wielded it, it made a loud crack.

"Now for a little farewell present," he said. "A chance to show you what a real whipping can be like. And afterwards we'll sample the pleasures of buggering that tight little backside of yours."

"No!" Charlie's cry was a forlorn one. She knew they would do what they wished with her. She braced herself as Zenski stood back and flicked the whip behind him.

Swish! Crack!

The lash came down across Charlie's unprotected back, the end whipping round and catching her flank, inflicting a terrible pain on the naked youngster so that she cried out aloud.

"Gag her," ordered Zenski. "We don't want them hearing her."

Ivan moved forward and, pulled a handkerchief from his pocket. He came up behind Charlie and forced it into her mouth. Then he removed his neckerchief and wrapped it about her head, tying it tightly behind her. He checked that it was secure and stood back. Charlie braced herself again.

Swish! Crack!

The whip lashed across her flesh once more, laying another red stripe across the smooth, white flesh of her back and bringing a muffled shout from her as the pain engulfed her.

Swish! Crack!

Swish! Crack!

Swish! Crack!

The pain was like nothing she had ever experienced, eclipsing that of any of her previous beatings. The strokes fell with a terrible regularity, each one biting into her whilst the end wrapped round her and bit into her side.

Swish! Crack!

Swish! Crack!

Swish! Crack!

Zenski showed her no mercy, his teeth gritted as he delivered blow after blow, whilst Ivan watched with obvious amusement, the bulge at his crotch indication the pleasure he was anticipating afterwards.

Swish! Crack!

Swish! Crack!

Swish!

But this time no blow fell. For a second longer Charlie remained braced for the pain. Then a cry of surprise and anger made her turn.

Zenski was standing where he had been, still grasping the whip. But the other end of the weapon was being gripped by someone else.

Zep!

Behind him were four more Spirits, two of whom had grasped Ivan's arms and were holding them behind him. Charlie gave a muffled cry of joy at the sight of her rescuers, her embarrassment at her nudity momentarily forgotten as she tugged once more at her bonds.

The other two bikers moved to grab Zenski, but Zep held up a hand.

"No! Leave him to me."

He gave a sudden tug on the whip, snatching it out of the hand of the astonished Zenski. The handle travelled high in the air and looped down, straight into Zep's grasp.

At once Zenski's hand dropped to his belt and he pulled out a bike chain.

Swish! Crack!

Zep moved so fast that his adversary had no time to move, the tip of the whip cracking down on his hand and making him drop the chain at once.

Swish! Crack!

This time the whip came down across Zep's face, making him scream with pain as a bright gash opened across his cheek and began to bleed.

Swish! Crack!

Another blow lashed across Zenski's body, bringing another anguished cry from him. Then he turned and began to run.

Swish! Crack!

A final blow caught him across the back of the neck as he ran. Then he was crashing through the forest, his screams ringing in the trees.

Zep turned to Ivan who had stood white-faced, watching his companion's beating. Now he struggled with his captors, whimpering in terror.

"Let the bastard go," said Zep. "We know where they're going. Our guys will catch them and strip them of their colours before they're halfway to their bikes. These two are finished with the Diablos."

At once Ivan was off after his fellow Diablo, but not before receiving a searing lash across the body from the whip.

For a moment all was quiet. Then Zep dropped the whip and turned to where the naked girl was still hugging the tree, her pale skin striped with the marks of her beating.

He cut through her bonds, using his axe to split the chain

that held her wrists. Then unknotted the scarf and she spat out the handkerchief.

"Their bikes," she said. "They left them in the bushes down the track."

"I know," said Zep. "We found them. They're going to have to dredge them out of the river I'm afraid. If they can find them."

He took the young girl in his arms and she turned her face up to his. Kissing him full on the lips, letting his tongue into her mouth and licking hard at his. He slid a hand down her belly and penetrated her, and she knew he would feel the wetness engendered by the whipping. He pulled back his face as Charlie tried to hide the passion his fingers were arousing in her. He stood back and, taking her by the shoulders, turned her to face the other four bikers, whose eyes were fixed on her bare breasts and sex.

"Don't you think you should thank your rescuers too?" asked Zep quietly.

Charlie was momentarily shocked as she realised what he meant. Was her honour really so cheap now? She glanced from face to face and saw the expectancy there, and she knew that it was. She was a bikers apprentice and Zep was her master. He was giving her to these men, and she must obey.

All at once a tremor of excitement ran through her. She looked up into his eyes. His face was stern, and she knew the others were watching him, evaluating his control of his young charge. She dare not disobey him now.

Her heart pounding she slipped from his grasp. She looked about her. She would have preferred to find some cover, some bushes at least, but she knew her capitulation must be a public one. Her heart hammering, she crossed to a patch of thick, lush grass. She threw Zep one more glance, then carefully prostrated herself on the ground. Slowly she spread her legs, raising her hips and offering her sex to the men in the most blatant of gestures.

"Whatever you say, Master," she whispered.

Chapter 25

Charlie gazed out from the stage in the Spirits' headquarters over the tables below. As usual the clubhouse was crowded with bikers, both male and female, sitting about the tables swigging beer and laughing and joking. For a second she felt a pang of envy as she surveyed their relaxed demeanour, wishing that she herself could be a part of it. She glanced down at her body. In contrast to the leather-clad bikers, she herself was completely naked, her hands tied behind her back. She was kneeling up, her legs slightly apart, at the edge of the stage so that her breasts and sex could be seen by all. It was a position that she should have been growing accustomed to by now, but still she felt an overwhelming sense of shame at the way she was forced to show herself so blatantly.

Charlie had been with the bikers for well over a month now. Since returning from their trip abroad, she had lived in the cell upstairs in the club, where she had been subject to a strict regime.

Mamba insisted that Charlie wore no clothes. Her emotions swung between acute embarrassment and extreme arousal as she went about her daily duties in the clubhouse, cleaning, cooking and generally making herself useful whilst all the time her charms were perfectly displayed to anyone who wished to see her. And plenty did. Bikers from clubs all about the country had heard about the Spirits' little naked apprentice, and it wasn't at all uncommon for visitors to come to the Spirits' headquarters to see her at first hand.

Often Charlie would be made to wait on their tables in the clubhouse, enduring their lewd comments and their wandering hands, feeling her up as she leant over their tables, delighting in the way her juices flowed so easily. If the visitor was a more senior biker, he would often take her upstairs and fuck her, making her come back down to the clubhouse afterwards, the spunk leaking from her whilst he regaled his companions with stories of her lasciviousness.

There were conventions and parties as well, often held outdoors, Charlie would be allowed a shirt to wear in transit to these, but on arrival would be made to give it up and would sometimes spend days at a time naked amongst groups of strange bikers.

Zep was now her master. Garth, Zep told her, had been expelled from the gang after the fiasco in which he had lost her to the Diablos and very nearly to total slavery. Charlie had grown to love Zep even more during the weeks of her captivity, though he was a strict taskmaster and brooked no dissension from his young charge. Other bikers would come to him, requesting to use Charlie and he would be careful to ensure that she was not mistreated, though he seldom refused a biker who asked to fuck her. Some afternoons at the conventions she would find herself tied to a tree in the woods whilst a succession of bikers would be sent to find her and take her. The anticipation on such occasions was both frightening and delicious, listening for the footfalls in the wood and knowing that she was powerless to prevent ravishment once found. Often five or six men would seek her out, and when Zep came for her in the evening he would find her exhausted, her thighs streaked with sperm, her body sometimes bearing the marks of the bikers' belts where they had whipped her.

Zep himself never screwed her, despite the fact that she longed for him to do so. She knew, though, that this wasn't because he didn't want to. His sense of duty made him control her without indulging himself, and she guessed that, were he to cease to be her master, he would want her as much as the next man.

Charlie had all but forgotten her former life as wife and housewife. This was the only thing she knew now. Nudity, whippings and being fucked by friend and stranger alike were her way of life and, despite the terrible humiliation of it all, she revelled in her situation and was always totally submissive, much to the delight of her captors.

Now, as she looked out at the faces below, she reflected on her situation. They often placed her like this, up on the stage, her hands tied behind her whilst they drank and talked below. The thrill of all the eyes on her bare body never ceased to excite her, so that after an hour or so her sex was wet with desire. To-night a tall gang leader from the North called Tiger was visiting, and Zep had already told her she would be sharing his bed at the end of the evening. Now, as she looked down at the strong man with shoulder-length dark hair and two day's growth of beard on his chin a shiver of anticipation ran through her at the thought of having his cock inside her.

All at once she heard voices to her left, and looked round to see Zep walking onto the stage. She smiled at him, then the smile froze on her face as she recognised the man who accompanied him.

It was Jon, her husband.

Charlie stared at him, her eyes wide. What was he doing here? She had almost forgotten about him, though she had known in her heart that one day he must come back and find the house deserted. Now he was here, staring down at his young wife as she knelt naked on a stage in front of fifty people, her body on view to all.

"Jon!" she gasped.

"So it's true then, Charlotte." His voice was stern, his countenance grim. "The boys at the garage said I would find you here, but I must confess I didn't believe them."

Charlie didn't reply, her throat dry.

"They told me they had a little rendezvous with you there a few weeks ago," he went on. "Is it true that you turned up naked, sucked off the security guard and then gave yourself to both of them? They told me you were a good fuck. Not exactly what a man wants to hear about his wife."

Charlie dropped her eyes. There was nothing she could say. He obviously knew everything.

"Well?"

"It's true."

"And I gather there have been other men?"

"Yes."

"How many?"

"I don't know. Lots."

"And what the fuck do you think you're doing now? Why

don't you cover yourself? Everyone can see you."

"I can't. I'm a biker's apprentice. You know what that means."

Jon shook his head. "You fucking slut."

"And what have you been doing in Mexico?" said Charlie, suddenly angry. "I know you've got another woman there."

"That's different."

"Why?"

"Because I'm a man. And anyway she's a proper lady." Suddenly he stood aside, and Charlie realised there was a woman with him. She was tall and olive skinned, with large breasts and a slim waist. Her eyes were large and brown, and she was grinning down at the young girl.

"I'd like you to meet Paula," Jon said. "She's been my mistress for some time. I brought her home so that I could finally come clean with you."

"So this is your wife, Jon," the woman said in a Latin accent. "Hasn't she any shame?"

"Apparently not any more," said Jon. "It seems the Spirits have made a complete slut out of her. We'll have to see what we can do to get her back on the straight and narrow."

"You want her back?" asked Zep.

"I suppose so."

"You'd let me go back to him?" said Charlie to Zep, dumbfounded.

"He's your husband," said Zep. "Only he can relieve you of your apprenticeship. You can go back home with him right now if you wish."

"Of course she's coming back," said Jon. "It'll be some time before I can forgive her of course, but meantime she can keep house and cook for me and Paula. After all, it's her duty as my wife."

"You want me to come home, Jon?" asked Charlie.

"It's your duty," said Jon. "I'll be sharing my bed with Paula of course, but I reckon a bit of celibacy will do you good after the way you've been behaving. Perhaps when you've shown a little contrition I might sleep with you occasionally."

Once more Charlie remained silent. She was shocked by her

husband's arrogance and presumption, but the shame and humiliation of her situation preventing her from replying. Then Zep crouched down beside her.

"Charlie," he said. "Listen to me."

Charlie gazed into his eyes. He hardly ever used her name when talking to her, and she felt suddenly close to him.

"Look, Charlie," he said. "I'm not sure you're cut out to be a biker. You're not aggressive enough. A biker has to be a fighter. That's just not you."

Jon grimaced. "A fucker maybe."

Zep threw him an irritated glance, then turned back to Charlie. "There's an alternative, though."

"What?"

"What you're doing. You could stay on as an apprentice to serve the gang and others."

"Don't be so fucking insulting," said Jon. "She'll come back and serve me like a wife should. What kind of woman would want the kind of life you're offering?"

"She might."

Jon turned to Charlie. "They forced you to join, didn't they? Didn't they? Didn't they make you join by threats?"

"Yes."

"Then they've got no right to keep you. Now get on your feet. You're coming home with Paula and me to take on your rightful duties."

She turned to Zep. "Can I leave if I want to?"

"I've said so haven't I? After all, you've practically served your time, and after what you went through with the Diablos I couldn't fault you for wanting to leave. You're free to go."

"What if I stayed?"

"You'd serve the bikers in any way they asked. As you are now."

"Naked?"

"Yes."

"Would you remain my master?"

"Yes. But you wouldn't just stay here."

"Where?"

"There's a gang in Spain have heard about you. They want to have you for three months. Now that the summer's coming to an end it'll be warm down there. They can keep you naked without fear of the cold harming you."

"Would they treat me well?"

"You'd still be whipped and made to fuck who they told you to. You'd still be a virtual slave."

"For how long?"

"You would be a captive for a full year. After that we'd review it. Meanwhile you'd go where we send you."

"Would you come?"

"Sometimes. But you'll be on your own as well."

"Don't be bloody stupid," interrupted Jon. "She's coming with me."

"The decision's her's," said Zep.

At that moment a tall, dark figure appeared beside Zep. Charlie's heart leapt as she recognised the visiting biker, the one to whom she had been promised this evening.

"Hey, Zep," he said. "I'm too horny to wait any longer. I'm dying to get my dick into this little beauty. Come on darling."

He took Charlie's arm and yanked her roughly to her feet. "I hope you like sucking cock," he said.

"Wait!" said Jon. "She's not going anywhere."

The biker turned to him. "You wait your fucking turn," he growled.

Jon stepped forward. "I'm warning you..."

Zep held up his hand. "Whoa," he said. "The lady's been given a choice here."

Charlie stared at Zep, then at Jon, then at the biker. She glanced down at her naked body and thought of the life she would lead as a slave of the bikers, kept forcibly naked, whipped at their whim and given to any man they wished. She knew that, once her choice was made, her freedom would be lost, possibly forever. She knew too that she would get no second chance.

"Release my hands please, Master," she said to Zep.

Zep hesitated for a second, his expression bleak. Then pulled a knife from his belt and cut through her bonds.

Jon stood, a grin of triumph on his face, as she stepped toward him.

"See? I told you she'd realise her duty," he said. "Now get some fucking clothes on, you slut."

Slap!

The blow took him by surprise, the flat of Charlie's hand smacking onto his cheek and making him stagger backwards. She glared at him for a moment, then turned and approached the biker, dropping to her knees in front of him. She pulled down his zip and reached for his cock, like the true biker's slave she was.

BONUS PAGES BEGIN OPPOSITE

Our next title will introduce a new author, Charles Arnold, with THE PENITENT. This is one not to be missed, and this is the first chapter:

Kathy was still half asleep when she heard the sound of chains clanking. She rolled over on her side and put both hands between her legs, pressed hard against her pubic bone. Her hands were together as if in prayer except that her fingers pointed down. The edges of her hands rubbed slowly between her legs.

She was a little girl in her dream, sliding up and down against a hickory post in her uncle's dark basement.

It seemed to her she had always lived in the rectory with her uncle, who was the village priest. Like in the other dreams, she was aware of his shadowy figure behind the cellar stairs, watching her. He was always there, watching. She began to whimper in her sleep. Her hands moved more quickly, and her pelvis ground against them in a circular motion.

Before she had a chance to climax, there was an explosive roaring in the street. She woke up, trembling, and went to the window.

Outside, a man stood next to his rumbling grader and pissed on the steel treads. His stream ran down a crack between two treads and dribbled onto his shoe. He pulled twice at his long flaccid cock before stuffing it back in his jeans.

She couldn't actually see the man's cock, but she knew what he was doing. Her nightgown was bunched up around her waist as her small fingers stroked her clit. As she came, she stood on tiptoes and pushed her open cunt against the window. But the man's back was towards her. She sat down on the bed, shaking. She remembered her uncle's cold blue eyes and her fumbling attempts to pull up her panties, and his voice, always the same, admonishing, 'Shame, Katherine, shame. God will punish, God will punish.'

It had been something like a game between them, a contest that had never been resolved. She knew he would watch her. She was obvious about going to the basement. She waited until she felt his presence there on the top step. Knowing he was there made it exciting in a way she could not understand. Knowing he would say 'shame' and 'God will punish' caused a fluttery feeling in her stomach and made her wet between her legs. She would take down her panties and rub herself against the post. After awhile, he would step out of the shadow saying, 'Shame! shame! God will punish!' Then she would run to her bedroom, fall upon her knees reciting the catechism while waiting for punishment neither her uncle nor God ever administered.

Outside, the grader started up again with a roar that shook the house. All morning the huge yellow machine lumbered back and forth, cutting a wide flat clearing in the brush and scrub oak of the vacant land across the street. This was the way such things begin: with a tall, solitary man and his machine pushing over trees and disturbing the morning with smoke and noise.

It was quiet when she crossed the street. She held a cold bottle of Iron City with both hands. Her cutoffs were tight. She could feel them pressing the dampness of her cotton panties into the crease of her ass and the crease of her pussy. Her nipples pushed against the loose tee shirt she wore.

John Wallowitz sat in the shade beside his grader. His shirt was soaked with perspiration. He could feel the sweat in his crotch, and the seat of his pants stuck to the bony flatness of his ass. His lunch box was open beside him. Too fucking hot to eat, he thought, and threw the sandwich back into the box. When he looked up she was standing before him holding out a bottle of beer. "Goddamn!" he said, "you surprised me."

But he didn't look surprised. He squinted his eyes and looked up at her, seeing long dark hair, the brown eyes, small delicate face, full mouth, the quick rise and fall of her breasts, the tiny waist, the way her shorts molded her firm ass and crept into the crack, her beautifully shaped legs and small hands and feet. She looked like a little girl with a woman's tits and ass. He could feel his cock slide in sweat against his leg. He still hadn't reached out for the bottle.

"I - I thought you might be hot," she said, and immediately reddened. He raised one eyebrow and smiled. She noticed that his teeth were yellow stained and the front one was broken. A dark purple scar extended in a half-circle from his right eye to the edge of his mouth. She continued to blush and stammer, "I mean..."

"You mean you felt sorry for old Wally out here in the sun and decided to bring him something nice."

"Yes, well, I thought..." He reached up and took the bottle from her, quickly twisted off the cap, and drank. She watched his Adam's apple bob up and down. Some of the beer spilled over his chin.

"Ahhh!" he sighed, holding up the half empty bottle, "that's where the gusto is supposed to be, right?" She smiled and nodded her head. He leaned forward and clamped his big hand over her foot. She was wearing thongs, the callused skin of his hand suddenly tight against her bare foot shocked her. She tried to draw back, but he held her firmly. She could feel her toes curling, and the grit on his hand was like sandpaper against her flesh. "Do you really think that's where it's at?" he asked. "I mean the gusto of life?" He studied the bottle. "No," he continued, "it ain't in a bottle." He looked hard into her eyes, then let his gaze drop slowly and settle on her crotch.

Suddenly it seemed as if there were a movie playing in her head. She saw her fingers lightly tracing the horrible scar. Then she was bending over him, holding his face between her hands. She kissed his eyelids and the pink tip of her tongue followed the livid curve of the scar, lovingly, tasting his sweat. Then she slipped her tongue into the corner of his mouth feeling it explore the yellow teeth, rubbing it against the edge of the broken one. The movie stopped. He released her foot and she almost fell. She was trembling and breathing hard. Her mouth felt dry.

"Thanks for the beer," he said. "You know, after work I usually stop down in Hawthorne and have a couple more. I owe you one."

"Oh, no!" she said. Her voice sounded strange, as if she were hearing someone else do a bad imitation of her. "I'm married you see -"

"Wally," he interrupted. "My first name's John but everyone calls me Wally." She nodded. "It's the only bar in Hawthorne," he said. She started to go. "Hey!" he yelled, "what's your name?"

She turned back to face him. "Kathy," she said.

"You have nice legs, Kathy." The colour rose to her cheeks. He smiled, "Harry's Bar." She walked quickly, then half ran toward her house. "In Hawthorne!" he shouted.

Later in the afternoon it began to drizzle, one of those August rains that go on for days, muggy and hot. She wore a nylon blouse and a slim tan skirt. She was about to put on her raincoat, but she returned to her room and, from deep in the corner of a dresser drawer, pulled out a silver chain. Attached to the chain was a Saint Christopher medal. She placed it around her neck and fastened the clasp. Before backing the car out of the garage, she removed her bra and panties and stuffed them into her purse. On her feet were white high heels.

Hawthorne was ten miles down route eighty-six in a depressed area of the county. Long ago the coal mines had been worked out and the freight depot closed. Harry's Hotel Bar was seldom frequented except for alcoholic pensioners and itinerant construction crews.

She pulled into a parking space and got out of the car quickly, not allowing herself time to think. In her stomach was a hollow, sinking feeling. Five men were grouped together at the bar, and one old drunk slept at a table in the far corner. The light was dim. An overhead fan turned lazily. Her heels clicked on the bare wooden floor. All of the men at the bar turned toward her.

"Hey, well Jesus H. Christ!" shouted Wally. "I told you guys she'd show!"

She stood before them now. Except for one man, the rest had swivelled around to stare at her, but no one had moved to offer her a seat. "Harry, you better ask for proof," someone said.

"Yeah, Harry," Wally laughed, "looks like you got a minor here." His eyes were bright. She could see that he was excited. "Hey, what's your name again?"

"Kathy," she said, feeling her face grow hot and red.

"Right, Kathy." He turned to the huge black man on his left. "Look at them legs, Cliff. She's got the best damn legs I ever seen!" He waved his arm toward two empty tables. "Kathy, walk around the place. Let the boys have a look."

"No, please!" she began.

"Go on, do it!" Wally said. "Stuff like you never pays us a visit here in Harry's."

No one smiled. The men continued to stare at her. The only sound was the soft whirring of the paddle fan. Kathy looked down at the floor. After a moment she walked over to the sleeping drunk and returned. She knew that they were undressing her; that they were pushing their cocks between her bare legs. "You're all right!" Wally shouted. He was confident now, arrogant and drunk. He stood up. She hadn't realized how tall he was, or how thin. Through her mind flashed a picture of her on her knees in front of him. She would need a stool to kneel on or pillows, like a little girl at communion. The thought startled her. She had never touched a man there with her mouth, not even her husband.

"Kathy here ain't no shanty Irish," Wally was saying. "She lives up in Cedar Grove, big house, couple hundred thousand, right, baby?" He put his arm around her waist and reached up to cup her breast in his big hand.

"Yes," she said, "it cost about that." She wanted out of here. These men were ugly and mean. They had been drinking. Wally was the worst of them. But his hand was hot on her breast. She felt her nipples swell.

"And little Kathy here brung old Wally a cold beer in the middle of the morning and damned if she wasn't wearing the tightest shorts you ever seen." Wally shook his head and grinned.

Cliff, the big black man, sipped his beer, but did not take his eyes from her. His head was shaved. There was a gold ring in his left ear. Wide leather straps were buckled tightly around his thick wrists. There were metal studs and heavy loops embedded in the straps. The wide bracelets could easily circle her ankles. A cord could be put through the loops to pull her legs apart, to open her.

Wally tapped the arm of the man at her right, the one who had not yet swivelled around to look at her. "This here's Ezra Stein," Wally said. "He's a fat, dirty old bastard, but smart. Ezra reads a lot." The fat man nodded as he turned lazily to stare at her. His little eyes were set deep in his face. His belly hung over his belt. Several buttons were missing from the lower part of his shirt. She could see the pale flesh of his belly and a trickle of sweat. His hands were soft and puffy, the spatulate fingers swollen at the joints. His pig-eyes glanced first at the Saint Christopher's medal, then rose to meet hers. She felt, all of a sudden, very cold and frightened. She tried to look somewhere else but couldn't. He smiled slightly. The pudgy hands twitched. He turned his back to her.

Wally pointed to the empty stool between Cliff and Stein. "Sit here," he said, and took his place standing behind and to one side of her. The cracked plastic seat felt damp and sticky against her bare legs. She ordered a beer and paid for it herself. As she lifted her glass to drink, Wally's hand slipped under her raincoat. She drew in her breath and quickly put down the glass. She glanced toward the door, but did not move to get up. She wondered if he would unbutton her blouse and rub his rough hand across her breast. The men, except for Stein, watched Wally's hand as it moved beneath her coat. "Jesus," Wally said, squeezing her breast, "they ain't big but they sure are perky." He laughed, looking around at the others and winking. "No bra, neither," he said. The colour rushed to her cheeks.

Cliff reached for her hand. She pulled back, upsetting her purse on the bar. Wally spotted the panties and dug them out. He waved them back and forth. She clenched her hands in her lap and stared down at them, her face red. Wally held her panties over his head. "And, Goddamn, nothin' under her skirt!" he laughed. "Who wants a sniff? Only one buck for a sniff!" He put them to his nose. "Ahhh, a real lady!" The men began laughing and shouting.

"I'll take them," Cliff said, and held out a ten-dollar bill.

"They're yours for free!" Wally shouted. Cliff stuffed the panties in his pocket. "I pay," he muttered quietly and placed the ten in Wally's hand.

"No!" Kathy cried. "Please Wally!" Suddenly, under her coat, his fingers gripped her nipple. He dug his fingernails into it. The unexpected pain was sharp and searing. She gasped. He swung her around, still cutting with his nail into her nipple. She was about to scream, but a look in his eyes stopped her.

"It's Mr. Wallowitz," he said squeezing tighter. "Mr. Wallowitz," he repeated. Tears came to her eyes. Stein still had his back to her, but the others watched silently. In spite of the pain, she felt a hot rush between her legs. "I ain't givin' you leave to call me Wally. Who the hell do you think you are? Just another rich bitch in heat, right? Ain't that right?"

"Yes!" she gasped.

"Yes, what?"

"Yes, Mr. Wallowitz."

"Tell the boys why you're here. What you want from Mr. Wallowitz." He eased the pressure on her nipple. She caught her breath and forced back the tears.

She couldn't think.

"Speak up, Goddamn it!" He twisted her throbbing nipple. "Tell them."

She looked up at him. The ugly scar had deepened. The pockmarks were angry red. "I - I want you to -" she paused. "I want you to come to my house and -"

"Say it right!" he shouted. The men waited.

"Do it to me," she whispered, looking down at the bar, her voice on the edge of breaking.

He tore open her coat and ripped her blouse down the front. Her hands flew up quickly to cover her bare breasts. Wally took both of her wrists in one hand and held them against the bar. "Show," he said, nodding to the men at the bar. He let go of her wrists. Still not looking up, she slowly lifted her hands to cup each breast. She held them out first to the men at her left, then turned to the fat man. Stein placed his hand lightly on the breast closest to him. His white flesh was cold and wet, yet his touch left a burning sensation that caused her to tremble. He slid his hand under her breast and lowered his head toward it. She thought he was going to take the swollen nipple between his thick lips. Instead, he spit on it. His spit was cold. She watched it slide, like a pale yellow snake, over her nipple and down the side of her breast.

"Ohhh," she said, softly, "ohhh!"

Wally spun her around to face him. He placed her tiny hands on each side of his face. She pulled him down to her, pressing her bare breasts against him. Before their lips met, her mouth was open to accept his tongue.

Wally's face between her hands was rough, his skin bumpy. Her fingers found the scar. She followed it with her fingertips. Wally shuddered and pulled away, shaken. With her right hand, she reached up and jerked violently at the Christopher medal breaking the chain. The room was silent as she closed her coat and fastened its belt.

"Friday night," she said, trying to keep her voice under control. The men knew she was hot. They could smell her heat. It hung in the humid air. It was as penetrating as the soft rain which whispered against the plate glass window. "Friday," she repeated, "around nine. My husband won't be back until Saturday."

"I'll be there," he said.

Turning toward Stein, she placed the medal next to his glass. He stared straight ahead, ignoring her. She picked up her purse and walked quickly to the door, knowing that behind her were at least four hard cocks. As for Ezra Stein, she wasn't at all sure.

Now A VICTORIAN SCRAPBOOK - Vignettes from a sterner age, by Stephen Rawlings, author of 'Jane and Her Master': Third extract:-

THE PURCHASE OF A SLAVE.

In January 1850, Samuel, later Sir Samuel, Baker, a forty nine year old widower, who had confided his teenage daughters to his sister's keeping while he accompanied the young Maharajah, Duleep Sign, on a tour of Europe, arrived in the Turkish river port of Middin on the Danube, in what is now Bulgaria. There, in the slave market, he bought a beautiful young blonde Albanian virgin. Her name was Florence, and she was just seventeen. Although there is a certain amount of mystery about the transaction, enough is known about the details of the local slave trade and traders for us to recreate how she came to be there, and the nature of her enslavement, preparation and sale.

The slim girl with the golden mane did not lack courage, as she was to show time and time again in later life, during her travels in darkest Africa. She kept up a brave front before the foster father who had cared for her when her parents had been lost in the death of the short lived Hungarian republic of 1840, but inwardly she quaked. Part of the price that the community had to pay for its defiance of the Turkish authorities in 1840, 'the year of revolutions', was the so-called 'blood tax'. One nubile girl from each household must be given up to be sold in the slave market, to pay for the very forces that had so brutally suppressed their efforts to gain their freedom.

A pretty girl would be purchased as a toy by some rich Turk, to give him pleasure, or be made a birthday present to his son, or given to a neighbour to whom he owed a favour, or sought some advantage from. She would expect to spend the rest of her life being used sexually by men who did not care for her, except as a receptacle for their lust, and would have her aborted should she fall pregnant or, at best, take her baby from her so that she might be ready for their bed again without delay. There were ugly rumours too of treatments to ensure the master was never deprived of a soft belly and pert breasts.

Now Florence waited for the tax collectors to call. Her pride sustained her and she wore her best dress, a long robe of fine red wool, embroidered with gold thread and black jet beads, little golden slippers on her dainty feet, her gleaming golden hair worked into twin thick ropes, wound around her head like a crown. She flinched when the knock came, but held her ground, while the men presented her foster parent with the official tax demand. Her composure was further threatened when the collector enquired if she were virgin, since such fetched much increased prices than once used goods, and, on being assured the no man had entered her, demanded proof. With flaming cheeks, she was made to lie on a low couch, and raise her legs and her robe, so that the collector might probe her most intimate place, and satisfy himself she possessed an unruptured membrane.

Finding her intact, he gave her 'uncle' a receipt for her person, witnessing that he had paid his dues on behalf of the family. When they ordered her to put out her wrists she obeyed quietly while they were bound with cord, then followed docilely behind them, keeping her head high. In the street she was added to a line of girls already bound, and, as the tax-collector and his escort passed through the town, others were added, until there as a file of some thirty of so young women of all sorts and sizes.

At last the day's quota was reached, and the collector delivered his haul to the house of one of the local slave merchants, with whom he had an 'understanding'. In the courtyard he handed over his charges in exchange for an official receipt and an unofficial purse of gold coins.

If the collector earned a 'present' so did the escort. Just as the executioner had the right to the clothes of those he hanged or flogged, so the soldiers shared the clothes of the girls they had guarded. The unhappy line was ordered to strip. There were many tears and protests, but these changed to screams and cries as overseers moved among them with their whips and lashed any girl who delayed to bare herself. One stubborn young woman who resisted had her clothes ripped from her, and was flung face down on the floor. While men stood on her arms and legs to hold her down, the chief eunuch of the house stood beside her and flogged her across her back with a thick leather whip, until the blood ran down her sides. It was not good business to damage the goods before their sale, but one was sacrificed to impress the others, and there was no more disobedience. Each stripped off her garments and added them to the pile at the escorts feet, seeming thereby to signify their final and irrevocable separation from their families and their lives to date.

Florence bared herself with the rest, scorning to make a fuss. Under the embroidered robe she wore a short cotton shift and, when she had pulled this over her head and stepped out of the little slippers, she was naked but for a strip of fine cloth she wore wound round her hips, and passed through her legs. One of the soldiers held out his hand for it ad she looked him in the eyes as she unfastened it on her hip and drew it from between her thighs. Again he gestured and she put her hands to her head, lifting her small firm breasts, and pulled out the pearl headed pins that held her hair, letting it cascade down her back and shoulders to the jut of her pert buttocks.

He stepped towards her, and she flinched from his touch, but he only lifted the small silver cross on its fine chain from around her white neck, the only thing she had possessed of her dead mother's. This time she sobbed. All around her other girls wailed and wept their own sorrow. Now they had no link with their families, no property of their own: now they were property themselves and, as property, they had to be marked.

One at a time, the girls were seized by the soldiers and bent over a stone block. The trader satisfied himself that those described as virgin were indeed intact and then, as they screamed and writhed, the eunuch pressed an iron into their flesh, on the base of the right buttock. As it withdrew it left the government mark, a crescent and star three fingers wide, deeply impressed in seared flesh.

Florence did not struggle as she was bent over the block, and unfeeling fingers explored her vagina, but the agony of the branding was too great to endure in silence, as she had promised herself she would, and she let out a long high whine of anguish as the hot iron burnt her.

As each girl was lifted writhing from the block she was passed to another of the slave-traders men, who placed an iron band about each ankle, joined by a short chain, and hammered the rivets that closed them tight.

The formalities were now complete, and the weeping girls

shuffled into the house, still naked, the brands flaming against their skin. Even the dark complexions of the Arabs and Egyptians showed them clearly. On Florence's pale buttocks the cruel crescent stood out black and angry. It was evening now, with the light about to go, and they were given a simple meal and left in a locked stone chamber to get what rest they could on the crude mats that strewed the floor. For their other wants a large stoneware jar with a wooden lid must suffice.

In the morning Florence's 'processing', to ready her for sale, began in earnest. First she was taken outside to the well, where two men doused her with water and scrubbed her with coarse soap and rough cloths. She was made to endure the humiliation of rough male hands forcing themselves between the cheeks of her bottom and soaping her cringing anus, then transferring their attentions to her front, working a lather in the thick tight curls of her maiden bush, then rubbing the soap over the lips of her vulva, and on the delicate tissues between them. The crude lye soap stung and burned, and the man laughed as she flinched. "You'll squeal louder when the prick goes in," he mocked.

She was humiliated, but not afraid for the moment. The men would not dare harm her. Her beauty and her virginity would bring the trader a fine profit, and the man that spoilt the goods would get short shrift from his employer.

Scrubbed clean, she was given over to the old women who did the actual preparation. Stretched on her back on a heavy table, a thick strap around her waist holding her down, her arms above her head, held there by cords, her knees drawn up and draped over brackets on short posts attached to the table, her legs splayed wide open, Florence could see, through the vee of her thighs, a pot heating over a small brazier.

The old woman brought it over and started to ladle the contents onto the crease of Florence's right thigh, just along the edge of her golden curls. She gave a small yelp of pain. The pot contained coarse sugar, heated until it softened; hot enough to make her jump, but it would not damage her tender skin.

The old woman pressed the sticky brown mess into her pubic hair, rubbing it deep into the roots. When a strip of her fleece an inch wide was thoroughly coated she laid a strip of open weave cloth over it and pressed it down firmly. It was left a few minutes to cool, then the woman took hold of one end of the strip, at the bottom of Florence's fork, and pulled upwards on it sharply, peeling it all the way up to her belly. As the cloth strip was yanked up it tore the hairs to which it was stuck cleanly out of the skin, roots and all. Taken by surprise, Florence shrieked aloud.

It was just the beginning; strip by strip, an inch at a time, the short curly hairs of her sex where ripped out. The pain was horrible, unbearable. Not the terrible agonising pain of the brand, but that had been over in seconds, and not repeated. This was, with great deliberation, enabling her to anticipate each new assault while she lay with the sugar cooling on her fur, waiting for the next ripping depilation, while the pain was also mixed with a belly churning extra ingredient that made it impossible to bear it in silence - she felt her dignity being stripped from her with the hair and, when it was over, and the domed hill of her mons shone pink and bare, she felt her soul had been stripped naked.

Once it was done she expected to be released, but the woman left the room and returned with the trader. With an impassive face, he stood by to supervise the next part of the preparation. The old woman had exchanged the spatula she had used to spread the hot sticky sugar for a set of three small wooden rods hinged together at their centres in such a way that drawing one set of ends together forced the other three points to open up. While the slave merchant watched, she carefully parted the labia around the vaginal opening, and gently probed the soft pink slot with the bunched points of the rods, until she found the small opening in the hymen. With infinite care she squeezed on the outer ends of the rods, and the inner ends began to stretch the delicate membrane open.

Florence could feel herself being stretched; at first with no discomfort, then a slight smarting sensation which made her wince.

"Careful, old woman," the trader growled. "If you burst her maidenhead I'll fill your old gap with boiling oil."

"Patience Master. I've not split a girl yet. This one's tight, but I can manage."

Keeping the rods gripped in her left hand, the woman reached down and came up with a long quill, bent at right angles at one end to form a leg an inch or so long. Florence flinched again a she felt the tip enter her vagina and scrape down the delicate inner wall, where nothing had ever passed before.

"Keep still girl," the old woman snapped. "Do you want me to split you? You'll be no good for anything but the sailors brothel if you can't go to the block virgin. Be quiet now, and let me finish."

Under the threat, her body trembling, the girl clenched her fists and let her head fall back, trying to keep still. The sensation was awful. The hard sharp end of the quill scratched as it progressed, then began to probe around the depths of her virgin sheath. It seemed to be scraping around some particular tender spot that the old woman wanted to plumb, then she screamed as a unbearable sensation, part pain, part her body's rejection of penetration in such a spot, convulsed her belly.

"Quiet, quiet," the old woman said, trying to calm her. "The danger's over. You won't be split now," and she felt the rods withdrawn, though she was sure the quill was still inside her, and penetrating into her womb itself.

She lay back panting, while the woman made more preparation. As the girl lifted her head to look through her spread thighs again, trying to make out what was happening, she could see the woman had now got a small bladder in her hand, filled, it would seem, with some form of liquid. She was fastening it to the outer end of the quill. Suddenly Florence screamed again, and went on screaming. A terrible searing burning agony filled her belly, almost as if the hot iron that had marked her irredeemably on her buttock had now been pressed into her womb.

The iron at her buttocks had taken a mere five or six seconds to do its work, burning through her delicate skin and flesh to leave her permanently marked, but this seemed to go on forever, until she sank into merciful unconsciousness.

When she woke she was lying on the matting in the room where they were kept. Her belly still ached, but the hurt was containable now, though she hugged her abdomen trying to make it ease. All around her she could hear the groans and cries of the other girls, as they lay curled up in their own misery.

"What have they done to us?" Florence croaked to the girl who lay beside her in her pain.

"They have burnt our wombs with lye," the girl sobbed, "so that our bellies will not swell from our masters' seed, and deprive them of the pleasure they take from our bodies. If our bellies were full, and our breasts heavy with milk, we would not please them so

213

much as if we remain barren."

They were left to recover from the wounds on their buttocks and in their bellies for the rest of that day, but the next morning, still sore and aching, they were paraded in the courtyard and prepared for their sale. To show them to best advantage, and hence raise the best prices, they were to be trained to walk, to dance in their fetters, to stand and display their bodies.

All day they circled the yard, or stood on a small raised dais, moving to the beat of a drummer, urged on, and their mistakes corrected, by stinging slashes of a supple cane. By the time they were allowed to seek their mats, and collapse, they were all totally exhausted.

Two days later they were driven to the monthly auction of slaves in the town market.

Florence was roused early, and scrubbed all over, her hair too. The old women dried it on a cloth, brushed it out, rubbed it with a piece of silk until it shone like burnished gold. They went over her pubis with tweezers in their hands, and drew out the few stray hairs that had escaped the painful depilation with hot sugar, and oiled her vulva and anus. Putting her on a marble slab they spread the scented oil over her whole body, stroking it in carefully, massaging her skin until it glowed. Then they sat her up and outlined her eyes with kohl, rubbed rouge into her lips, brightened her eyes, and expanded the pupils with belladonna. Finally they gave her a plain white robe to cover her nakedness The garment felt strange on her skin after nearly a week of total nakedness.

The market was traditionally held in the mornings and the women were herded through the chilly streets, not yet warmed by the sun, shivering in their thin garb with cold and fear, and lodged in the holding pens behind the auction block. One by one they were taken through and, as the door opened and closed, those remaining could hear the hubbub of male voices, and the jeers of the crowd, and shuddered.

When her own turn came, Florence was momentarily stunned by the noise and the lustful stares of the men, the jeers and sexual innuendoes, the cruelty in the faces that surrounded her. In this intimidating atmosphere she was made to drop the only covering she had and stand before them naked. The auctioneer waited for the roar to subside a little, then banged on a great gong to gain attention. Avid for the sale to begin, the men gave him enough quiet to proceed.

He hawked his wares in crude and uncompromising terms. Florence cringed to hear her body discussed as if it were meat, her virginity offered as it were a tasty sweetmeat, her breasts, thighs and limbs given the same treatment as, all the while, she stood in her nakedness, feeling their eyes burning into her, as the trader told how she might grace any man's bed, how her young flesh might receive a man's lust, and give him joy.

When the bidding began she became aware of just what kind of men might possess her, and shuddered. A fat Turk, his little close-set eyes and wobbling chin speaking more eloquently of cruelty and vice than any words; a great dark giant, his rich clothes and costly weapons fouled by dirt, his person stinking; a sleek Armenian brothel keeper with a whip at his belt; and others equally frightening.

As the sale wore on it seemed the choice of masters for her tender body fell between the Turk and the brigand. Just as it seemed the Turk might possess her a new voice called from a side of the room she had not been watching. Turning her head she saw a tall European standing against the wall in company with a young dark skinned man who might have come from Persia, or even further East, India itself. The very strangeness of his appearance had the fear of the unknown. Besides, he might have been bidding for her on behalf of the oriental, from a land where cruelty was a way of life. On the other hand, she might be sure life as the Turk's possession would be hard.

With bated breath she listened to the bids mount and nearly fainted when the Turk threw up his hands in disgust, and the European smiled in triumph.

And now our serial, ERICA (expanded version), by Rex Saviour. This is episode 7 but that need not stop its enjoyment by new readers: Rex is trying to cure Erica of her fear of being touched, beaten, etc. by desensitisation, that is exposing the patient in gradually increasing doses to what she fears most - so far it is not working out too well!

2-4

I finished my coffee, paid the bill, visited the gents, and pondered on the rest of the evening. I was determined to make Erica's birthday a memorable one, a milestone date.

Outside, I found her beside the locked Rolls, positioned as I had taught her, on tiptoe, feet apart, hands clasping opposite elbows behind the back. She stood very straight, upright and motionless. Fortunately the bra and knickers that she had removed in the restaurant were held behind her, but even so her rather nice pose had attracted quite a crowd.

As I watched, one of the young football fans raised the hem of her skirt. She was crying silently, but she kept her arms behind her back and hardly moved, just shrank away - she was more frightened of disobeying me than of the youths who surrounded her in so ribald a fashion. It was unfortunate, perhaps, that the match had been so frustrating...

I waited, wondering how long her resolution would hold. Her lips were parted, the tip of a pink tongue just showing - I had forbidden her to hide it completely when not speaking. When one of the youths started to kiss and fondle her, her control snapped and she ran off down the street. The bottom waggled beautifully, because of he cord cutting into her crotch. A policeman was approaching, and the youths turned away, disappointed.

I took the keys from my pocket and walked round to my door.

When the engine was running smoothly I overtook her. I opened her door and she climbed in rather hastily.

"You moved."

"I'm s-s-sorry, Uncle. It was because -"

"You will be even sorrier soon. You will have to be punished severely for such disobedience."

"I know, but it was because -"

"On top of what you had coming already."

"I know, I know!"

"I think you need a drink first. We'll drop in at the Fox on the way home."

"Oh God!"

I took out my little black book. "Blasphemy. Five marks."

"I - I thought it was one."

"It used to be. It's five now you are nineteen."

"Oh God!"

"Six."

"Oh God!"

"Really, Erica!"

She burrowed her head into my lap, knowing that that sometimes makes me more lenient. "Sorry, Uncle Rex, I know I have to
be beaten but not the pub first, not the Fox, please not!"

"And you just broke rule 1 about saying sorry."

"Yes, but not the Fox, not the Fox!"

I felt timid fingers at my flies and decided to humour her this
time.

"Very well," I said.

She raised her head.

"Are we going home now, then?"

"No, but we'll try a different pub, since you don't like the Fox."

She had my flies open now, and her head dropped into my lap
again. "Home, oh please, straight home. I mustang go into a pub
like this."

So that was it, she was concerned about the short skirt.

"I'm glad you are modest, my dear," I said. "I'm trying hard to
teach you to be, as you know."

She had freaked out once when people got a glimpse of her
pubic hair, but that was due to the special mini skirt I got her when
she was eighteen. There had ben dancing at the Fox that night, I
remember. I had to punish her for crying about it. I always punish
crying, but maybe I shouldn't have spanked her there and then,
over a bar stool. Anyway, we had a pleasant time after that: I allowed her to dance with quite a few men, and they all enjoyed
themselves. In any case, I have started to shave her again, so there
is nothing to see now.

"You have my permission to stay up a little longer," I said,
"this is a treat, so don't worry about the outfit. Maybe it is a bit
sexy, but I'm sure it will be admired."

She said nothing, but I felt her tongue upon me, avid in its
hunting. Desperation sometimes inspires her.

We were cruising up New Road, just coming to the Wheatsheaf.
I turned past the idlers on the corner into the car park, and she sat
up to look through the windows. The pub was rather full, almost
all male, almost all black, some, it must be admitted, rather siz-

able. She actually whimpered.

"Oh Uncle, no, no, let's go to the Fox after all."

"What's the matter?" I asked. "Don't you like black men?"

I knew very well that she didn't, because of Big Willie, her neighbour for so long. It is just another thing she and I have to work on together, and here was a chance for a little desensitization.

I took the car out again. It was just that it wouldn't be safe too near that notorious pub, but Erica misunderstood.

"Oh thank you, thank you, Uncle. I'll be ever so nice to you, I promise!"

She would be in any case. She is quite a bright little minx. She knew very well that the quality of her evening would depend upon my mood.

"Oh, I'm not depriving you of your treat," I said. "Let's see what it's like, since you complain about the Fox."

"But I like the Fox better." Her troubled little face was very appealing: she can't help the saucy look, which is so misleading. "I do, I do!"

"You certainly have more friends there," I said. "But I expect we shall make plenty of new ones here."

"Oh God!" As I made another note in my little black book she burrowed her head deep into my lap again.

I parked in New Road, maybe a hundred yards from the pub. I had to pull Erica's head away from me before I could get her out. The plaits being tied together made a good handle.

"Bring the bra and knickers," I said. "We may need them!"

She blushed at the wolf-whistles as we passed the loiterers on the low wall of the street corner outside: this is where the pot smokers go for their gear. It is on the edge of the ghetto, that part of the city we laughingly call multi-cultural.

"At least you needn't worry about the police here," I said. They never go in the Wheatsheaf. They don't want another riot. Erica connects policemen with prison and avoids them, so that should have been a relief to her.

"In!" I said, "or it's the cellar after your beating."

"Oh please, I can't go in there, not like this!"

"The cellar then?"

"No, no, no - can I put my knickers back on?"

"Certainly not. Not now you are ready for your beating. You must carry them. It might be best to keep them out of sight." It was good advice, but not practical, as she had no bag, no pockets, no way to hide anything. "Well, are you coming or is it the cellar? All night?"

"Oh God, I'm coming -"

Our entrance caused quite a sensation. Erica was clinging to my arm, and several of the loiterers were following us. I have never known her to be so upset. This would be very good for her, she needs to acquire poise.

"Don't let them touch me, oh please please please, oh God they're all staring at me -"

She stood by my table, very upright, very self-conscious, trying to hide her knickers and bra behind her back, not a very good thing to do as there were people all round us. I hadn't quite realised exactly how short that skirt was, or how tight the jersey. They affected even me!

There was a hush, then:.

"Hey, man!" A tall lean black with a wispy little beard wandered over, loose limbed, and sat on the edge of our table. He patted Erica's pert little bottom approvingly, winking at his cronies when nothing happened. I don't permit her to react to anything like this: I feel it is part of my responsibility.

"Smart chick for a honky girl!"

It was interesting that he thought her white. I suppose, to him, she was. In actual fact, of course, she is this lovely shade of olive brown - all over that is, no white patches and deliciously smooth. It is due to parentage, not to the sun.

"And the stockings," I said. "Feel that. Pure silk."

"Oh man, oh man!"

I was watching over her carefully, of course, in case he went too far. I am very protective with Erica. She is not allowed to talk to strange men but unfortunately she can't help being a temptation to them. I blame the way she shrinks from the slightest touch, the very thing that I am trying to cure her of. But I don't want to put her off men altogether. It is a very delicate balance I try to maintain. It's OK, I think, for a stranger to feel the silk, but I draw a line at fingers so far above the stocking tops as his were at that moment. After a while I coughed, and he took his hands away reluctantly.

"Call me Yankee," he said. "What you havin'?"

"A glass of wine, thanks, Yankee." A realisation struck me. Here, if I had needed it, was a way into, at the very least, a free drink situation. It would make a good game, I thought, for Erica and I. She likes some of our games more than others, and I am always trying to think of new ones for her.

"And you, honey?" he asked Erica.

"Nothing," I answered for her. "I don't let her drink." I was into the game already. No need to strain the punters' pockets. "She fetches, we drink."

"Right on, man. Pint of bitter for me, honey."

I watched her wriggle through towards the bar, trying to avoid appreciative hands. She had been too uptight to think of the money, she'd have to come and ask Yankee for that. The bar was crowded but it still gave the others a chance to see her. They were staring already, much less inhibited than the rather snooty crowd at the Fox.

She was soon out of sight as the throng at the bar closed in behind her, though I could still hear her squeals - maybe she got a pinch or two. Little things like that are good, they teach her how to handle situations. I knew she would thank me in the future. As a matter of fact she would thank me tonight. I decided to make that part of her training.

Suddenly I wanted to get her home.

"We can't stay," I said. "Send her out to me, would you, Yankee?" I found out later that although everyone calls him Yankee he is in fact Jamaican. "One of your friends can have my drink."

"Oh man!" He licked his lips. "Five minutes?"

It would take her five minutes to fetch the drinks. "No more than ten," I said. I didn't want him to stretch it out too long, I was pretty eager to get her home.

2-5

As I waited in the Rolls, parked some hundred yards from the Wheatsheaf, I knew that Erica's desensitization would be continuing inside. I was pleasantly relaxed about it. Her fear of black men must be overcome, even if she found the treatment unpleasant in the short term.

After thirty minutes, however, I did begin to get a little uneasy, and after another ten I seriously thought of going back for her. I was actually on the point of getting out of the car, despite the light drizzle that was now falling, when I heard the wolf whistles and knew she was on the way.

Some youths were following her, and she ran the last few yards before scrambling into the car.

"Why were you so long? You knew I was waiting out here."

"Oh, Uncle, they wouldn't let me go, it was horrible, so horrible!"

It was hard to hear what she said for sobs.

"You smell of beer, girl!"

"One of them s-s-spilt it over me!"

I decided not to make an issue of this. Indeed, I put my hand on her thigh to comfort her, and as usual she squirmed under my touch.

"My dear," I said, "where are your stockings?"

"It was the one called Yankee. You're going to be cross! Oh God! His friend said Yankee needed them for his girl friend -"

I felt further. "He took the suspender belt too?"

"Oh - well - yes -"

"Well, really, you'll have to pay for those." I switched on the overhead light at the last traffic lights before we left town. "Look at your skirt!"

"It's only a little torn, Uncle!"

"It stinks of beer!" She could see I was getting more and more cross as I examined it. People were looking in from the bus beside us. "Out!" As she scrambled into the road I raised the electric aerial. "Now, off with the skirt, quick, before the lights change. Knot it round the aerial, back in, quick."

But it was no good. The lights changed the bus got away before me.

"Now look what you've done," I said.

"I'm very s-sorry, Uncle."

"More black marks! And give me the belt, I'll need it as soon as I can find a place to stop." The broad red leather belt she wears round her slim waist is quite heavy but nice and supple, ideal for beating her at short notice. That is why I make her wear it.

I kept the light on to get a good look at her. I was pleased that they hadn't taken the silver chain from her neck: it had not even come away from the nipple rings. Probably the men in the pub had liked the look of her with head and breasts up.

She spoke again, blurting out more useless excuses.

"There was such a crush at the bar, all those hands, oh God I couldn't stop them, truly I couldn't - please let's not go there again."

"We'll see," I said.

"   Oh but please -"

"What are you complaining about? You weren't a virgin, were you?"

She blushed.

"You were raped as a child, before you came to me?"

She nodded

"Frequently?"

"Yes," she said, in a very small voice.

"By your father and all his friends?"

"Yes."

"So you're used to being screwed most days?"

"Yes."

"In fact I'm the only one who has not fucked you when he could have done?"

She nodded again.

"You see!" It was the first time she had admitted all this. "Were you buggered as well?"

"What's that?"

"Up the arse," I said crudely. "From behind."

"Oh! Like a boy!" She was crying now. "Daddy made me dress up in trousers like a boy one day, and he gave me a big cap to pin my hair up under. He said the man would like a pretty little boy and he would take me home for the weekend and be kind to me... It was worse next time, because I knew what was really going to happen..."

"Did that man beat you as well?"

"Oh yes, most of them did."

"Well then!" I said. "Don't complain now!"

I speeded up to overtake the bus, but had to drop back again because of a bend looming ahead.

"Uncle -"

"Well?"

"You'll find a hole in the back of my skirt where my bottom g-g-goes -" It was a big effort for her to tell me that, but of course she would have known it would be even worse for her if I discovered it for myself. "One of them had a pair of scissors, he said it was pretty material, he wanted a piece of it, they made me stand on a chair while he cut it out and they all laughed and crowded round and - they each wanted to put his finger in the hole -"

"That was an expensive outfit!" She must have quite ruined it. I tried again to overtake the bus and again failed. "Well, go on!"

"They t-told me to dance - up on the table -"

"I trust you didn't do any such thing!"

"They got some reggae music going and they were clapping to it, they made me clap too, with my hands above my head while one or two of them clapped on my bottom with a newspaper and I had to wiggle in time, and then one shouted out 'skirt up, honky girl' and I had to hold the hem in my hands and still wiggle, higher they kept shouting, higher, higher, higher - oh God, I can't tell the rest - oh, don't hurt me, I'll tell, I'll tell - oh God, it was horrible -"

She was almost hysterical as I overtook that dammed bus at last. I slapped her face and shouted at her. "Whatever it was they did, it must have been your fault, egging them on, dancing up on a table, shameless! Never behave like that again! I've told you not to lead men on, it's not fair to them."

"I didn't, I didn't, I didn't want to -"

"Don't argue with me, girl! Aren't you in enough trouble already? Why else would they touch you up like you've been telling me, make you stand on a table and flaunt yourself? They did all that didn't they?"

"Y-yes."

"And more you haven't told me yet?"

"Y-y-yes."

"Then of course you led them on!"

"Oh God, no -"

"And you shall be punished for it, never fear. Now tell me the rest, and be quick about it."

"Well, they were touching me - you know, feeling me where my skirt was lifted, up... oh! ... there were lots of them, as many as could get near enough, they were all pushing and laughing and drinking at the same time - all those hands, so greedy, crawling all over me, some were into me -"

"I'm not surprised, egging them on like that. It was blatant provocation. That sort of behaviour is dangerous for you. You know I absolutely forbid it. You know I would get the blame if you are hurt. Really, it is most inconsiderate."

She was almost silent.

"Go on," I said.

She started to cry again. "Then - someone shouted out - screw her - screw her good - they all shouted and whistled - they wanted an auction - but Yankee said I was for him. He - he did it on the floor. He got on top of me, and the others cheered him on, they called me Yankee's doll, give it her man, screw your doll good man!"

"Did he use a condom?"

"Well -"

"Did he or did he not?"

"N-no!"

"Really, Erica, this just won't do. I hope that's all?"

"No, well -"

"NO?"

"No - oh God - Yankee had a friend. He tried next, it was him who spilled beer on me, he smelled of it too, he was very heavy, he heaved about on me but he couldn't do it, not for a long time until the others held me, they were all cheering and laughing, he got in in the end -"

"Well really," I said, "you actually let two of them screw you, is that what you're saying?"

"Well, yes, I suppose -"

"That was most inconsiderate! What about aids and everything? Now we shall have to have you examined. You know I dislike taking you to clinics."

There was no risk of pregnancy, I had put her on the pill in good time, and hardly any of aids at that time, but it was extremely inconvenient. I pulled into a lay-by and dragged her from the car by the handle in her hair.

"Bend over the bonnet."

The metal was very hot, so I let her lean forward over it with her legs apart, back to the road, hands clasping elbows behind her. She had to be careful not to let her breasts touch the bonnet as the belt cracked down again and again and again on her squirming bottom and little gasps came from her.

When I had finished, I climbed back into my seat, lit a cigar and listened to some music, leaving her bending over the bonnet. How was I to know the bus would pass? When she stopped sobbing I touched the horn, and she climbed back into her seat, resting her bottom gingerly on the cold leather.

"Thank you for my punishment, Uncle Rex."

Fortunately for her, she seldom forgets to be polite. I restarted the car and drove off.

"That was nothing to do with your main punishment," I said. "That still comes later."

"I know!"

"It's lucky I have Mr Smith to help!"

She didn't reply to that, but I could see that she didn't like it.

2-6

We drew up at the outer gates of my charming old mansion, a country house that was very isolated yet modernised and luxurious. I looked at the girl sitting beside me, apprehensive, quiet as a mouse.

"Here we are."

"Yes."

I showed her my black book. "Nearly punishment time."

"Yes, Uncle Rex."

"It's very full - cellar or beating?"

I have recently created a replica of her father's cellar. She knows about it but hasn't been inside it yet. Pure selfishness on my part: I prefer a more physical approach. However, I suppose I shall have to use it one day, if she is to be cured her of her phobia about being locked up in darkness, but I knew what she would say now that she was given the choice..

She drew in her breath. "Beating please!"

I opened the massive gates. To do this one also needs the special key that turns off a small section of the electric fence, which I had installed to discourage burglars. It runs right round the property some half a mile from the house at its nearest. It's the latest thing, state of the art, something I am really proud of.

"I expect you wish you had been more obedient?"

"Yes, Uncle Rex. It was just that pub. If we could go to the Fox next time -"

"Well, maybe."

"Th-thank you, Uncle Rex."

"After you've been back to ask Yankee for your stockings and garter belt back."

"Oh God no!"

"More blasphemy. I intend to deal with it less leniently in future." I noted it down in the black book, then drove through and locked the gate from the inside, turning the electricity back on as well. All this must make Erica feel very safe. I decided to drive over the fields instead of using the track. There is nothing harmful in the grounds, cows and sheep wandering around, that sort of thing, frogs I suppose, bats and moths and owls, but Erica does hate being out there in the dark, another timidity she must be cured of. After all, although there are grass snakes they don't come out at night. She ought to know that, being so interested in snakes.

I stopped in the middle of nowhere.

"Out!"

I thought she was going to protest, but after a glance at my stern face she got out and took up her usual position over the bonnet. Her skirt still dangled from the aerial: I walked round and felt her bare bottom, warm and smooth and flinching from me. There were hardly any signs of the belting I had given her in the lay-by. Fortunately she doesn't bruise easily, and I have this excellent cream I rub in after I beat her. It seems to sting a lot, but it works wonders - that is to say it is very good at preventing bruising though I rather suspect that repeated applications have increased her sensitivity.

"Well?" I said.

She looked round at me, eyes big with fright. "What is it, Uncle? What should I do?"

"Where's the belt?"

"Oh God!"

She just can't seem to be able to cure herself of blasphemy despite the punishment it invariably brings and what I had just said about being less lenient over it.

"Ten black marks for that!"

"Ten! Oh no, no -"

"Twelve, then. Any objection?"

"No, Uncle, oh no." Panic stricken, she dived into the car and brought the belt to me. I could see her trying to make up her mind whether or not to kiss it, not knowing the correct procedure for this situation: in the end she kissed it once before handing it to me and taking up her position again, leaning over the bonnet with feet apart, hands clasping elbows behind her back. She looks good like that, but the moon was low and would soon disappear - it was too dark to see properly, though when I raised the belt her buttocks clenched.

"Relax," I said. "You don't think I'm going to do it out here in the rain, do you? But you need to stay a while, you need a good washing to be rid of those beer fumes." I unstrapped my watch. "Stand up, put this on. It is now ten o'clock exactly, right?"

She nodded. The watch was safely on her wrist.

"Back in position!"

As soon as she was leaning over the bonnet again, with her hands folded up behind her back as before, I snapped the catches on her wrist bands to the rings on those above the opposite elbows, thus folding her arms tightly into the small of her back, straining her shoulders back. I stroked her bottom with the belt and then put it between her teeth. I got back into the car and backed off a little way, into a nettle bed, until she was picked out in the headlights, leaning over nothing.

"Wider!" I shouted. She manoeuvred her legs further apart with difficulty, but then she made such a delightful picture that I got out my camera to honour the occasion.

When I touched the horn she was commendably quick to come into position over the bonnet where it had moved to. I let the electric window down, and she edged along until her face was level with mine. Her legs must have been very wide, anxious to please no doubt, for her shoulders and head were braced further back than I had seen before, the collar chain tugging at her nipples. Tears glistened in her eyes. I couldn't see her arms, of course, but I knew they were satisfactorily secured high up behind her back.

"You've had a lovely treat," I said. "It's almost punishment time now. It seems to be raining quite hard, so we needn't delay too long. Shall we say half an hour?" I saw the dismay in her eyes: if she went back to the track it would take longer than that to walk to the house, so she'd have to cut across the fields. I edged forwards from the nettle bed and got out into the rain - she came to me meekly so I could run my hands up and down her slippery legs. She has such lovely smooth skin I can't resist it.

I raised each leg in turn and took her shoes off.

"You'll walk easier without these. Don't worry about the frogs, I know they jump about at night but they're harmless, and so are the slugs and worms. I don't think the foxes have rabies, but be careful of them. Report to the bathroom in half an hour. Be very careful not to lose the belt, I shall be needing it." She wanted to say something, probably that her watch was on her wrist and her wrist was fastened behind her back, but dare not drop the belt from her mouth. "I shall be very angry if you don't keep to time. Half an hour exactly. Exactly, mind you, or the punishment is doubled. At least doubled." Her eyes were almost popping out of their sockets, but still she dare not drop the belt. "Oh, whatever you do, don't disturb the bull."

We only have cows, of course, but she doesn't know that.

An owl hooted, a white spectre on a low bough of a nearby tree. I caught her look of extra alarm, but it was too late to stop.

I drove back to the track, then on to the house. Without lights it looked a gloomy pile, creepy even without the bats that swooped round it at dusk and dawn. I stopped for a moment on the gravel to listen to the rustling of small creatures in the ivy, then the big garage door rose to my infrared command and lowered behind me when the car was safely within.

The garage communicates directly with the house. I switched on the landing light and stepped onto soft carpet. The rain was pelting at the windows now. I lit the fire in my den and laid out a few implements.

I went upstairs, switching off the downstairs lights behind me, and started my bath running. Erica's job usually, but one can't have everything.

As I lay and luxuriated in the hot soapy water for an hour or so, my mind went forward in anticipation of a delightful evening to come.

2-7

My bath lasted a little longer than I had intended. It was such a luxury that wild night, to imagine Erica, her soft skin whipped by the rain, facing the front door, expecting it to open on my wrath at any moment.

When I was dry I went to the bedroom window and opened it. Sure enough, there she was, legs wide apart, her arms behind her back, crossed and secured high up, the neck chain emphasising the squared shoulders and upward thrust of her firm breasts. As I leaned out, she looked up, the belt still in her mouth.

"Well, come in," I shouted. "You're late! How much longer must I wait?"

She opened her mouth and dropped the belt. I slammed the window down on her despairing cry - no doubt she would be asking how to open the front door with no arms.

I put on the dressing gown which is all I need in the warm den and went down to check on the fire and have a glass of dry white wine. Everything was fine. I love that room, with the subdued lighting and tasteful decor and our collection of erotic pictures, and whips and ropes and other objects, and the solid leather sofa, strong arm chairs and thick soft carpet: Erica and I have spent many happy hours there.

Eventually I went to the front door and opened it. She was on the lowest of the three steps, looking up at me from her lower position: it was as if the old mansion had been built specially for such a situation.

"Well," I said roughly, "why are you late?"

She had somehow managed to get the belt back in her teeth, but now she dropped to her knees in front of me and released it again so she could kiss my feet.

"The den," I said. "Immediately."

She got up and swayed gracefully down the corridor whilst I shut and locked the door. When I reached the den she was in place in the corner, facing into the room, legs wide apart, toes turned slightly inwards.

The way her arms were fastened high up behind her back straightened her shoulders nicely and the chain round her neck from the nipple rings was also well strained, and the few strands of hair twisted round the chain at the back held her head well up too. She was in exactly the position I had taught her, so that her eyes, wide open and apprehensive, were fixed on the crossed whips that surmounted the riding crop on the wall over the fireplace. I think the fact that I had never yet used them on her made her particularly interested in them. She was closely shaven, of course, but the lips of her sex were moist. The cruelest thing you can do to my Erica is to deprive her of her daily beating.

I settled myself, lit a cigar and picked up my drink.

"You were late!" I said, as I revolved in my fingers the cut glass that held the fine wine, admiring both it and the frightened girl so splendidly posed in the corner.

She knew better than to make excuses, she just came and knelt at my feet, head raised, tongue between her teeth, then began kissing and licking, first my feet then coming slowly upwards between my thighs, so reluctantly, delicate and delicious, pushing my dressing gown away with her head.

At that moment the intercom from the front gate rang. I pushed the button to open it for the car.

"That must be John, Erica dear. You'd better go back in the corner."

She took up her position gracefully.

"Tip toes."

"Oh G - yes, Uncle."

When I heard the car pull up outside I went to the front door and let John in. Precise at work, he seemed larger now, casually dressed, a great powerful bear of a man with more than his fair share of belly. When I led him into the den he sucked in his breath at the sight of Erica and almost whistled. However, he took his cue from me and said nothing about the naked girl shrinking from him.

"You asked me to assist at a punishment session," he said, "and to bring my own, ah, instrument. Is instrument the right word?"

His legal mind at work, I suppose. It was something I had never considered. "Appliance perhaps?" I said. "Since you intend to apply it?"

"Yes," he said. "I certainly do!" Erica's frightened eyes were on the strap he was flourishing as he cracked it down hard on the leather arm of a chair, and we both saw her jump. "Will this do?"

"Excellent," I said. "A glass of wine?"

"Thank you, yes, nice."

"Do sit down." I handed him his drink and got out the chess board. The specially carved pieces came from the Far East. "Care for a game?"

"Sure. Why not?" His big hands manipulated the pawns with delicacy, but his eyes were glued to Erica's naked bottom since I had I told her not to listen to private conversations or stare so rudely. Now she faced the corner, still on tip-toes, arms secured high up, legs apart. And I had fitted her ear plugs. She was always as still as a statue in that corner for fear of attracting my attention: sometimes she didn't hear me coming on that thick carpet even without the ear plugs. I won the game fairly easily, although John can usually beat me if he is concentrating. It took maybe half an hour and she never moved a muscle.

"Another?" I asked.

"Well -"

"Rather attend to Erica now?"

"Well, yes." He stirred to ease his crotch. The poor fellow was getting quite uncomfortable.

"She's got a lot more black marks since this morning."

"Indeed?"

"Yes, I'm afraid so ... Erica, come here dear."

Nothing.

"ERICA!" I shouted. "COME HERE!"

I motioned to John and he walked up behind her. She visibly stiffened when she felt his breath on her neck, and squealed when he put his hand between her parted legs to get a grip to turn her round.

He removed the ear plugs and returned to his seat. His crotch was troubling him even more than before.

Now she came to us, standing close and opening her legs again, as she had been taught. Her head was adjusted upwards so as to keep her eyes on the whips above the fireplace, as she had been taught.

"Say hullo to John, Erica."

"Hullo, good-evening, Uncle John, I hope you are comfortable?"

"And will help with your punishment."

"And will help Uncle Rex to punish me, Uncle John."

I reached out to stroke her. "I like that slightly golden skin, don't you? And the smoothness of it?"

"Ah! Yes, yes, nice ... and the handle you've made in her hair, very fetching ... I notice she keeps her lips parted?"

"A tip I got from 'Story of O', didn't I dear?"

"Yes, Uncle Rex."

"I see." John licked his lips. "And being shaved, I like that too."

"Oh yes, She's specially smooth under her arms and there, down there, aren't you my dear?"

"Yes, Uncle Rex."

"John might like to feel for himself."

"Yes, Uncle Rex."

She presented herself, but no verbal invitation. I held him back with a hand on his arm.

"Don't forget your manners, dear."

"Oh God -"

I got out my black book. "I don't believe in blasphemy," I told John. "It adds to her punishment. Looks like being a record tonight, specially if she isn't polite to you."

"Points for blasphemy? A legal matter, eh?"

"Quite. Well, Erica?"

"Oh - Uncle John - I am smooth there, my - between my legs, truly I am, please feel for yourself - oh oh!"

Perhaps he did make a bit of a meal of it, but all this was still rather new to him.

"Tears," he said. "Tears already, and we haven't even started."

"Strange that, she's usually pretty good about it. Anyway, enough of this fooling around. What she needs now is a good beating, eh dear?"

!"Yes, Uncle Rex."

"Hardest so far."

"Y-yes, I suppose so."

"So where is the belt?"

"Oh God!"

"Really, Erica!"

"It must be outside the front door where I dropped it, Uncle Rex!"

"Unfortunate." I turned to John. "Shall we use the whips instead of your strap and her belt? OK, then. It will be the first time you've felt them, won't it dear?"

"Oh no, please may I go and fetch the belt please?"

"See, John, she really dreads the whips. I told her they'd hurt a lot more."

"I suppose they will. You'll have to reduce the number of strokes."

"I'm afraid not, I have all that worked out and written down."

"I see - where is she going?"

Erica was standing facing the study door, like a cat waiting to be let out.

"I think she wants to go and fetch the belt - would you like to go with her? Take your strap if you like."

John gave her quite a touching up as she waited by the door. It was good to see how quickly he got into the mood. Eventually he opened the door and followed her down the passage to the front door, not sparing the strap.

When the door was open she went down on her knees and started to search around in the dark with her mouth for the belt. It is black, and would not be very easy to find, specially if it had slipped down the steps. I went back to the den. From the sounds I heard it was obvious that John was beginning to feel quite at home and wielding the strap with more confidence.

When they came back, Erica was crawling on her knees, the belt in her teeth. At the door of the den John gave her a particularly vicious crack of the strap, and she fell forward on her face, then came wriggling across the thick carpet on her stomach. It was an interesting sight, impeded as she was by the way her arms were fastened up behind her back and the belt between her teeth. When she dropped the belt he drove her round the room before he allowed her to pick it up again.

John had great potential as a therapist, I thought. I must use him again in the future.

At last Erica arrived at my feet with John still strapping away at her tail with undiminished enthusiasm. She dropped the belt and started to kiss me, trying to wriggle upwards.

I spread my legs and let her come. There seemed no particular hurry to start her punishment. We had the whole evening before us. John and I sat at ease. We had progressed to the brandy now, and sat slowly sipping it, gazing at the erotic sight before us.

There was no need to hurry, every reason to savour the moment. I got out the cigars, and offered one to John.

233

Erica stood very erect before us, her splendidly lithe young body within touching distance. She was naked except for the jewellery and a broad band of red velvet at her throat, her arms secured high behind her back, head and breasts alike held up by the neck chain. She clenched the belt between her teeth and stared wide-eyed at the crossed whips above the fire, not daring to move a muscle.

Except she was shivering slightly. No, the lavishly appointed room was too warm for that. It was a delicious little tremble that ran right through her. And was that just the faintest hint of the beginning of a whimper, nearly smothered by the broad leather belt in those beautiful white teeth of hers?

"Tip toes," I said. That was even better. There was a slight sheen of sweat coming upon her, making her already entrancing body glisten like amber crystal under the subdued lights.

I turned to John. "She's never had so many black marks as she has tonight," I said, leafing through my black book. "On her birthday, too. I tried to give her a treat, and what thanks do I get for it?"

"It must be very aggravating when someone you are trying so hard to help is so ungrateful," said John, stretching out his fat legs and easing the damp bulge at his crotch at last.

"It is, yes. The book gives me the minimum punishment, I usually add a few licks of the strap for luck."

"And to keep her guessing?"

"That too," I agreed. "It does seem to make her more apprehensive before a beating, even her regular ones."

"Yes, but why do we need the book at all?" asked John as I refilled his glass. "Isn't that an unnecessary restriction?" He was well into his legal mode now, and he is an excellent lawyer when he concentrates on it. "Who makes the rules anyway?"

"I do," I said. "One must have rules."

"Rules can be suspended by mutual agreement," said John, "so I propose that you as her step parent and I as her legal representative hereby suspend them. Let us just assume the, er, the subject of the correction, that is to say the young person Erica" - I think the brandy was beginning to carry him away a little - "needs to be dealt with severely and use our discretion in the matter."

"Extremely severely."

"Extremely, yes. Extremely severely. Understood."

I looked at Erica. Tears were welling up in her eyes, almost ready to overflow. She seemed much tenser than usual before a punishment, and was trembling more, and the whimpering was quite easy to hear - and obviously very stimulating to John, who had not heard her whimpering before. It is one of the things I like best about punishing her, something that I am very familiar with, but it was getting to me even more than usual. Yes, quite rousing. I think it was having John there that made the difference.

He saw me looking at him and shifted in his chair. "I'm pretty strong," he boasted.

"You'll really let yourself go?"

"Oh yes, I guarantee it. But -"

"Yes?"

"Well, perhaps it would put the matter on a sounder basis is I knew of what she stands accused."

"Certainly," I said. "A good point. Will you tell him, Erica, or shall I?"

She dropped those lovely brown eyes to me, so dark and shiny they are, puzzled as well as very frightened now, not knowing if she should open her mouth and drop the belt.

"Here," I said. "Come over my lap while you tell."

She did. Her weight for so small a person is quite surprising, but not unpleasant. Definitely not unpleasant! The feel of her of her trembling is good, too, and it is especially pleasant when her arms are secured with her wrists up behind her neck, as now. I usually put a palm under a breast and hold a nipple, ready to twist it or nip it now and then, and stroke her bottom with the other hand. This time I took the belt from her teeth and did the stroking with that. John stood beside us and did his own stroking, with the splendid strap he had brought with him.

"Now, tell us what you are to be punished for."

"Oh God!"

I gestured to John and he gave her a taste of his strap.

"Oh! Oh!"

"Erica dear, you know not to blaspheme."

"Oh God oh oh oh - yes Uncle!"

"That was for the blasphemy. Say thank you."

"Th-th-thank you, Uncle John, for correcting me."

"So what are we going to punish you for?"

"F-for fidgeting - oh oh - is this my punishment?"

"Of course not, you know it's just to decide what you've done."

"Yes Uncle - please Uncle - tell him -"

"Well John - did you think this was her punishment?"

"Yes, sorry. No harm in warming her bottom up, though, is there? After all, athletes warm up before action. I am somewhat surprised that you do not do it always. As her legal representative think I must suggest you do so in future."

"Very well," I agreed. It was a new experience to have someone strap her as she wriggled over my knee and I was quite enjoying it. "Very well," I repeated. "Start again, Erica."

"F-for - for fidgeting - oh oh - and -"

"Don't fuss, girl. Fidgeting, yes. And?"

"For fidgeting - oh - I daren't go on if Uncle John is going to strap my bottom every time I say something!"

"Repeat after me, then. Fidgeting -"

"Oh - oh God, I'll say it all myself. And crying - oh oh!"

"From the beginning, dear."

"It's not fair! Uncle John is hitting me even if I've said it before!"

"The sooner you get it right the better, then."

"Yes, yes - oh God - oh - for f-f-fidgeting - oh - and blasphemy - oh oh - and crying - oh - and spoiling my skirt - oh - and leading men on - oh - and - oh oh!"

"And losing something? And lateness?"

"Oh God - oh oh oh - for fidgeting - oh - and blasphemy - oh oh oh - and crying - oh - and spoiling my skirt - oh - and losing my stockings - oh - and losing my garter belt - oh - and leading men on - oh - and being late for punishment - oh - oh God - oh oh OH!"

"Yes," I said. "I think that's about it."

"Six for luck then?" asked John.

He gave her more than six. She very nearly fell off my lap, but she knows not to do that: she has found out the hard way.

"Right," I said. "Stand up, my girl!"

She stood in front of us, her bottom still squirming, tears flowing from her eyes, but she managed to be absolutely still and silent apart from that. She had been learning fast recently.

John and I had another glass of that excellent brandy each whilst I considered what to do next.

"After punishment," said John. "I fancy screwing her."

"OK," I said. "Straight after punishment or in the middle, that should be good."

"Do we toss for first go?"

"No, you. She sleeps with me, gives me plenty of chances. Want to borrow the belt?"

"OK then, thanks. It is a bit heavier than my strap."

"I've always found it satisfactory."

Erica had was whimpering loudly now the belt was out of her mouth. This is something I have not been able to cure her of. If I nominate a certain time for punishment, the whimpering sometimes starts as much as half an hour before, so she had done quite well that night.

"Upstairs my girl," I said. I released her arms. "Wait by the bed. You're going to like this one, John."

After another drink or two we followed Erica upstairs. She was standing by the bed at attention. "Position four," I said, and she lay down on the bed on her back and then raised those slim but shapely legs over her head and pushed them into the snap-catches on the bed head, very wide apart.

"Beautiful!" said John. She did indeed present a splendid target as she looked apprehensively up at us from between her legs. But she had not finished. She wriggled her body a bit further down the bed, then raised each wrist to the bed head in turn and snapped it into its catch, just inside those for the ankles. Now she lay still, her bottom raised and presented, entirely helpless. It was a position I sometimes ordered when I might not be ready for an hour or two, as it was one she could take up by herself but not release herself from.

"I like it," said John, bringing the belt down on her bottom with a grin of anticipation. The whimpering got louder. "Yes, very good, I like it! I do approve of your household, Rex."

"Good of you to say so, John. I hope you'll drop in again soon. Tell you what, Erica and I have a game where she stands in a corner for an hour or two, blindfolded and wearing ear-plugs. Sometimes I prepare a surprise for her. One day it could be you!"

"Great. And maybe I could bring a friend? I know someone very discrete who'd just love to come."

"That'd be fine ... oh, by the way, I've got this ointment to rub in after a beating. Like this."

I rubbed a generous portion into her bottom: it's remarkable how she squirms from it these days, more than she used to. Maybe increased sensitivity is a side effect. The formula is something I laboured at for years before I gave up research chemistry to be a writer. The firm I worked for know nothing about this: I told them I had failed. Maybe I'll market it one day, after it's been thoroughly tested.

"See how quickly it reduces the marks? Like magic, isn't it? Put some more on as soon as you've finished, would you, so she's clear when I come to bed? Don't economise, I've got plenty more. OK then, I'll leave you to it."

"Right!" He had taken off his jacket and was rolling up his sleeves, his eyes flashing, not at all the prim but beefy solicitor I usually saw. "Plenty of severity, eh?"

The whimpering was quite loud now. "Yes. She's been told not to scream, by the way. If she does, the punishment should be doubled."

Myself, I don't usually bring on the screaming. It would deprive her of all reason to hold back. John, I fancied, would be less subtle.

"And what about the screwing?"

"Up to you. It's easy to release her, or leave her as she is if you think it would be more convenient."

I had been back downstairs for at least twenty minutes before the first scream. After another quarter hour or so they stopped. I heard the bed creaking: he would be fucking her now. I thought of her past, the horror it had left her with of the touch of a man, specially the intimate touch. Soon I heard thosenmistakable little mewing noises that come from her only at moments of great distress.

Letter from a reader:
You will have to reprint Circus. I lost it. MW., Italy

Out of print titles

All titles (including above) are available plain text on
floppy disc
£5 or $8.50 postage inclusive
(PC format unless Mac requested)

or can be downloaded from
www.thebookshops.com/silver
e-mail james@jamesbrown.com
Credit card Teleorders/Fax orders (UK) 0113 293 0654

All our in-print titles (listed overleaf) can be ordered from any bookshop in the UK and an increasing number in the USA and Australia by quoting the title and ISBN, or directly from us by post. Credit cards show as EBS (Electronic Book Services - £ converted to $ and back!): Price of book (see over) plus postage and packing UK £2 first book then £1.30 each; Europe £3.50 then £2; USA $6 then $4. Please make US cheques payable to Silver Moon Books Inc.

TITLES IN PRINT

Silver Moon

ISBN 1-897809-03-4 Barbary Slavegirl *Allan Aldiss*
ISBN 1-897809-08-5 Barbary Pasha *Allan Aldiss*
ISBN 1-897809-14-X Barbary Enslavement *Allan Aldiss*
ISBN 1-897809-11-5 The Hunted Aristocrat *Lia Anderssen*
ISBN 1-897809-16-6 Rorigs Dawn *Ray Arneson*
ISBN 1-897809-17-4 Bikers Girl on the Run *Lia Anderssen*
ISBN 1-897809-20-4 Caravan of Slaves *Janey Jones*
ISBN 1-897809-23-9 Slave to the System *Rosetta Stone*
ISBN 1-897809-25-5 Barbary Revenge *Allan Aldiss*
ISBN 1-897809-27-1 White Slavers *Jack Norman*
ISBN 1-897809-29-8 The Drivers *Henry Morgan*
ISBN 1-897809-31-X Slave to the State *Rosetta Stone*
ISBN 1-897809-36-0 Island of Slavegirls *Mark Slade*
ISBN 1-897809-37-9 Bush Slave *Lia Anderssen*
ISBN 1-897809-38-7 Desert Discipline *Mark Stewart*
ISBN 1-897809-40-9 Voyage of Shame *Nicole Dere*
ISBN 1-897809-41-7 Plantation Punishment *Rick Adams*
ISBN 1-897809-42-5 Naked Plunder *J.T. Pearce*
ISBN 1-897809-43-3 Selling Stephanie *Rosetta Stone*
ISBN 1-897809-44-1 SM Double value (Olivia/Lucy) *Graham/Slade**
ISBN1-897 809-46-8 Eliska *von Metchingen*
*I*SBN1-897809-47-6 Hacienda, *Allan Aldiss*

Silver Mink

ISBN 1-897809-09-3 When the Master Speaks *Josephine Scott*
ISBN 1-897809-13-1 Amelia *Josephine Oliver*
ISBN 1-897809-15-8 The Darker Side *Larry Stern*
ISBN 1-897809-19-0 The Training of Annie Corran *Terry Smith*
ISBN 1-897809-21-2 Sonia *RD Hall*
ISBN 1-897809-22-0 The Captive *Amber Jameson*
ISBN 1-897809-24-7 Dear Master *Terry Smith*
ISBN 1-897809-26-3 Sisters in Servitude *Nicole Dere*
ISBN 1-897809-28-X Cradle of Pain *Krys Antarakis*
ISBN 1-897809-30-1 Owning Sarah *Nicole Dere*
ISBN 1-897809-32-8 The Contract *Sarah Fisher*
ISBN 1-897809-33-6 Virgin for Sale *Nicole Dere*
ISBN 1-897809-34-4 The Story of Caroline *As told to Barbie*
ISBN 1-897809-35-2 Jane and Her Master *Stephen Rawlings*
ISBN 1-897809-39-5 Training Jenny *Rosetta Stone*
ISBN 1-897898-45-X Dominating Obsession *Terry Smith*

UK £4.99 except *£5.99 --USA $8.95 except *$9.95